KNOCKED UP BY THE BOSS

A SECRET BABY ROMANCE

ANNIE J. ROSE

CHAPTER 1

ANDREI

I ran my hands through my dark brown hair and sighed.

Wednesday was usually a fairly nondescript day of the normal business week. The whole concept of "Hump Day" might have made some people feel better, but to me it just felt like overcompensation. Making a big deal out of Wednesday sending you on the downward slide to the weekend seemed to emphasize that it was for the most part a mundane day.

Monday was the beginning of the week. Depending on the person, that could mean grumbling drudgery dragging out to the office to face another five days of work, or a fresh start and motivation to push for the goals set for the week ahead. Friday was the end of the week. That wrapped it up and funneled everybody into the weekend and two days of rest without work.

Mostly everybody. I was known to stretch my week out into Saturday and sometimes even into Sunday if there was enough to do. My company was the center of my life, and work took up the vast majority of my thought and energy.

Which was why most of the time Wednesday was just another day with a routine like any other. For me, that routine meant meeting Gus for lunch. My best friend, and sometimes my competitor as well, Gus was another first-generation American born of Russian parents in New York. That gave us a strong connection, and we stayed connected even when work was all we lived and breathed by meeting up for lunch every Wednesday.

It always went the same way. I finished up my work for the morning and checked over my schedule for the after-noon before heading out. Leaving the office building meant walking by my assistant Gina's desk, and I'd tell her to take messages while I was gone. She didn't need the reminder, but it was part of the flow of the day. Only that day, the routine got shaken up. I barely glanced toward Gina's desk as I walked past, waving over my head and calling out to her as I went. But what I noticed out of the corner of my eye was enough to make me stop and do a double take.

Gina wasn't the only one at the desk. Sitting across from her was the most gorgeous woman I'd ever seen, perched at the edge of her seat with her legs crossed and her hands draped over her knee in a way that was somehow at once demure and alluring. Like she was covering up and tempting me to take a glance at the same time. Figuring Gus could be patient for a few extra minutes, I walked over to the desk and leaned against it, looking over at Gina before turning my eyes back to the woman.

"Good afternoon," I said.

She glanced up at me with huge blue eyes that made my stomach clench.

"Hello," she said.

"Bridgit, this is Andrei Petrov, the owner of the compa-ny," Gina said, then gestured to the woman and looked at me. "This is Bridgit Holliday. I'm doing her follow-up interview."

Now that I heard her name, I recognized it as one of the three applications I'd gone over earlier in the week when Gina had presented them to me. She handled the initial screening of applications, then did a round of interviews at a separate location to pare down the pool to the most promising applicants. Not that the position I was hiring for was terribly grueling.

Gina was a great assistant and was perfect for the role when the company first started. It was still small, but had become far busier and more successful, meaning she was having more and more work piled on top of her. In order to keep up, I was in the market for an all-purpose secretary, and it looked like I was being served up a young, gorgeous woman as a potential option. I tried to remember her application, but it didn't come to mind. That could mean she didn't have anything that particularly stood out about her resume, or it could mean I was just too distracted by looking at her to think about much else. Either way, I was intrigued.

The longer I stood there, though, the more that intrigue turned to caution. I chatted with them for a few minutes, the conversation mostly shallow boilerplate exchanges, all the while trying to act like I wasn't checking her out. I didn't even realize I was doing it until Gina asked me a question said that I clearly didn't hear. All that came to mind was the curve of Bridgit's neck and the way she shifted her weight just slightly in her seat. I had to snap myself back into reality and remind myself this was my potential new secretary. Those types of thoughts weren't going to work if Gina decided to hire her on for the position.

"Well, I'm going to head on to lunch," I finally announced. "Good luck with the rest of your interview."

"Thank you, Mr. Petrov," she said, and I had to bite my bottom lip as I turned away and hurried out of the office.

I made my way to the subway and stepped through the turnstiles. This was the fastest way to get to the restaurant. Driving would not only take three times as long, but it would be an enormous pain in the ass to find a parking spot at this time of day. Born and raised in the city, I couldn't remember a time in my life when I didn't use the subway. By the time I hit double digits in age, my parents were bundling me off to activities or to visit other family who'd come over from Russia around the same time they did. I could navigate the system by myself as a young child and never lost my attachment to the train.

As I stood gripping the handle overhead, I considered texting Gina. There was still time for me to tell her not to hire Bridgit. If only for my peace of mind. With the way I'd reacted to her just sitting at Gina's desk and talking about essentially nothing for less than five minutes, I didn't know if I was prepared to handle seeing her around the office every single day. As my secretary we'd be working closely together, and there would be no way for me to get around spending time with her. That could prove inconvenient if my initial response to her was any indication.

I eventually decided against texting her. It wasn't fair for me to put the kibosh on Bridgit getting the job if Gina thought she was the best one for it. Just because I couldn't control my thoughts didn't mean she should have to miss out on the opportunity. If Gina decided to hire her, I would just have to learn to push all that out of my mind, swallow it down, and not acknowledge it. Eventually, it would go away, and she would be just another woman working at the office.

I hadn't totally convinced myself by the time I met Gus

at our usual restaurant. Our favorite spot for Russian food in the city had been a delightful discovery at the end of a long search. We'd met in school and automatically saw similarities in each other. Even though both of us were born in the United States, growing up in homes where Russian was the primary language gave us slight accents. We both also traveled to Russia frequently during our childhoods and lived in New York very much like it was an extension of our parents' homeland. That gave us a connection to a culture and way of life that set us apart from many of the other kids around us. But in the end, it was the food that really attached us to each other.

We hugged when we saw each other, patting each other firmly on the back and greeting each other in Russian like we often did. The hostess brought us to our usual table, and I immediately spilled everything about Bridgit.

"So, you might end up having a sexy young secretary to look at while you work every day. What's the problem?" he asked.

"The problem is I don't just want to look at her," I said. "Bridgit is the first woman I've wanted since my divorce. It happened that fast, and I don't know how I'd react to having her around all the time. Actually, I know exactly how I'd react to having her around all the time. It would be nearly impossible to get anything done with a fucking hardon all damn day. Not to mention, she'd be my employee and I'm just not that guy. It's unethical and creepy."

The waitress came by with coffee and handed us menus. We almost always ordered the same thing, but sometimes they offered a special that caught my eye, so I liked glancing over the menu just in case. There wasn't anything new on offer that day, so Gus and I ordered our usual spread, handed the menus back to the waitress, and waited for her to walk away before we continued with our conversation. I didn't want to get the creepy boss reputation at my favorite lunch spot.

"This is the first time in a while I've heard you even mention a woman in that way," Gus pointed out after a deep sip of his coffee. "Maybe this one is worth letting your guard down for."

CHAPTER 2

BRIDGIT

I knew my studio apartment was tiny when I moved in. The first thing I thought when the landlord showed it to me was it seemed barely bigger than my bedroom and walk-in closet from my parents' house. But it had never felt smaller than when I was sitting there the day after my final interview with Gina. I sat on the couch that dominated the tiny living area with my phone clenched so hard in my hands I wouldn't have been surprised if it cracked in my grip. I tried to tell myself to relax, but I couldn't even get my fingers to loosen up from around the phone enough to stop the aching in my knuckles. The longer I waited, the more it seemed like the walls were closing in around me and I was being suffocated by the miniscule apartment.

But I didn't have any other choice but to sit there and wait. I wouldn't have been able to concentrate on anything else, and there wasn't really anything else to do. That's what had gotten me into this position in the first place. No job. No hobbies. No more friends or family other than my brother. Speaking of my brother, he wasn't doing me any favors pacing back and forth across the open floor of the apartment. He was supposed to be there for moral support and make the waiting easier, but his inability to sit still was just ratcheting up my anxiety.

"What time is it?" he asked.

"Noon," I told him. "She said she was going to call between nine and noon."

"It's going to be okay," he said, but his steps quickened a bit and he made his pivots faster as he continued to pace. "It's really going to be okay."

I wanted to believe him. Steven and I had always been close, and I depended on him a lot. Especially now that our parents had turned their back on me and made it abundantly clear I no longer had a place in their family. Steven was the only one that had gotten me through that transition, and he was doing everything he could to help me figure out my life now and what I was going to do moving forward. I was completely indebted to him and loved him with my whole heart. Even if I was still shocked it was working out this way.

As close as my brother and I were, I would never have expected him to take my side in this situation. He was always extremely loyal to our parents and tended to agree with them on just about every issue and in every situation. Not to the extent it seemed worshipful, but also never compromising. Until now. When the disastrous situation I'd just dragged myself out of exploded, I figured I was on my own. I didn't want to admit it, but there was never really a question about how my parents were going to react or how it was all going to play out with them. I dared go against what they wanted for me and what they thought was right for my life. That rendered me essentially worthless to them, leading to me being blacklisted from the family.

It didn't seem too far a leap that Steven would be on their side and I'd lose him just as fast as my parents. But that's not what happened. Instead, he fought for me. He stood up to them and made sure they knew he not only didn't agree with the way they were treating me, but that he wasn't going to go along with it. He would still be in my life and wasn't going to just leave me dangling in the wind, woefully unprepared for anything on the outside of the privileged and sheltered life I grew up in.

It was only because of Steven I got the interview with the import company at all. It would be an understatement of fairly epic proportions to say I didn't have any qualifications or experience that really made me eligible for the position. But I needed it badly and was hoping Steven's connections would land it for me. For all the times in my life I tried to rise above the privilege of my upbringing and bemoan favoritism that left others in the dust, I was dearly hoping it worked out for me in this situation. If it didn't, it meant carrying on the way I had been since my parents cut me off, and I just couldn't deal with that anymore.

I hated living off Steven's charity. He tried to convince me that's not what it was. He even whipped out the old tried-and-true "it's not charity, it's family." If anything, it made me feel a little worse. Yes, I was family. The family who had been cast aside because I didn't fall into place with what was demanded of me. The family who went from pampered to pauper in ten seconds flat and was now stuck to him like a barnacle. Our family tree was officially ornamental, and I was the unwanted branches that got trimmed off to make sure it kept up proper appearances.

And Steven saved me. Every step of the way since that day, he'd been there to make sure I didn't end up in a gutter somewhere. It sounded dramatic and over-the-top, but it was true. After the final confrontation with my parents, I left with nothing. I moved into the itty-bitty studio with only the clothes he was able to smuggle out for me. My parents made it very clear everything in their home belonged to them, even if it was once mine, and there was nothing I could do about it. Even paying for my apartment for me was risky to Steven, and he chose something small and unassuming so the cost every month wouldn't raise alarms. And so eventually I would be able to pick it up for myself.

Which was what brought us to this moment, waiting impatiently in the living area of that tiny studio for the phone call that would determine the next steps in my existence. We were so invested in waiting, when the phone rang it startled both of us. My hand shaking, I pressed the answer button and put the phone to my ear.

"Hello?"

"Bridgit? It's Gina. I'm sorry for the delay. I got into a bit of a talk with the last call," Gina said.

"It's fine. How are you?" I asked, the words coming out as mumbled mess.

"I'm good. I'm just calling to let you know the position is officially yours if you want it."

It was exactly what I'd been waiting for, but I'd worked myself up about it so much I wasn't sure I actually heard it correctly.

"What?" I asked.

She laughed quietly.

"The job. You got it. I'm hiring you. If you're still interested, of course," she said.

"Yes," I said, possibly too enthusiastically. I drew in a breath to calm myself down. "Yes. I am still interested."

"Good. Let me give you a few details."

"Okay. Go ahead," I said, waving my hand at Steven and miming for him to find a piece of paper and pen.

Gina started giving me information about the company and the position, and I repeated it all out loud. Steven finally found the pen and paper and started frantically copying down everything I said.

"Tell Steven I said hello," Gina said when she was finished.

I cringed slightly and pulled my face away from the phone.

"Gina says hello," I told him.

"Hi, Gina," he called loudly enough for her to hear him through the phone.

She giggled, and it was everything I could do not to roll my eyes. The woman had just given me a job. This was not the time to start with that.

"Thank you so much," I said. "I'll see you soon."

Getting up from the couch, I crossed the apartment and flung myself down on my bed. It was small and lumpy, but at least it was mine. My brother came over and plopped down on the edge of the bed beside me. I pulled myself to sit up, and he took my hand, squeezing it. I didn't even have to say anything, and he knew exactly what I was thinking and feeling.

"Andrei will take good care of you. I've worked with him before," he said.

"You have?" I asked.

"Yeah. Did you get a chance to meet him at your interview?"

"Just for few minutes. Not long enough for me to really get an impression of him," I told him.

"He's a stand-up guy. A bit traditional in an old-school

Russian way, but he's fair. Plus, Gina will keep me updated," Steven reassured me.

"I'm sure she will," I teased.

He nudged me playfully.

"You're going to be fine. You can do this. I know you can. So, let's go get you some work clothes. And shoes. And a messenger bag."

I looked over at him and let out a deep sigh.

"I wanted a job so you'd stop spending your money on me," I pointed out.

There wasn't a lot of point in arguing with him. Not only did I know it wasn't going to do any good because he was going to get his way no matter what because he was the older brother and it was his birthright, but I really needed those things. This might be my first job, but I knew enough to assume the few pairs of jeans, shirts, and skirts Steven was able to smuggle out of my parents' house without them noticing weren't going to be right for the workplace. He'd already bought me the outfit I'd worn to the interview, but that wasn't going to be enough to carry me through to my first paycheck.

"If you have to, you can start paying me back after you start getting paid. But not for this place," he said.

"Steven, I have to pay my own rent," I said.

"No. I'm your big brother, and I want to make sure you're all right. Besides, it can be considered my good deed for the month every month," he told me.

If anyone else said it, I might have been offended, but I knew he was joking. The laugh that broke my tension made me feel better, and I nodded my agreement. It was all he needed, and Steven jumped up, grabbed me by the hand, and tugged me out of the apartment before I could start resisting again. We spent the rest of the day shopping, and by the time we were finished, I had a work-appropriate wardrobe, a tablet, and a messenger bag. It felt like getting ready for a new school year, but with an added layer of anxiety. Any humor I felt before we left was gone by the evening, and I returned to my apartment worn-out and melancholic, unable to even be excited about any of the new clothes or goodies he got for me. All I could think about was how much I owed him, even if he didn't want me to pay him back, and how different my life was now and would always be.

The worst part was I couldn't even just jump into the job and get distracted. I still had a few days to go until I started, and that meant much more sitting around in my shoebox questioning my life and its direction.

CHAPTER 3

ANDREI

"Come on, you can't be serious?"

The week was off to a fairly quiet start. I had several meetings scheduled for later in the afternoon, interspersed with handling paperwork, emails, phone calls, and various other tasks, but the morning was slow. Like I often did, I spent several hours of the weekend alone in the office taking care of work so it wouldn't roll over into the new week. Doing that gave me something to fill my weekend and keep my mind from rattling around in the relative silence of the rest of the day but left little to do on Monday mornings. That's why the beginning of the week was more often than not marked by sitting at Gina's desk with her, drinking coffee.

My assistant was one of the few people I'd encountered in my life who had quite the attachment to coffee I did. Gus drank his fair share, but he didn't even come close to my devotion and probably addiction. Just any coffee wouldn't do. I was very particular about my brew. Gina called it snobbery. Either way, Gina could handle the extra-dark, bitter coffee I preferred black and would sip it with me in the morning as we waited for the day to get fully underway.

That morning I was listening to her regale me with stories about her weekend. That was another thing I could rely on Gina for at the beginning of the week. She was always good for a story or two, and I usually found myself laughing as I made my way to my office after our coffee. Today was no exception. I took a sip from my second cup of coffee and tried to get it down before she said the next thing that would make me laugh. I barely made it and had to set my cup down on the edge of her desk and focus on swallowing.

"That didn't happen," I argued with her. "No one would do that in a bar."

She shook her head and took a sip of her own coffee.

"It must have been a long time since you've been in a bar," she said.

"A very long time," I agreed.

She nodded as she swallowed.

"Well, you would be surprised at what people will do." She shrugged. "I mean, I never am anymore, but you probably would be."

I scoffed. "What are you getting at?"

She shrugged again and looked off to the side as if she had no idea what I was talking about, then laughed. Still just under thirty, Gina relished the slightly more than ten years that separated us in age. We didn't really socialize outside of work, but not for any other reason than I didn't socialize with anyone other than Gus outside of work. Over the years we'd worked together, she and I had developed first a comfortable rapport, then a friendship. I trusted her, and it was good to have someone I felt at ease laughing and joking with even at work. It was a good relief, especially when things got busy or tense, as they were prone to do in this industry.

Before she had a chance to respond, the door to the office opened and we both looked up. My stomach clenched and my heart jumped in my chest when I saw Bridgit walk in. Despite the obvious anxious tension in her expression, she looked just as good as I remembered from her interview more than a week before.

The streamlined navy-blue pencil skirt and blazer she wore were subdued and made her look like the quintessential contemporary secretary while also deliciously hugging her ample curves. Her dark blonde hair was tied up in a twist at the back of her head, and the only jewelry she wore were tiny gold ball earrings. It was definitely a dressed-down appearance. Not that it took away from her appeal. Bridgit could wear burlap and she'd still be hot as hell.

She hovered at the doorway, seemingly unsure of what she was supposed to do next. Her eyes glanced between Gina and me, and I realized she probably thought we were in the middle of something serious. I stood and waved her over.

"Good morning, Bridgit," I said. "Gina tells me you're going to be my new secretary."

What I didn't tell her was I'd taken the last few days to try to come to terms with the idea of her working there and convince myself she wasn't going to be a distraction, that I could control what I thought and felt. That was proving to be a bunch of bull. It only took a few seconds of being in the same space with her for the attraction to surge back even stronger than it was the first time I saw her. Fantastic. Now I had to keep that all to myself and ensure she didn't catch on.

"Yes," she said. "Today is my first day."

Her lips pressed together slightly like she was internally chastising herself for stating the obvious. I was the owner of the company and her boss. Of course I knew it was her first day. I didn't acknowledge it.

"We're looking forward to having you on board," I told her.

"I am, too," she said.

"Do you have everything you need? You know how to get around the office and where everything is?" I asked.

"I think so. Gina gave me a rundown."

"And I'm going to show her around and make sure she is comfortable," Gina added.

"You're in good hands with Gina. She knows this place better than anybody but me," I said. Bridgit nodded, her hands gripping her messenger bag tightly in front of her. Her nerves were obvious, and I didn't want to make them worse. "Well, I guess it's time for me to get some work done. Welcome to the team."

I headed across the open area to my office. The building was set up so the warehouse was on the bottom floor with administrative offices and the mailroom attached to one side. Above that was the space dedicated to my office, including a large open area with Gina's desk and furniture for people to wait if they needed to meet with me. A hallway just beyond the door where Bridgit just came in led from the elevator while the glass walls of my office allowed me to look down over the operations inside the warehouse.

The glass walls were one of my favorite features of my office building when I designed it. This wasn't the first building where my company was located. When I got started, I was in a squat building shoved in a row of other offices with little in the way of amenities or identifying features. As my company became more successful and brought in more money, I decided it was time to create my own space that would set me apart. The first thing I thought of was having glass walls in my office so everybody knew what I was doing throughout the day, and I knew what they were doing as well. It created accountability as well as a sense of approachability I hoped would make my employees more comfortable.

Right now, all it was doing was giving me the perfect view of Bridgit as she settled in for her first day of work. I went to my desk and threw myself into work, trying to get absorbed in it so I didn't keep watching her. But I kept finding my eyes wandering up to her, following her as Gina showed her around, introduced her to the computer system, and got her settled at the new desk I'd bought so she'd have space to work.

The glass didn't do anything to conceal what was going on beyond it from my vision, but it did block the vast majority of sound from coming through. I could still hear the muffled sounds of the warehouse below, but the glass totally blocked Gina's voice from me and mine from her, necessitating an intercom system for us to communicate when we weren't in the same space. But that effectively meant all I could do was watch Bridgit. Small talk at least gave me her voice and Gina's contributions to latch onto and keep me more focused. Without being able to hear her now, the only thing I had was the visual appeal of her.

And she was undoubtedly appealing. Without me around, she seemed to loosen up slightly and was soon smiling at Gina as they talked. The smile warmed her face and brightened her eyes, making me even more helpless to do anything but track her every movement. Thank goodness she didn't seem to notice. My new secretary was already somewhat wary around me. The last thing I needed was for her to look up and find me staring at her. Throughout the day I forced myself to keep working, to tear my eyes away from her and try to pretend she wasn't there. I had to try to work like there was no one beyond the glass wall but Gina, that everything was the same it had always been.

And that was far easier said than done.

But it wasn't just my intense attraction to her that made me keep looking up at Bridgit. Something about the way she moved around the office and completed tasks Gina showed her seemed off, like she wasn't entirely comfortable in an office environment and didn't know what to do. I had to remind myself it was only her first day and she would get used to it. I remembered her application and resume seemed sparse, but Gina obviously saw something more in her and I trusted my assistant.

The amount of time I spent dedicated to watching my new secretary that day became more obvious as the hours wore on. By the time the warehouse was shutting down, I still had a long list of things I wanted to accomplish for the day. Gina knocked on the door, and I waved her inside.

"Do you need anything else before we head out?" she asked.

"No," I told her. "Thank you. Have a good night."

"Don't stay too late," she said.

"I won't. I just have a few things I want to finish up."

She left and I watched her lead Bridgit out. They were chatting and smiling with each other, and I could only imagine they had plans to celebrate her first day with a few drinks. That was the kind of person Gina was. She'd want to be supportive and encouraging. I was just glad to have them gone. The office was blessedly silent, and I could focus on finishing up work. But even without her there, I couldn't get Bridgit out of my thoughts. Soon, I couldn't take it anymore.

I locked up and headed home as fast as I could. I made it there with thoughts of her naked, her hair tumbling down her back and her hands reaching for me racing through my mind. I got inside and tossed everything in my hands onto the entryway table. I barely made it to my bed and kicked off my shoes before I was wrestling with my tie and my zipper. Loosening both, I stretched out on my bed and opened the fly of my boxers to release my aching cock.

Those thoughts kept fueling me as I wrapped my hand around my shaft and indulged the desires she woke up in me. My hand moved fast and unrelenting as the images of her in my head grew sultrier and more intense. It didn't take long before I exploded. I dropped back against the bed gasping for air and wiped sweat from my forehead with the back of my arm. I felt more relaxed and at ease when I climbed out of bed to get cleaned up and head into the kitchen for dinner, but there was the voice in the back of my head reminding me it was only her first day. She was going to be around every day, and I was going to have to figure out a way to deal with that without having to jerk off every night to relieve the tension.

CHAPTER 4

BRIDGIT

"I'm so sorry you have to keep showing me this," I said miserably.

Gina just smiled kindly.

I still didn't know what toner was. It was my third day on the job, and that bit of information had gone into my brain more times than I could count but tumbled right back out almost immediately. Gina just kept explaining it to me, showing incredible patience, and I appreciated my brother using his connections with her to lend me this job even more. As she showed me yet again how to use the copier, I glanced over at the massive glass walls that surrounded Andrei's office. My first day, he spent virtually the entire day in there behind the desk, emerging only twice for a few moments. But after that it was the opposite. In the last two days, I'd barely seen my boss at all. Honestly, though, that was probably a good thing since I was failing spectacularly at this damn job.

Who the hell knew being a secretary could be as complicated and challenging as this was turning out to be?

It was a closed-minded, privileged, and probably tone-deaf perception, but when Steven told me he could possibly get me a job with a friend of his who was interviewing for a secretary position, it didn't sound like that much of a stretch for my brain. I was still nervous about landing the role simply because I'd never had a job before, but I didn't think it would be difficult. After all, my experience with secretaries came largely from my occasional visits to my father's offices or their portrayals on TV and in movies. There was a lot of taking notes and typing up those notes, maybe answering a phone call or two throughout the day, but that's all I was expecting.

It turned out that was just another way I was completely oblivious to the actual world around me. By the middle of the second day I decided I needed to start a journal just so I could jot down all the revelations about life and the ways I needed to get my shit together. Starting with acknowledging what actually went into working and maintaining a job. It was much more complicated and involved than I ever would have imagined, and every hour I spent in the office seemed to present a new opportunity for me to fall flat on my face and demonstrate my cluelessness. At least Andrei wasn't around to witness the circus of failure playing out just beyond his office.

Trying to sound as casual as possible and not like I was at all concerned about his perception of me, I asked Gina why he wasn't in his office. She tossed a look in the direction of his office like she hadn't even noticed he wasn't there and shrugged.

"He's had a full schedule of meetings, and sometimes when that happens, he just stays in the conference room downstairs rather than bothering to come up here in between them. It's more convenient, and he doesn't have to waste the time riding the elevator and walking across the room," she said.

I looked at her strangely.

She laughed. "Andrei Petrov is many things. Capable of balancing his work-to-life ratio is not one of them. He would probably move in here and sleep in a cocoon hanging from his office wall if he could work out the zoning issues. Work is his everything. Pretty much literally. With the exception of the weekly lunches he has with his best friend, he does nothing." She pressed a few buttons on the copier and it churned to life. She let out a satisfied sigh. "There. I don't know what you did to this thing, but I fixed it."

"Thank you," I said.

"Ready for the next task?" she asked.

I nodded, determined to catch on this time and be able to wean off Gina's constant help. She'd been a godsend throughout those first few days. What started as her just showing me around and giving me the rundown of what was expected of me every day turned into her essentially holding my hand to guide me through everything.

I still felt like I couldn't keep up. By the middle of my third day, I was nothing short of defeated. Gina invited me to go to lunch with her, but I begged off under the guise of having brought my carefully meal-prepped lunch. It wasn't completely a lie. I did bring my lunch with me. But it wasn't the strategically planned meals the chef used to pack into tiny containers and stack in the refrigerator for me, so I had my exact nutritional plan laid out in front of me for every meal and snack every day. It was a peanut butter and jelly sandwich.

But I had prepped it. So, there was that.

Needing some time away from the office that was rapidly becoming the arena of my torment, I went outside to eat. The pavilion off to the side of the building was already occupied, and I wasn't feeling particularly social. Instead, I went around to the back of the building and sat down in the shadow of the loading dock. Fortunately, all the guys from the warehouse were also taking their lunch, and none found the idea of a cement picnic appealing, so I had the whole area to myself.

I took a bite of my sandwich and leaned my head back against the building. My eyes stung and I tried hard not to cry. It wasn't just the difficulty I was facing. It was what it represented. I wasn't oblivious. I knew the kind of world I grew up in and that being the daughter of an exorbitantly wealthy businessman and a woman who came from even more money meant that world was different for me than it was for other people. It offered perks and opportunities other people didn't get and shielded me from realities and challenges I didn't even know about. Being aware of that made me feel somehow like I was more in-tune than other people, like I was more aligned with reality than others I knew. But now I was having to come to terms with not only how much I *didn't* know, but how unprepared and complacent I had let myself be.

My first instinct was to blame my parents and cutting me off, but I stopped myself as those thoughts went through my head. Yes, it was their fault I was in the position I was in now in that they shoved me out of the nest knowing full well I was not equipped to fly. It was also their fault in that they allowed me to be overindulged, never accountable for anything, and with my only expectations being living up to what society expected of me. Beautiful, well-dressed, well-spoken, and primed for marriage.

But it wasn't their fault I let that happen. I could have pushed to be more involved in the world around me. I could have actually paid attention in school and pursued more of an education. I could have put effort into finding something in life I was good at and enjoyed so I could have a career or even a meaningful pastime. Hindsight. It's a killer.

A shadow fell over me, and I opened my eyes to find out who was interrupting my pity party. The bite of peanut butter and jelly slid down my throat as I swallowed hard. Andrei himself stood over me, looking down with his head at a tilt like he was both scrutinizing me and trying to figure out what I was doing. I tried to fix the expression on my face, to look casual and confident, but it didn't work.

"Struggling, huh?" he asked, his deep brown eyes taking me in.

There was a note in his voice I couldn't quite identify, and I didn't know how I was supposed to respond. He kept staring at me, and the hint of a smile on his lips suddenly made me irrationally angry and defensive. I set my sandwich down onto its bag beside me.

"It turns out when you're raised to do nothing but marry well, you aren't exactly prepared for the workforce," I said irritably.

My pride was already bruised, and I couldn't help lashing out, but as soon as I did, I knew I was wrong. It probably wasn't a good idea to snap at your boss three days into your new job. I waited for Andrei to respond, to scold me, to fire me. Instead, he gave an almost imperceptible nod.

"Ahhh. A tragic backstory, I see. Well, Gina is a saint, so she'll make sure you get it," he said.

With that, he finished walking down the loading ramp and headed toward a smaller building at the back of the property. I watched until he disappeared into the logistics center and then reached for my sandwich again. Finishing it in a few bites, I stood and headed back into the office. I didn't understand anything that just happened. Andrei wasn't angry for the way I spoke to him. He didn't get offended, he didn't reprimand me or try to put me in my place. But he also didn't seem intrigued or even thrown off by what I had said. I hadn't really intended to reveal that glimpse of my past to him, but as soon as I did, I wondered what he was thinking of me. I assumed he would ask me about it, demand to know what I meant by that. Yet, there wasn't even the flicker of interest in his eyes when he responded.

Either he already knew what had happened, which I highly doubted, or he had his own shit in his past and didn't make it a practice to delve into other people's. It wasn't that I wanted to spill everything out and confide in him about what happened to me. In fact, that was way down on my list of things I planned on doing anytime soon. Yet somehow it was almost hurtful he didn't seem even slightly interested. He was dismissive, almost flippant about it, and I didn't like it.

I rode the elevator up and walked into the office more determined than ever not to screw this up. I would give all my brain to the job and really focus on getting everything down. This was my reality now, my new world, and I had to shift my mindset to that. Embracing it would allow me to really focus and get over this hump.

Just like I knew she would be, Gina was right there to go over everything again, to explain everything and make sure I understood. She really was a saint, and I found myself happy not just to be working with her, but for the friendship that was growing between us. She would be the first friend I made on my own without the orchestration of my parents or their world.

By the end of the night I caught on to what she'd shown me and left work feeling a bit better about what I was supposed to be doing. I knew the next day would bring its own set of new challenges, but this time I was more prepared to face them.

CHAPTER 5

ANDREI

I didn't really expect my interaction with Bridgit to go quite that way. Of course, I also didn't expect to find her sitting on the ground outside the office eating a peanut butter and jelly sandwich for lunch, either. There was something about that image that felt off, and it went beyond just seeing a grown woman in business attire eating a sandwich by a loading dock. She struck me as far more put together than that, even in her anxiety and nerves as she started work. Her inability to catch on to what was expected of her also struck me as odd, but her snapped answer gave me a greater insight into that.

I wanted to know more about her and get a clearer picture of what was going on, but there was no way I could talk to her about it. Every time I got near her, Bridgit was either visibly nervous or on edge. After that conversation, it seemed I could add frustrated to the mix, none of which were conducive to a good conversation. So, I gave her a wide berth for the rest of the week, not wanting to make her uncomfortable or interfere with her progress. Whatever was happening with her personally, it clearly had a major impact, and I didn't want to possibly make anything worse for her.

But I was still curious and needed to know what was going on with my new employee. There was only one option, and that Friday I brought along my secret weapon. At the end of the day, Bridgit left while Gina and I were still working. That wasn't unexpected. Fridays often meant tying up loose ends from the rest of the week, which sometimes caused work to bleed over past the usual five o'clock end of the day. If Gina was disappointed with not being able to cut out and start her weekend early like many people did at other offices, she never let on. She always liked to get things wrapped up and signed off on at the end of the week, so she didn't have to deal with them anymore when the next week came. And that Friday I made sure she got the best of both worlds.

As she finished up some paperwork, I carried the beer I brought out of my office and over to her desk. Cracking one open, I set the bottle down on the desk in front of her and dropped down in the chair across from her. She didn't hesitate to pick up the beer and take a swig. I joined her in it with a draw from my own bottle before diving in.

"How's it going?" I asked.

She knew exactly what I was getting at. Gina had worked with me long enough to not need me to spell things out for her. Shaking her head slightly, she took another sip of the beer and leaned back in her chair.

"Bridgit is a nice girl, but she's a bit slower than I assumed she'd be," she said.

"Are you regretting hiring her?" I asked.

She immediately shook her head. "No. I stand by the hire. She was the right choice."

That answer made my ears perk up. It wasn't what she said, but how she said it that seemed not quite right. Gina wasn't saying Bridgit was the right choice for the secretarial position because she was the best qualified or the most experienced of the applicants. The tone of her voice said there was another reason she was the right choice. Just like I suspected, there was a story there, and I needed to hear it.

"All right," I said. "Spill."

"What do you mean?" Gina asked, taking another sip of the beer as if to stall.

"Don't play innocent. I know something's going on here. You had several other options of people you could have hired for this position, and I know for a fact some of them did this type of work before. I don't think any of them would have struggled so much figuring out how to use a copier or how to organize and file shipping records. Yet, you chose Bridgit. The other day I went to iron out an issue with an order and found her sitting out by the loading dock eating lunch by herself. She about bit my head off when I asked if she was having a hard time and mentioned being raised only to marry well. Now, I don't know about you, but that doesn't sound like a normal thing people tell their boss on a regular basis. So why don't you just tell me what's actually happening around here," I said.

She sighed and leaned forward to rest her arms on the desk.

"All right. I'll tell you. Bridgit wasn't exactly a fluke applicant," she confessed. "All the other applicants were completely legit, but she was a bit of a ringer."

"A ringer?" I asked.

Gina nodded. "I'm friendly with her brother Steve. You might remember him. You worked together briefly a few years ago. Steve Holliday."

I let the name tumble around in my head for a while, comparing it to various memories and trying to line it up with a face or a specific instance that might illuminate the connection. Finally, it did.

"Steve Holliday... we worked together about five years ago. We secured goods for that massive event his father was organizing, right?" I asked.

Now that I realized the connection, I could see how the two resembled each other.

"That's him. We've kept in touch since then and have gotten to be friends. He got in touch with me a few weeks ago and told me he'd heard you were looking for a secretary and needed a favor. His sister, Bridgit, was desperate for a job and really needed something fast," Gina continued.

"Their father is one of the most powerful businessmen in the state and their mother comes from an even more prominent family. How could she possibly be in such need for a job?" I asked.

"You know how families like that can be," Gina said. "At least to a degree."

She was right about that evaluation. Though I had the money and influence to be a part of the society circles, it never appealed to me. Most of the people I encountered weren't people I'd want to associate with, and even the kind ones felt like they were from such a different existence I couldn't connect with them. But for some, my opinion was the last thing they cared about. The fact that I wasn't born into my wealth and instead built it for myself after being raised by modest immigrants meant I would never be worthy of being a part of their circle. There was so much manipulation, coldness, and judgment, I couldn't see myself aligning myself with them. It was somewhat of a shock to hear Bridgit was a part of it.

"I do," I said.

"Well, Bridgit is a casualty of it. She told you she was raised for nothing but to marry well. That's genuinely the truth. Her parents saw their daughter as a commodity. Her marriage could create stronger alliances among powerful families, grant business connections and networking, and further position the family for influence and control. She was indulged and pampered her whole life, essentially groomed for marriage, then her parents chose the man they wanted her to marry."

This surprised me. Of course, the concept of a matchmaker wasn't foreign to me, but it still seemed odd.

"They wanted an arranged marriage for her?" I asked.

"More or less. That's the easiest way to think of it. Essentially both families were in agreement about wanting to combine forces, so the parents selected their son Grant to marry Bridgit. Only she refused to go along with it. Grant was extremely controlling and was showing signs of becoming abusive. Bridgit knew if she went through with the marriage it would be miserable and possibly even dangerous for her later. He wasn't someone she could tolerate being married to, even if it was what her parents and his wanted. So, she stood up to them."

"Good," I said.

Gina took another swig of her beer and shrugged.

"Good from a moral fiber perspective, yes. Not good from the perspective of how her parents reacted. They fully expected her to do exactly as they said just because. It didn't matter to them that they were fooling around with her future in such an egregious way. They didn't grasp that they weren't asking her to escort someone distasteful to an event or do a favor she didn't particularly want to do, but that would be over in a relatively short period of time. They were demanding she give herself over completely to a man she couldn't stand and who would never see her as anything more than property. He wouldn't respect her or try to do anything that might make her happy. Forget about loving her. She would be something pretty to have on his arm at parties and events, a step ladder to more success in his career, and the source of the next generation for both their families," she said.

"That's disgusting," I commented.

"It is, but that's not how they saw it. And even if they did, they didn't care. They demanded Bridgit marry him, dangling her family and her stability in front of her as collateral. If she agreed to the marriage, she'd be set for life, have all the luxuries she could ever want, and not lose favor with her family."

"And if she didn't?"

"Then she was completely cut off. She still refused, and that's exactly what they did. They kicked her out without anything, nowhere to go, no money, and no idea what she was going to do next. Fortunately, her brother took her side and has been helping her out. Including getting her the job here. Are you angry with me?" she asked.

I finished my beer and set the empty bottle heavily onto her desk, shaking my head.

"Absolutely not. Like you said, you did the right thing. That's horrible what they did to her. I can't believe there are people like that in this day and age."

It pissed me off to hear what her parents put Bridgit through. I was infuriated thinking about the pain, humiliation, sadness, and fear she was having to face. No wonder she snapped at me the way she had. A new surge of emotion rushed up inside me. Now I wanted to protect the woman nearly as much as I wanted to bed her.

"What are we going to do?" Gina asked.

I pried the cap off another beer and handed it to her, then opened one for myself.

"What do you mean?" I asked.

"You've seen her around here. She's a disaster. We can't just let her keep flailing around. Nothing is going to get done, and she might actually end up making a mess of things," Gina said.

"Then we figure out how we're going to get her up to speed better," I said.

We nursed our beers as we built a plan for how we were going to get this situation under control. It was obvious Bridgit needed this job, but like Gina said, we had to have her doing what she actually needed to be doing. We agreed we would both work together to make sure she was good, to help her figure everything out, and to encourage her. Mostly importantly, we agreed we weren't going to make a big deal out of it. I didn't want her to know I'd dug into her past and knew what was going on with her unless she decided to tell me. I didn't want to embarrass her or make her feel like a charity case.

When everything was settled, I dropped a kiss onto the top of Gina's head and left, heading to the gym. I had a lot on my mind and knew the best way to combat the raging thoughts was to work out.

CHAPTER 6

BRIDGIT

The rhythmic knocking on my apartment door sounded like something out of a bad caper movie or TV show. There wasn't any question about who was on the other side of the door, but I still hesitated in the middle of the studio just to see what would happen. The pattern grew more complicated but didn't manage to accurately repeat itself. After the third series of knocks, I smiled and crossed to the door, disengaging the series of locks Steven insisted on installing after I moved in. Considering it was my first time living on my own, he wanted to make sure I felt safe and secure.

The locks finally undone, I opened the door and laughed as my brother dropped to the ground and rolled across the floor. He hummed a spy theme as he jumped to his feet in a low crouch, and I noticed something bulging in the front of his shirt. Laughing, I shook my head and shut the door.

"What are you doing?" I asked.

"A mission," he told me, getting up and reaching under his shirt. "Ta-daaaa."

In one swift motion, he yanked a tight roll of clothes out and presented them to me. I took them from him and went through them happily.

"This is great. Thank you," I told him. "I have to admit, that was quite the entrance for bringing me a drawer's worth of clothes."

Steven brushed his hand back over his hair, leaving it standing up on end, and grinned.

"Oh, I have a couple of suitcases and a box in the car," he told me. "But I couldn't do the spy roll if I was carrying them."

"Of course you do," I laughed. "Thank you for smuggling for me. I really appreciate it."

"Any luck getting into your bank accounts?" he asked.

"No," I told him with a deep sigh as I tossed the clothes onto my bed so I could put them away later. "They are still officially in deep freeze as ordered by our parents."

"I just can't believe they're going this far with it."

"I can. Nobody says no to the illustrious Mr. and Mrs. Holliday when they want something. I said no, so I'm dealing with the consequences," I told him.

And there were definitely consequences. The truth was, I was still shocked with the extreme nature of their reaction to my refusal of the arranged marriage. If someone had told me they were capable of doing it, I wouldn't have hesitated to agree with them. It was just the type of people they were. But I hadn't ever really thought they would completely cut me off. Get mad at me, sure. Restrict my access to the family accounts or some of the other privileges I was accustomed to, absolutely. I was fully anticipating them having a bad reaction when I told them no, and knew I was going to be punished for it. But I figured it would only last a few weeks, and then I'd be back in their good graces. Or at least be on the way toward them.

But that didn't happen. Within hours of them telling me I had to leave the house, my bank accounts were frozen, my credit cards were cancelled, and every service professional I was accustomed to using from drivers to personal shoppers knew not to associate with me. I went from the top of the world to nothing in the blink of an eye, and it seemed to only be getting worse.

"Well, I'll keep sneaking you stuff as much as I can," Steven told me.

"Thanks. Can I get you something to drink?" I asked.

"What do you have?"

I walked over to the tiny kitchenette area of the studio and gave a futile glance into the refrigerator.

"Tap water," I told him.

He came over and looked over my shoulder into the almost bare refrigerator.

"Is this all you have?" he asked.

"There's a jar of peanut butter in one of the cabinets and a couple of cans of soup," I told him.

"You haven't been grocery shopping?" he asked.

"I haven't gotten my paycheck yet," I admitted.

"Come on," he said. "I'm taking you to the store."

"No," I told him. "When I got my job, I told you I was going to be taking care of my own basic needs. You insist on paying my rent, but I need to do something to take care of myself."

"You can't live off soup and peanut butter for the next week," he pointed out. "I didn't realize it would take this long to get your first check. You need food."

I hated giving in, but he was right. My plan so far had been to raid the break room every morning in hopes of coffee and donuts, then skate by on the meager food I had left over until I could get to Friday. It was far from ideal. Steven brought me to the grocery store and loaded me up on supplies that would last well more than the week ahead. It seemed like every time I put one item in the cart, he had three or four to accompany it. His big-brother protective instincts were in full force, and he wanted to make sure I had everything I could possibly need to carry me through. It was heartwarming, but I wish he didn't have to do it. I didn't want to have to rely on him and have him feel like I was a burden. I was determined to drag myself up by my bootstraps so he could just go back to being my big brother rather than my caretaker as well.

When we finally got back from the store, he helped me put the food away in the little kitchenette. Soon it was stuffed full, and I had to admit a sense of relief came over me. Even if Gina did decide I was too hopeless of a mess to keep my job for now, at least I'd survive long enough to find something else. We each grabbed a snack and a drink and went over to the living room area of the studio. Dropping down onto the couch, we rewarded ourselves with chips and cans of soda.

"How's everything going with you?" I asked, turning my head to look at my brother. "You've been doing everything for me. How are things with you?"

We caught up a bit, but I started steering the conversation in another direction when Steven drifted toward talking about my old social circle. I didn't want to hear the gossip about all my old friends, the people who dropped me as soon as I didn't have money anymore. By now there was no doubt each and every one of them knew the details of my failed relationship, likely with a good amount of embellishment to ensure my parents came out of it looking like the good ones. And yet not a single one of the people who once considered themselves closest to me had even bothered to reach out to me. They didn't try to contact me to hear my side of the story or find out what was going on. I just disappeared in their eyes. And they were fine with it. It made me realize that I had been alone for far longer than the past few months.

Not wanting to think about them, I shifted over to talking about my job. I hadn't gotten a chance to tell him about it yet and I thought he'd appreciate the update considering he was instrumental in getting me the position. I made it a point to steer clear of the sort of burgeoning crush I had on Andrei. It wasn't something I'd spent a lot of time thinking about and knew it was stupid, anyway. Crushing on your boss never turned out well, and I would never do anything about it, but it was definitely there. That didn't mean I needed to open up that can of worms with my brother. I'd rather just tell Steven about me stumbling around the office incapable of figuring out how to do anything and let him have a good laugh at me.

It was reassuring that was my brother's reaction. He didn't seem at all concerned about me or the future of my position. He told me Gina wasn't going to fire me just because I wasn't an amazing secretary right off the bat. They'd give me plenty of time to figure myself out.

"How are you getting along with Andrei?" he suddenly asked.

Could he know? Had I given myself away somehow?

"It's fine," I told him, staying as neutral as possible. "We haven't really interacted very much."

The truth was, we'd interacted more over the last

several days, and he was proving to be more than I would have ever expected. I never would have thought someone who looked like Andrei to be such a teddy bear, and yet that's exactly how he was with Gina and me. It's what was fueling the crush I was trying my hardest not to acknowledge.

Even if Steven had gotten a hint that my feelings for Andrei were drifting beyond respect and civility, he didn't say anything else about it. We talked more about my work and then started chatting about ideas for the summer months ahead. We didn't mention the obvious detail that we wouldn't be having our usual family trips, but it was still fun talking about simpler things like cookouts or going to the local theme park we hadn't visited since we were children.

Steven stayed long enough to order us in a giant pizza, and we propped up my tablet to watch some streaming TV. A few episodes of a nonsensical obstacle course reality show were all I needed to decide internet-based TV as an alternative to usual cable was one of the greatest developments of our time. After he left, I took a shower in the miniscule bathroom that was the only separate space of my apartment and crawled into bed. I lay there staring up at the ceiling, trying to honestly evaluate my life.

It was easy to try to put on a brave face and act like everything was fine. That was my stubbornness and pride talking. I didn't want anyone to see my weakness or question my ability to handle things. I'd never really had to manage anything or deal with any adversity in my life, but always resented when people implied the same. I noticed when people were given special treatment and liked to talk a big game about it being immoral and unfair, not recognizing just how extensively I relied on that same special treatment in my life. Now I wanted to prove to people I didn't need all the pampering and indulgence to get by. I was just fine on my own.

But that wasn't exactly the truth. I wasn't doing great. But it definitely could be worse. I could be without Steven and everything he'd done for me. I could be without the job he got me, without Gina and without Andrei. That would leave me in a much more serious situation than I was. I missed my friends, or at least I missed when I had people I thought of as friends and the fun we used to have together. I missed my home where I grew up. What I definitely didn't miss was my parents or their expectations. But then I felt grateful for the burgeoning friendship I was cultivating with Gina, and even Andrei. Something told me, they were the real deal when it came to friends.

After a while, I fell asleep with hope for this new life I found myself in and was starting to accept as my own.

CHAPTER 7

ANDREI

It was almost time for lunch, and I walked out of my office to check in with Gina about my schedule for the rest of the day. It turned out one of the meetings planned for the afternoon had already been rescheduled for later in the week by the other people. The second wasn't of major significance, just a check-in with a client about a major event they were coordinating in several months.

These clients could be very particular and sometimes insisted on several meetings in the months leading up to the event to ensure everything was still on track. While this could be tedious sometimes, I actually very much enjoyed that element of my business. It was unique and kept my work interesting and different. I also believed it was one of the main reasons my company was as successful as it was. I was able to find things people had no idea how to locate and at unique, special touches to important days. It was more than just jars of caviar or bottles of rare specialty liquor. It was memories they would think back on for years to come. For some that might seem like just a small detail, but I liked knowing I could help people create their vision for their event.

This particular client, however, was taking their need to stay in touch a bit to the extreme. Every week they came in wanting to check the progress of their order, add something, or change a detail. The event was still months away, so I was looking ahead to many more of these meetings.

I was just starting back to my office when I heard the elevator open in the hallway and then moments later the chattering I knew so well. The voices grew louder as they came down the hallway. My parents' voices carried, and I could clearly hear them going back and forth in Russian. Hearing that made me feel happy in a way not much else did. It was familiar and reassuring, a throwback to my childhood and a reminder of not only my roots, but the strength of the family I had behind me. My parents had been married for almost fifty years, and while they bickered and picked at each other like the little old couple they were, they also still cuddled and loved on one another like they were still dating.

I loved just listening to them go back and forth in Russian; some of the words and phrases were far more meaningful in the native tongue than they would be if they tried to translate them over to English before they said them. That was one of my favorite parts of speaking both languages fluently. I could tell the distinct differences and what things meant when they were spoken in their intended language versus the other. Sometimes English just didn't do justice to what a phrase would mean in Russian, and sometimes there just wasn't a way to put into Russian what I could in English slang. It wasn't unheard of for my family to carry on conversations that bounced between the languages even in midsentence.

Finally, the main door to the office floor flew open and my parents walked in. I opened my arms, and my mother slid into a hug. She kissed me several times on each cheek, pressed her hands to my face and pulled back to look at me, then pulled me back in for several more kisses. Somehow, she was always able to make me feel like I was still a little boy and she needed to make sure I was all right.

We exchanged a few words in Russian, and then I turned to my father, who was waiting for his own hug. A tall, strong man, he was where I got most of my looks as opposed to my small, somewhat doughy mother. Her hugs were soft and pillowy, comforting in a way that could get anyone through any difficult situation, or make them feel like the most important person in the world. On the other hand, my father's hugs were strong and firm, sturdy and reassuring in a way that made it seem like everything was fine and would work out even if they seemed bleak. But when things were going well, both types of hugs were just warm and happy, and I was always happy to see them.

"Gina," my father said, opening his hands as he walked toward her desk.

My assistant stood and came toward him. Dad cupped her face and kissed her on each cheek. Gina greeted him, then went for a hug from my mother. They had both become very fond of my assistant over the years and made it a point to visit with her whenever they came into the office. From across the room, I could see Bridgit eyeing them curiously as she pretended to be working on the copier. Now wasn't the time to introduce her. I needed to get my own thoughts about her under control before I risked talking to them about her. They weren't exactly subtle or discreet, and there was always the chance they would say something to her.

"Have you had lunch yet?" I asked my mother and father. They shook their heads. "Then let's go. I'll shut down for the day."

"Can you do that?" Mom asked.

"Of course. I own the company," I said, putting my arm around her. I looked over at Gina. "You two take the rest of the day, too. Just cancel my meeting for this afternoon. Tell Mrs. Johnson she can come in next week and we'll talk about everything."

Gina grinned. "Sure thing."

Bridgit hurried over to her desk and grabbed her bag, then went to Gina's desk and picked up a coffee travel tumbler. She flashed a quick smile at me, and I swore I could feel my mother's questioning look. I didn't look her way or acknowledge it. That wasn't going to stop her, but it might keep her from saying anything until Brigit was gone. We waited in the office while she left, and I couldn't help but notice my father follow her with his eyes as she swept past, then look at me with questioning in the raise of his eyebrows.

Gina made the phone call to cancel the meeting while I went into my office to get everything I needed before leaving. We said goodbye, and I locked the office door. Just as I turned around, Mom pounced.

"Who is the new girl, Drei?" she asked.

"That's Bridgit. She's my new secretary," I answered. "Things were getting busier and we needed more help around the office."

"She's a pretty one."

"Gina hired her," I clarified, hoping that would put them off my scent.

"She's just your type, son," Dad said.

And there it was.

I sighed as we made our way down the sidewalk. I wanted to deny it. I wanted to be able to just say that had nothing to do with anything and I didn't have a type, but it would have been futile. My parents knew me and were always able to tell when I was lying to them. Besides, it would be ridiculous to even try to deny it, considering how much Bridgit looked like my ex-wife. A younger, less jaded version, perhaps, but very much like her. But that was definitely where the similarities ended. Both might have been my type with their appearances, but they couldn't have been more different in their personalities.

I let my parents choose the restaurant where we would have lunch and wasn't surprised when Mom chose a little Chinese place around the corner. She still cooked for her and my father every day and was very picky when it came to the traditional foods. The Russian restaurant where I ate with Gus didn't appeal to her, but she thought of Chinese food as a guilty pleasure. It was funny to see her talk about it like it was some sort of illicit thrill.

After lunch I had no intention of going back to the office. Even though I saw my parents fairly frequently, it had been a while since we'd spent more than a brief time together, and I wanted to spend the day with them. They tended to be homebodies, preferring to spend most of their time in the heavily Russian neighborhood where I grew up, so when they ventured out to see me, I liked to bring them on adventures. They told me what they wanted to do, and I made sure it happened for them. That day became a sequence of museums followed by a long walk around Central Park. Mom delighted in a horse-drawn carriage ride even if it made me feel silly, and Dad sat happily staring into the fountain for half an hour. It was early evening by the time we started toward their house.

"Call Gus," Mom told me. "Tell him dinner will be ready in an hour."

She said it casually, like it was a foregone conclusion my best friend would be coming for dinner. She had all but adopted Gus as another son when we were much younger, so she always figured he would be there with us. I called him, and he didn't hesitate to agree. Mom had already done some of the preparation for dinner before they came to my office, and the lingering scent of the food made my mouth water. She disappeared into the kitchen where I knew she was tying on her favorite apron and diving into cooking a massive family meal. I had to smile. This was her intention all along. Coming to the office was just a ploy to lure me home. Not that I minded.

Gus got to the apartment, and Dad welcomed him with a shot of vodka. We sat in the living room talking while Mom finished cooking and loaded the big dining room table with platters after platter of food. The vodka kept flowing throughout dinner, and I knew I'd feel it in the morning. I wasn't as young as I used to be, and the vodka hit me harder now. But that didn't deter me. I loved sitting there at the table with my family, laughing and sharing.

My father seemed immune to the effects of the vodka, and I wondered if that would come with age. Until then, I was just very glad I owned my own company. If I woke up in the morning wishing I could take my head off and set it aside for a few hours, I didn't have to worry about my boss firing me for not showing up to work on time. The worst I might face is Gina making fun of me.

CHAPTER 8

BRIDGIT

It turned out time went by much faster when I had a better grasp of what I was doing at the office. I wouldn't go so far as to say I'd gotten it all the way down and was excelling at my new position, but at least I wasn't causing mini catastrophes at regular intervals throughout the day. That week flew by, and before I knew it, it was Friday and we were getting ready to sign off for the day. I didn't have any plans for the weekend, of course. There wasn't really much to do when you had no friends outside of the people you worked with and no money to do anything with. It probably meant two days of sitting around my apartment in grungy clothes and binge-watching shows about auditioning for professional cheerleading. That was something about watching that competition that both inspired me and made me feel terrible about myself. In short, the gaudy reality TV version of Oscar bait.

I was actually starting to look forward to getting home and diving into my weekend as a couch potato. I might even break into some of the meat stuffed into the back of my freezer for emergency provisions to make tacos. I didn't know why, but that sounded strangely delicious and applicable for my watch party of one. As I was heading out, I stopped by Gina's desk. She had been busy throughout the day, and we didn't have as much time as we usually did to chat.

"I'm heading out," I told her. "See you Monday."

"Actually, I need you to hang on for a second," she said.

I was surprised she was stopping me. Usually if we didn't leave together, I was the one trying to linger on at the end of the day because I was trying to figure something out or just didn't feel like going home to The Emptiness of my apartment, and she was the one hurrying me out. Her waylaying me felt almost ominous. Maybe I wasn't catching on as fast as I thought I was and had screwed something up so royally I needed to stay after and fix it. Could they give detention at work?

"Everything okay?" I asked, trying to stay casual despite the nervousness now creeping up my spine.

"Just give me one second," she said, getting up from her desk and disappearing through the door that led to the hallway.

I could probably have escaped at that point. If she was going out into the hall, that meant she was heading down to the offices and it would take her a few minutes to make her way back. But I figured that wasn't the best plan. She'd notice I was gone, and if I actually had done something, it would make it worse. I waited there until she finally came back in. The smile on her face took away some of the nervousness, and I noticed her hand behind her back.

"We don't do direct deposit since we're so small. But here, welcome to the family."

Gina's hand shot out from behind her back toward me,

and I saw she was gripping an envelope. I took it from her and took out what was inside. My heart jumped a little when I saw my first paycheck. I'd forgotten today was payday, and this was the best surprise I could have asked for. I stared down at it trying my best not to cry.

We'd talked about money, of course. It was part of the second interview and then was finalized when Gina called to offer me the position. But there was a difference between the abstract sum in my head and actually seeing a paycheck with my name on it. This was mine. I'd earned it. And for all I knew, it was fairly good. Regardless, it was the first time I'd ever seen something like that, and I was happier than I even thought I would be. Sniffling, I choked back the tears and forced a broad smile to keep them at bay.

"I'm totally celebrating!" I said.

Gina nodded, smiling broadly. A couple days before, she'd finally admitted to me Steven had told her everything when he asked about getting me the position with the company. As much as I have wanted to keep my past to myself, I figured she needed to know the details if he was going to ask her to do that for me. And in a way it was good knowing I wasn't keeping something from her. That made it mean even more when she smiled, seeming truly happy for me. She knew this was a monumental moment for me and wanted to be a part of it.

"Let's go," she said, flashing the keys to the office. Andrei had taken another half day, so it was just the two of us. We headed out, and she locked up the office. "Where do you want to go? There's a really cute bar I know that's not too far away."

"That sounds great," I said, then stopped her. "Actually, there's one stop I need to make first. Is that okay?"

Gina shrugged. "Sure. It's your big moment. You decide how to celebrate."

I laughed. "Well, it's not exactly part of the celebration, but it's something I've been needing to do. Now is the perfect time to do it."

She followed me as I led her down a few blocks to the closest bank. All my life I'd only ever had access to bank accounts filled and controlled by my parents. They monitored every transaction and were able to close it down as soon as they kicked me out of their lives. Setting up my own account that was just mine and couldn't be messed with by anybody was another step toward independence.

We got into the lobby just in time before they started to close, and one of the bankers waved me into her cubicle off to the side. I filled out all the paperwork and started the account, happily handing over my paycheck as my first deposit. The banker handed back a few bills I requested, and I tucked them into my pocket. It wasn't much, but it felt good to have money in my pocket again, especially since it was actually mine.

We left the bank and caught a cab to the bar Gina was talking about. It turned out to be just down the street from my apartment, though I didn't mention it. We walked inside, and the vibrant energy of the space immediately filled me with excitement. It had been a long time since I'd felt alive and excited like this, and I looked forward to enjoying the evening with Gina. We sat down at the bar, and a few seconds later the bartender walked up to us.

"Can I get you something?" he asked.

"IPA," Gina ordered.

"Whiskey sour for me," I said.

He nodded and slid a food menu across the bar toward

us before walking away to make our drinks. I perused the offerings, deciding to splurge a bit and order an appetizer.

"What looks good?" Gina asked. "I'm buying."

"Nope," I said. "This is my treat."

"I want to celebrate," she said. "It's to congratulate you."

"And I want to thank you for everything you've done for me. No one else would put up with everything I've put you through since you hired me, and I appreciate it. I know you hired me as a favor for my brother, but it means the world to me and I really do want to get to the point where you feel like it was a good choice."

"I already do," she said.

I smiled and an idea popped into my head.

"Let's call Steven! He should be here for this, too."

Before I could even get my phone out, a man sidled up to the stool beside me and sat down. The bartender set my drink in front of me, and the man pointed to it.

"I'm buying that," he said.

"No, he's not," I said quickly, then looked at him. "I appreciate it, but no, thank you."

"Come on, don't be like that. Let me buy you a drink," he said.

"I said no, thank you," I reiterated. "I'm here with my friend."

It was meant to be a polite, gentle way to tell him I wasn't interested, but he wasn't getting the hint. Instead, the man looked around me at Gina and looked her up and down like he was evaluating her.

"I'll buy her a drink, too, so she'll have something to keep her occupied while we talk," he said.

"Excuse me?" Gina asked, understandably offended by the statement.

"Just calm down," he said.

I held up a hand to stop the man from saying anything else.

"Don't tell her to calm down," I said. "Don't talk to her like that."

"Look, you don't need to get so worked up. I tell you what. Why don't I buy both of you drinks, we'll get to know each other, and see what happens? Then maybe I can find somebody for her and we can enjoy some time just the two of us," he said.

By now the bartender had been listening into the conversation and took a step toward us. I thought he was about to get involved, but he suddenly stopped, his eyes snapping up over the man's head. Before I could turn to see what he was looking at, two huge hands dropped down on the man's shoulders. They squeezed tightly, and I immediately felt the tension and discomfort ease from me. I knew those hands. I'd stared at them and wondered how they'd feel on my body more times than I cared to admit.

"The lady told you to fuck off," Andrei growled.

He didn't need to raise his voice to ensure his intentions were very clear. He was sheer alpha intimidation, and the man on the stool beside me immediately cowered. All his swagger gone, he slid off the stool and backed up, his hands held up in front of him in surrender.

"I didn't mean any trouble," he said.

Obviously not interested in having any more of a confrontation with the great bear of a man hovering over him, he ducked away and disappeared into the crowd.

"Are you okay?" Andrei asked, looking right at me.

I nodded, the flutters in my heart having nothing to do with the unpleasant showdown with the man.

"Thank you for that. He just came out of nowhere," I told him.

"Are you going to tell me you've never had something like that happen to you?" he asked with a smirk that said he didn't believe it.

As flattering as it was to know he obviously thought I got hit on all the time, I couldn't pretend I was prepared for the unwanted attention. I shook my head.

"Actually, no. Believe it or not, I haven't spent a lot of time in bars like this. Up until now most of my socialization has been in country clubs and at parties where everyone had a proper stick up their ass."

I knew how it sounded, but there was really no other way to put it. At least he was decent enough to not make fun of me. Instead, he reached out and grabbed my drink. He gestured at the bartender, who nodded in return.

"Come on. Come sit with us," he said.

Without waiting for me to answer, he started away from the bar. I didn't know what to say, so I fell into step behind him and followed him to a booth at the back of the bar. Another unfairly attractive man was sitting there sipping a beer, and he smiled as we approached.

CHAPTER 9

ANDREI

I felt better having Bridgit away from the bar and at the booth with me. Whether she was used to being hit on or not, there were enough leering eyes throughout the bar that night to make it obvious if she was going to be spending any time in bars from now on, she needed to get used to it. I, for one, was not a fan of that idea. We got to the booth, and I ushered her in front of me, gesturing at Gus.

"Gus, this is Bridgit. Bridgit, this is Gus, my best friend," I introduced.

"Oh," she said. "It's nice to meet you."

Gus nodded. "Nice to meet you, too. You all right?"

She nodded, waving her hand like she just wanted to get the whole idea of that guy and what she just went through out of the air.

"I'm fine. Thanks. Rude, offensive guys at the bar are kind of a trope, so I guess it was about time I experienced it."

She laughed and I saw Gus's eyes flicker over to me, like

he was acknowledging what I'd told him about her. I gestured at the booth.

"Go ahead and sit," I told her.

"How you doing, Gus?" Gina said as she joined him on the opposite side of the booth.

"Doing good. How about you, Gina? Keeping this guy in line at the office?"

"Doing what I can. You know him. Last week it was all I could do to stop him from eating all the caviar and dancing on the conveyor," she said.

It was a comfortable, easy exchange, and I had to laugh. The two of them were like peas in a pod. They only knew each other through me, and never saw each other in any context that didn't involve me, but when they got together, they were like old friends. Their mutual love of teasing me helped keep the momentum going.

Bridgit slid into place, and I sat down beside her, moving close enough to make sure any other assholes who might be lurking around the bar knew she was with me. When I first looked up and noticed her sitting at the bar with Gina, it was amusing, but not that much of a surprise. This was one of Gina's favorite spots. In fact, she was the one who'd introduced me to it during one of her campaigns to get me out of my personal funk.

When I noticed Bridgit sitting there, it was a chance to show her to Gus so he would understand my reaction to her. I didn't know if I was going to even go up to them. They seemed to be having a girls' night, and I didn't want to interfere. But when that guy walked up to her, it caught my attention. I didn't move immediately, but I watched carefully. Bridgit was holding her own at first, and I tried to keep myself calm. But then he pushed too far, and I saw red. She was trying to get him away from her, and he kept trying to force his attention on her. That wasn't going to stand with me. Whatever I had tried to tell myself about my spark of jealousy just being a need to protect a female from an overly aggressive douchebag, went out the window. I didn't want that asshole, or any others anywhere near her.

Gus encouraged me to interfere, but I didn't need the push. Nothing would have stopped me. It took every bit of control I had not to pulverize the guy as soon as I got my hands on him, but I managed, and he got away. I immediately took Bridgit away, not wanting her to be on her own for another minute.

Now she was there sitting beside me, and I felt far more comfortable. She was safe with me, and I had the chance to be close to her. Admittedly, it was a sticky situation, me being her boss and all, but I shoved that out of my mind and just enjoyed feeling the heat coming off her against my side. I wasn't going to question her easing closer to me across the bench or the easy way she fit into the group.

Forcing the anger of the confrontation and the strange dynamic of wanting to protect her out of my head, I tuned in to the conversation she was having with Gina and Gus.

"How have you been enjoying working at the office?" Gus was asking Bridgit.

She nodded. "It's been good. I still have some to learn, but I'm getting there. It's definitely better than some of the alternatives I considered."

Gus looked at her strangely.

"Alternatives?" he asked. "Like what?"

"Toll collector. Parking meter enforcement. Crime scene cleanup," she answered without hesitation.

Gus and I laughed.

"You really thought this out, didn't you?" I asked.

"Desperate times," Bridgit answered. "But none of those worked out for me."

"Why not?" Gus asked.

"Cold. Creepy," she answered.

"Which one?" Gus asked.

"Kind of all of them," she said.

Gina reached across the table and squeezed her hand.

"Well, I'm glad they didn't work out. Their loss. I'd rather have you at the office with me, anyway," she said. "And I am especially glad to be here with you today while you celebrate."

"Celebrate?" I asked. "What are you celebrating?"

Bridgit blushed and looked down.

"You're going to think it's silly," she said.

"No, he won't," Gina said.

"Tell me," I nudged.

Bridgit let out a sigh and looked over at me.

"Today was payday and I got my first paycheck. As in... my first paycheck of my life," she told me. "I've never actually had a job or gotten paid for anything, and it was really exciting to earn my own money. I went to the bank and opened the first bank account I've had that was just in my name. It might sound ridiculous, but it was really exciting for me."

Some of the same defensive edge she had in her voice when I found her having lunch out by the loading dock had crept back into the words, and I wanted to settle her down again.

"I don't think it's ridiculous at all," I told her. "That's very exciting. I remember when I first started making money, and it was a big deal. Congratulations. You should be proud of yourself for standing on your own two feet."

She looked at me for a second, and her soft lips turned up into a smile.

"Thank you."

The smile lighting up her eyes made the anger burn in my chest. All the rage from before came rushing back now that I knew the asshole had bothered her when she was here doing something so pure and innocent as celebrating her first paycheck. Just like I told her, it was a big deal for her. Knowing her backstory, I wasn't at all surprised to find out she had never gotten a paycheck before. Being out on her own for the very first time was probably scary and earning money for herself was a major step. She deserved to feel great about it and be proud. And she deserved to celebrate without some arrogant ass getting in her way and trying to force himself on her.

Right then, I vowed to myself to make it up to her.

Lifting my hand above my head, I got the attention of a passing waitress. She came to the edge of the table, and I saw her look at both the girls, a flicker of disappointment crossing her eyes. Gus and I had been on our own the first time she came by and had openly flirted with both of us, to no avail. Now she was seeing two women with us brought a droop in her posture.

I ordered another round of drinks and several types of food. Talking to the waitress gave a break in the conversation that let me steer it toward less sticky topics. Bridgit didn't need to be scrutinized anymore or feel like she had to talk about things that probably weren't the most comfortable for her. Instead, we talked about movies and books and ate our way through plates of nachos, burgers, fried cheese, and potato skins. Out of the corner of my eye, I watched Bridgit unabashedly dive into the food and enjoy every single bite. It was a major turn-on.

I'd never liked the withering type of woman who acted like she never ate or would only pick at salads when out in public. I loved to see a woman enjoy eating and not feel uncomfortable about it. The four of us kept talking, laughing, and eating, and by the time I realized how late it was getting, I was glad we were only partway through a third round of drinks. Only a few sips out of her glass, Bridgit sat back and let out a sigh. I looked over at her.

"You okay?" I asked.

"Just a little tired," she told me. "I think I'm ready to head home."

"Let me make sure you get there safely," I told her. "I'll call you a cab."

She shook her head. "You don't need to. I actually live just a couple blocks from here."

I slid out of the booth and glanced around to make sure no one was paying attention and might have heard her say she lived close, then reached in for her hand to help her out onto her feet.

"I'll walk you," I told her. "Gus, Gina, have a good night."

Gus was grinning at me, and I could see a smart comment forming in his head, so I herded Bridgit away before he could. She waved at Gina, and we headed out of the bar into the cool night.

CHAPTER 10

BRIDGIT

As we left the bar, I could feel the alcohol running through my veins, warming me up and making my head feel a little lighter. I definitely wouldn't go so far as to say I was drunk. I hadn't drunk enough to compromise my thinking or put me in any danger. Just enough to loosen me up a tiny bit so I felt more relaxed. The drinks took away my inhibitions and made me more willing to go along with what I was feeling. Which in that moment meant bringing Andrei into my apartment with me.

That wasn't the intention. I never wanted anyone but Steven to see the tiny studio and know it was what I called home. Obviously, I appreciated what my brother did for me, and I knew if I told him it made me uncomfortable, he would do everything he could to find me a new place. But I didn't want to put him out any more than I already had. Staying here meant he could keep flying under the radar with our parents and they wouldn't know where I was. It was worth it for that, but I still didn't want to open that part of my life up to new people, especially Andrei.

I looked around the sparse studio populated with the few pieces of furniture and hanging rack of clothes that represented all my worldly possessions. Embarrassment quickly took over. I really, really didn't want my powerful, sophisticated millionaire boss seeing this. I couldn't even imagine what he was thinking as he surveyed the murphy bed I always kept pulled down rather than tucking it back into the wall and the patio table I'd snagged when a neighbor was moving out. It was humiliating, and I couldn't help but wonder if what he thought of me changed as soon as he saw it.

Just thinking that way brought up a whole new set of feelings. It was upsetting that I'd be this wrapped up in material things I'd worry Andrei would change his entire perception of me based on where I lived and what I owned. Both as my boss and just as another human being. It was another product of the way I was raised I never really thought about before, but that was brought into laser focus by my change in circumstances. Now that I was living a totally different life, I had to look at myself in a new light.

I tried to wish away the feelings, to push aside the discomfort and embarrassment. But I could see him cataloguing the space and evaluating it. I wanted it to stop. This wasn't why we were here. To be honest, I didn't know why we were here. I didn't make a conscious decision to bring him back to my apartment or to let him walk me inside. I definitely didn't mean to shut the door behind us and let him come further in.

But we were here now, and I knew what I wanted. There was one surefire way to get his attention, and I wasn't going to hold back anymore. The buzz was starting to leave me, but my crush on Andrei was simmering just below the surface. It wasn't going away, and if I was ever going to be a time to do something about it, now was it. I took a deep breath and took a few steps to close the space between us. Rising up on the balls of my feet, I wrapped my hands around the back of his neck and kissed him.

I didn't know how he was going to react, but I didn't need to wait long to find out. He instantly kissed me back, and I couldn't help but let out a little sigh. The sound was enough for him to pull me closer, crushing his mouth against mine for a harder kiss. Suddenly, he pulled back. The loss of the warmth of his lips on mine was disappointing, and I strained to find more of it, but Andrei kept me at bay, tilting his face until he met my eyes.

"Are you sure about this? It will change things," he said.

His eyes searched my face, trying to figure out what I was feeling and thinking. I nodded.

"Yes. I'm totally sure."

I would have said anything to get his hands back on me. Fortunately, it didn't take any more than that.

Strong, thick fingers wrapped around my waist and pulled me in tight. I could feel his cock twitch inside his pants as his body rubbed against mine, and I pushed my hips forward to meet it. His scent was intoxicating, and I found myself moving my lips from his to his neck and running my own delicate fingers across his muscular chest. Suddenly, I felt cool air on my legs as he pulled my dress up over my hips. His intense grip seized my ass and picked me up so I could wrap my legs around his waist, and he walked me to the small murphy bed.

I giggled as he tossed me onto the bed, and I bounced. Getting up on my knees, I pulled the dress up and over my head, finding his kiss searching for mine as soon as it was off. I fumbled for his buttons and began to undo them as he reached behind me and unsnapped my bra in one fluid motion. It slid down my arms, and my heavy, perky breasts spilled out and into the cool air of the room.

Kisses trailed down my neck to my collarbone as his hands filled with my breasts. I let my head hang back and focused on the warmth of his lips on my skin and the tingling sensation between my thighs as he worked his way down. His tongue slid between my breasts, and a hand slid into my wet panties. I moaned, clutching his hair and clawing at his back with my free hand. He licked my sensitive nipple, and a finger found my core and immediately sought out my clit. An explosion of intense pleasure rolled through my body as he twirled the pad of his middle finger around my clit and gently, but firmly, encouraged it out.

Slowly he worked his way down my stomach, and I pulled him up by his chin to crush another kiss onto his lips. As I did, I was finally able to work his shirt completely open, and he tore it away from himself, tossing it into a corner of the room. I ran my palm down his chest and down the crease of his pants, feeling the shape of his engorged cock beneath the layers. My breath hitched at the anticipation of it inside me, filling me. Eagerly I unzipped him and tore at his belt until it loosened, and I could unbutton the pants. As they fell away, I shoved my hand into the elastic waistband of his boxer briefs and wrapped it around the base of his massive cock.

As I began to stroke him, he moaned, and the vibration rattled from deep in his chest and straight through into me. Just hearing his involuntary reaction of pleasure at my touch was tantalizing, and my body broke out into goose bumps despite feeling hot and slick with sweat. I pulled on the waistband and let his cock spring out, and a smile stretched across my face. My eyes met his and I scooted down, lying on my stomach as I stroked him and placed my lips at the tip of his head. I stretched out my tongue to swirl around it, letting it linger on the sensitive area underneath before I took him into my mouth. Easing him down into my throat, I relished in the sensation of his thick erection growing even harder as my tongue slid around him and I tasted the salty sweetness of his skin.

One of his hands slid into my hair, and he began to guide me as I bobbed back and forth on him. The other reached down to cup one of my breasts, and I moaned at his touch. The vibration of my voice on his cock only seemed to amplify his pleasure, and he began to rock into me, taking control, and I let him completely dominate me. I slid one hand underneath to massage his balls as I tried to relax and let him get as deep as possible.

With a gentle but firm motion he pulled out of my mouth with a pop and turned me so that I lay on my back on the bed. His mouth crashed down onto mine as he pulled aside my soaking panties to expose my pussy, and a finger slid through my folds and deep into me. I cried out and temporarily lost control as the pad of his thumb made slow circular motions on my clit as his finger penetrated deeper inside me. I knew I wouldn't be able to control myself for long and desired his enormous cock to be buried deep in me soon.

Suddenly, I felt the wave of an orgasm begin to wash out over me, and I reached down to grab his wrist, holding him in place while my hips bucked. Having his finger inside me, his thumb pressing into my clit sent me over the edge, and I climaxed hard, my body writhing on the bed and leaving me breathless and temporarily dizzy. I lay back as he spun me around, pulling my legs to the edge of the bed and then resting my ankles on his shoulders. Before I had a chance to prepare, he plunged into me, his cock stretching me wide and bringing me perilously close to the edge between pleasure and pain. I rode that line as he rocked back and slammed into me again and couldn't stop the cries that bubbled up from my chest.

He thrust into me over and over, his hands gripping my hips as he fucked me deeply. I tried to breathe and let my body relax to open for him, to stretch for him as his cock brushed areas inside me that brought new waves of ecstasy. I clenched my fingers over his elbows as he began to slam into me faster, grunts of effort and pleasure rumbling from his chest. I was overwhelmed by him, consumed by him and his scent, his taste, his dominance of my body. I could think of nothing but the hunger for his body to be inside mine, for my slick juices to cover his cock and welcome him inside me. He took that invitation with gusto, and soon I felt myself trembling as another epic orgasm began to build.

I looked up to watch him as he focused on my body, his eyes tracing the curvature of my breasts as they bounced with every thrust. I felt beautiful and sexy and desired. My toes curled as I let the wave wash over me, and my body clenched around him. Suddenly he roared out and slammed deep inside me, his cock throbbing as he came. My body milked him until he was empty, and he shuddered and rocked a few more times as he spent every last drop of his seed into my eager body. He collapsed into my arms, and we lay there in the remnants of our sweat on the crumpled sheets.

Half an hour later, I lay on my side, my hand propping up my head as I watched Andrei get dressed. I didn't regret a single second of what happened between us. In fact, the most prevalent thought running through my head, other than how incredible he looked without clothes, was wondering when we could do it again. Being that forward about something like that wouldn't be something I'd usually do. I wasn't used to having to exert myself or be bold in situations like this. But that was the past. Now was different, and I wasn't going to let other people dictate how I thought or went after what I wanted.

Pulling up to a sitting position, I eased closer to the edge of the bed and reached out to run my hand down Andrei's chest.

"When do we get to do that again?" I asked.

He grinned at me and buttoned the last button before leaning down to kiss me.

"We'll work it out," he promised. "But this stays out of the office, okay? Nobody knows about it but the two of us."

I nodded, not at all put off by the conditions. If anything, I was relieved. There was enough upheaval and change going on in my life, and I'd already had my fair share of scrutiny and judgment. The last thing I needed was for the people at work to find out I was sleeping with the boss. This was for me, and I just wanted to enjoy it without it getting more complicated or dramatic. I reached up and pulled Andrei down for another kiss to seal the agreement before he left.

CHAPTER 11

ANDREI

I wish I'd spent the night at Bridgit's apartment. It was the first thought that went through my mind when I got home after leaving her place, and it was still there when I woke up the next morning. That was strange for me. I was never the sleepover type of guy. Especially when it came to women I wasn't in a relationship with. Of course, those parameters didn't give me a whole lot to work with considering my experience with true relationships was slim. I'd only dated a few women before Katya, and then we got married fairly quickly. It was what was expected of us. After the divorce, I tried to jump back into the dating game, but that was a failure right from the beginning. It turned out getting my heart put through the grinder of my marriage ending wasn't exactly conducive to finding love again. Or even a casual fling.

It didn't take long for me to realize I just wasn't interested in trying to be with anyone else. The need for emotional attachment wasn't there, and the libido wasn't there. It was just easier to go about my life on my own. But now I found myself alone in my empty house, wishing I hadn't left her there in the crummy murphy bed in the tiny studio apartment. Despite the unbelievably limited space and spartan conditions, I'd actually rather still be there with her than in my big, comfortable house without her. Not the least reason being I liked the idea of rolling over after a couple hours of sleep and finding her naked body there waiting for me. That was better than counting sheep any day.

I woke up to the sound of my phone alerting me to a new text, and my first thought was hoping it was Bridgit. Of course, that was ridiculous. She didn't have my personal cell number, which I intended to change, and she didn't strike me as the kind of woman to call first thing in the morning the next day. She was the kind of woman who would make it clear she was interested in more but wouldn't have to reassure herself by checking in immediately. That made her even more appealing, and I found myself wanting to be the one to call. But I stopped myself. We weren't in high school, and we'd done nothing wrong. I didn't need to check in and make sure everything was all right between us.

Besides, the alert on my phone was from Gus telling me to get my ass in gear and meet him for breakfast at the diner. I forgot we'd made those plans. I needed to get to the diner and face what I was sure was going to be a royal ribbing from my best friend.

From the second I walked into the diner and saw Gus, I knew I was in for it. There was no way I was going to be able to skate around what had happened the night before. The expression on his face was smug as hell, and it seemed he was primed and ready to hear the whole story. I didn't even bother to act like nothing happened. I could have. I could have just sat down across from him and had breakfast like absolutely nothing had gone on just to piss him off. But it was obvious he already knew something had happened, and the truth was, I wanted to talk about it.

"You don't look like you got a lot of sleep last night," he said when I slid into the booth across from him.

"That would be because I spent a good portion of the night not sleeping at Bridgit's place," I told him.

He laughed and leaned back in his seat.

"Not even going to play coy? I have to admit, I'm disappointed in you. I thought at least you'd have the decency to pretend you were a gentleman. You know, protect her honor and whatnot," he said.

"I was a perfect gentleman. I did exactly what I said and made sure she got home safely," I told him.

"Atta boy," Gus said boisterously.

The waitress came by with coffee, and we placed our order. When she was gone, I held up my cup in a toast and took a deep sip.

"And as a bonus to the whole situation—she is the one who instigated it," I told him.

"Seriously?" Gus asked. "How'd you manage that?"

I laughed.

"It's not like I planned it. I didn't pull up my skirt to show off my garter and try to seduce her," I told him. "We were just in her apartment and she kissed me."

The waitress brought us our breakfasts, and we took a few seconds to smear butter and jam on our toast, stab the yolks of our eggs, and sprinkle salt on our potatoes. As we ate, I told him about the night with Bridgit. I didn't give him details, but he didn't push, either. We could talk about the fact that it happened but weren't going to sink into the crudeness of specifics.

When I'd told him the whole story, Gus turned to the inevitable next step of the conversation.

"So, what's next?" he asked.

That question was going to come. It had to. I couldn't just tell him I'd slept with the gorgeous new employee I'd been lusting after since the first second I saw her and not expect him to want to know how I planned to move forward.

"We haven't really decided that," I told him. "It's not like we had a debriefing at the end and talked everything through. We definitely don't want it to be a onetime thing, though."

"I know you, so I know you're not going to make her a mistress, but you are going to keep it out of work, right? Keep it separate from everything else?" he asked.

I nodded.

"Absolutely. That's one thing we did establish. Both of us were in agreement we didn't want to bring it with us into the office. Whatever is going on between us and whatever else it leads to, we didn't want anyone at work to know about it. That could bring up all sorts of drama and complications I'm not interested in dealing with right now. And, yes, I'm definitely not planning on making her my mistress," I told him.

"Why does it sound like there's some hesitation behind that?" he asked.

I ate a few bites of my eggs, trying to come up with exactly how I was going to explain what I was feeling. I couldn't really figure it out for myself. It was so unexpected, I didn't know what I was going to be thinking or feeling in the next moment, or how I could reconcile all the different thoughts going through my mind.

"It's not that I want her to be a kept woman. After what

71

she's been through, that's not something she would want, anyway. You heard her yesterday when she was telling us how happy she was about getting her first paycheck. It was a huge deal to her to finally have earned her own money."

"That's right," Gus said, nodding as he set down his glass of juice. "What was that all about? You didn't tell me her story."

"I didn't actually know it until Gina told me a few days ago. It turns out this is her first job because she comes from a really wealthy and powerful family. Do you remember when I worked with the Holliday family a few years ago on that event?" I asked.

"Vaguely."

I nodded. "That was her family. I never met her, but I worked with her brother. Her parents tried to force her to marry some guy, and when she refused, they cut her off. They just threw her out without anything and not caring what happened to her so they could save face. So, her brother Steven got in touch with Gina to see if she would hire Bridgit. That's why she was so excited to celebrate her first paycheck. She's never gotten one before, and it's the first time she's had a chance to feel like she was really doing something for herself."

"That's crazy. I can't believe parents would do something like that to their own child," he said.

"Neither can I. Especially growing up with parents like we had. But that's exactly why I could never put her in that kind of position. She wouldn't want me to take over and start paying for everything. She wants to be able to take care of herself and feel like she's standing on her own two feet. Even more than that, she wants to feel like she's able to make her own choices and not have to answer to anyone. If I was taking care of her, it would be little different than being under the control of her parents. She would feel like she wasn't really leading her own life, and that's the last thing she needs right now."

"But?"

"But you should have seen her apartment. I know my parents aren't wealthy and we both grew up in modest circumstances, but her place is not even close to that. It's like a landing pad for broke college kids who flunked out and don't want to work. She didn't complain about it, but maybe there's something I can do about that for her," I said.

"Without it getting in the way of anything else?" Gus asked.

I nodded.

"We agreed it won't interfere, and I'm going to keep up my end of that because I'm definitely not done with her yet."

I grinned and Gus shook his head, laughing as he went back to his breakfast. When we were finished eating, we talked about some upcoming plans before going our separate ways. I opened my phone to check my to-do list. There were several things I needed to get done that day, starting with picking up a few groceries. Gina always told me I could afford to have someone do things like that for me, but I didn't see the point in that. Just because I had money didn't mean I was helpless. As my assistant, there were things Gina took care of for me related to work, but outside of that, I preferred to handle things on my own. My parents wouldn't want me to become one of those spoiled rich people who took advantage of others, and I didn't want to be that type of person, either.

I spent the rest of the day catching up on errands and then headed into the office to take care of some work leftover from the week before. The half days I'd taken over the last couple of weeks weren't the norm for me, and I was feeling the effects of more work lingering on undone than I usually had. I wasn't behind on anything—my deadlines were still days or even weeks away—but I didn't want to get even close to them. I preferred to stay well on top of my work so I never felt the crush and could manage any curve-balls that might come my way.

Saturdays at the office were usually particularly produc-tive because I was the only one there and could focus completely. That day it was harder. I was alone at the office, but my thoughts weren't on work. Every few seconds they drifted to Bridgit and the night we'd spent together. By the time I finished the work I wanted to do, it was well into the night. But the memories were definitely worth it.

CHAPTER 12

BRIDGIT

I didn't immediately open my eyes when I woke up on Saturday. There were those few moments in between sleep and consciousness when I remembered what happened the night before and tried to determine if it was real or just a dream. I absolutely could have believed it was a dream. Those were the types of things my imagination would have conjured up to fill the long night. My attraction to Andrei had only grown over the last few days and seeing him at the bar had brought it to a whole new level. I never wanted to think of myself as somebody who needed rescuing or who had to rely on a man to protect me in a sticky situation. But I had to admit having him swoop in to get that guy away from me was a nice relief. If he hadn't been there, I would have found a way to get away from him and been able to move on with my night, but it was far more enjoyable the way it turned out.

Seeing my boss suddenly burly and intense was a new side to him. The first time I saw him I noticed how big he was and knew he was probably intimidating to many people, but that had never been his personality. There was nothing gruff or aggressive about him when he was talking to Gina or to me. As soon as he got near that guy, though, something primal kicked in and he became protective and even more powerful. It was an adrenaline rush that was both exciting and a turn-on. I'd be lying if I didn't say that was when the desire for him started. Seeing that guy run away from Andrei as fast as he could and then having Andrei usher me to his private table sent a shiver through me that settled right between my thighs.

Maybe I'd taken all those feelings and mixed them up with the drinks I'd tipped back over the evening and rolled them up into an incredibly sexy dream. That thought didn't last long. It only took a few seconds for me to realize without a shadow of a doubt everything I remembered from the night before had actually happened. I could still feel him, still smell him around me. I wanted to just lie there and relish in it. This wasn't like me, and somehow that made it even better. And even better than that was him admitting to wanting more. Just the thought of another visit from him woke my body up and filled me with craving.

I allowed myself the weekend to savor the memories and enjoy thinking about Andrei. Monday morning, I forced myself to put all that to the back of my mind and started pretending nothing happened. I went into work determined to be professional and not let on to anyone what happened between me and the boss Friday night. It was the agreement we'd made, and I still wholeheartedly believed in it. I had my own reasons for it beyond avoiding gossip and drama at work.

This job wasn't just a bridge. It wasn't just something to tide me over until I could figure something else out. It was the first step in my new life, and I was determined to do it the right way. I didn't want to put my position with the company at risk and didn't want to put anything between Gina and me. She was becoming a good friend, and I was learning so much from her. I didn't want the possibility of losing any of that, especially after Steven went to bat for me. It would toss me right back down into that dark place where I didn't have anything or anyone and had no idea how I was supposed to move forward with my life. But it would also hurt my brother and disrespect everything he did for me and how much he put himself out there. I was determined to keep it to myself and not let whatever was going to happen between me and Andrei outside the office to impact anything that happened inside.

I put everything I had into working hard that day. Trying to remember everything Gina told me and all the ways she had to correct me in my first few weeks, I pushed myself to perform at my best and be as productive as humanly possible. As I did it, I kept looking over at her, scrutinizing every time she glanced my way and everything she said to me. I wondered if she somehow sensed something had changed or if she could read the expression on my face and thought something might be going on. Even if she did, she didn't say anything or make any indication of her suspicions. When I wasn't looking at her, I was looking through the glass at Andrei's office.

I couldn't help but notice he didn't spend much time at his desk that day. Instead, he climbed the short metal staircase to a large catwalk that extended out over the warehouse. It allowed him to watch operations below and keep up with what was going on. As soon as I saw it the first time, it gave me *Charlie and the Chocolate Factory* vibes. It reminded me of the spoiled little girl who stood up on the balcony with her father watching the hundreds of hired workers frantically unwrapping chocolate bars to find the coveted golden ticket. Only this time there wasn't a small army of identically dressed women shoving aside paper and foil as fast as their fingers could move. And I couldn't imagine any of Andrei's employees having the same level of fear those workers had.

I wondered what brought him out onto that platform for so much of the day. He wandered out there a couple of times a week to check in on the warehouse and make sure everything was going well. If there was a particularly large order coming in or complicated logistics being managed, he might spend more time out there and even use the staircase leading up from the warehouse floor to go down and talk to the rest of the team. But that Monday he spent far more time out there, and it wasn't lost on me he may be doing it to avoid interacting with me.

Finally, after lunch, he used the intercom on my desk to call me into the office. He didn't say what it was about, and it was difficult to decipher the tone in his voice. I agreed and walked over to Gina's desk.

"Do you have any idea what this could be about?" I asked.

"No idea," she said, shaking her head. "But don't be too worried about it. If something was wrong, I'd probably know about it first."

She winked at me, and I tried to find reassurance in it. I made my way into the office and closed the door behind me. Andrei was back at his desk, and he gestured at the chair across from him. I settled down, wondering what was going on. He hadn't told me I needed to bring my computer to take notes or find any files for him.

The walls of the office were solid glass, which meant we definitely wouldn't be doing anything sexy in here. I couldn't do anything but sit there and wait for him to say something.

"Bridgit, I wanted to talk to you about our arrangement," he said without introduction.

His hands folded on the top of his desk, and his eyes were trained directly on me. Every word he was saying was carefully thought out and specifically chosen to make sure it clearly communicated what he was intending to say to me. Only, I still didn't know what that was. I blinked a few times, then tilted my head to the side and shook it.

"Our arrangement?" I asked. "I don't know if I understand what you're talking about."

"Our arrangement," he repeated as if hearing it another time would somehow make it clearer to me what he was talking about. "What happened between us."

It hit me and I felt struck by his choice of words.

"Oh," I finally managed. "That arrangement."

"Yes," Andrei said. "I think it's important for us to discuss the terms to ensure we're on the same page about everything."

The words made my stomach start to turn. I didn't like the sick feeling that was forming in my gut, and I tried to fight it back. I knew we were keeping what had happened out of the public eye, but the way he was talking now sounded rather clinical. I didn't care for it. Before we did anything, he was very careful to ask me if I was sure and specifically said if we went through with it, things would change. I agreed to it. I didn't even hesitate. I was sure about what I was doing, and so was he, so there was no going back on that now. Still, it felt wrong.

"You're right," I said, giving a resolute nod and doing everything I could not to let any emotion show on my face.

"We need to make sure we are in agreement about everything."

"Perfect. I'm glad you feel that way. We've already agreed not to allow anything personal between us to impact work. That includes not talking about it with anyone who works here or showing any special attention to each other while we are here," he said.

I swallowed the bitter taste rising in my throat.

"Absolutely. I wouldn't want anyone to think anything is happening or that it may be influencing my position here," I told him.

"Good. We will see each other when it is convenient for both of us. I will pay for any activities, meals, or other costs. And speaking of which, I know you're just getting started on your own. If you need anything, don't hesitate to let me know. I'd be happy to help you."

I nodded woodenly but didn't argue or walk out. After all, this was what I'd agreed to. I agreed no one would know and everything would change. Really, it wasn't all that surprising. It just meant Andrei was just like all of the other guys I'd known. There was no such thing as just having a relationship. It was all about the give-and-take, the terms that ensured each side got something out of it and was properly covered. I'd already learned there was little room for love in most pairings in my social circle. People had sex for fun and got married for society and business. Not that affection didn't sometimes develop over time, but that wasn't the primary goal. I had thought he'd be different and had to try hard hide my disappointment.

I suddenly realized that I couldn't work with him anymore. It was too uncomfortable now, too awkward. I hated the mention of me needing things and the hint at slipping me perks, essentially paying for me like I was a kept woman. That wasn't something I could deal with. It was obvious I needed to move on, but that would take some time. I decided right then I would keep my distance while I saved money to get out from this position.

Resigned to my decision, I did the one thing I appreciated my mother teaching me—I smiled at Andrei like nothing was wrong.

"Is that it?" I asked. "I have some work I need to finish."

"Yeah, I guess. Unless you have something you need to add," Andrei said.

I shook my head. "Not that I can think of. It sounds like you thought it all through."

"I'll talk to you later?" he asked.

I nodded and walked back to my desk wondering how we went from a relationship to a business transaction, but I couldn't figure out where we went wrong.

CHAPTER 13

ANDREI

The conversation I had with Bridgit on Monday didn't go exactly the way I thought it was going to. I wanted to make things straightforward and transparent between us. There was nothing ambiguous about what had happened between us or if there was consent. While I knew both of us had been drinking that night, it wasn't enough to create even a question as to whether either of us were in our right mind or if we could be trusted to make that sort of decision. We'd even made the point to verbally confirm that consent to each other, and when I pointed out to her things would change between us, Bridgit didn't hesitate. Both of us knew what we were doing and what it would mean, and afterward we were both willing to agree to keep everything out of the office. It was only the professional and responsible choice. There was no need for anybody else to know what went on between us, or to be involved in however the relationship unfolded.

That was the thing. Not talking to the people at the office wasn't about being sneaky or because I had any sort of shame about Bridgit. It was an unusual and potentially awkward situation, to be sure, but I didn't regret a single thing that happened between us, and I wasn't embarrassed about it. But if we opened up to the people around us or even just let something slip and anybody at work, from Gina to the guys in the warehouse, guessed what was happening between us, they were instantly a part of it. Especially Gina. Bridgit and I had no idea what was going to happen between us. We both said we wanted to see each other again, but maybe that would be it. Things would fizzle out and we'd realize there was a tremendous amount of sexual tension, but now that we'd broken it, we could just continue on.

I highly doubted that. The little taste of her I'd already gotten only worked to rev me up and make me want her even more. Before it was all about imagining and wondering what it would be like to touch her and hold her. But now I knew exactly what it was like, and all I could think about was how much I wanted more of it. That didn't mean I wanted to hear anybody else's opinion or let our arrangement have any impact on my company.

That's why I wanted to talk to her and clear the air. With a little bit of time separating us from our night together, we'd be able to talk it through. I knew I didn't want that to be our only night together, and she had the same thought, but we didn't talk about anything else. With my history and what she'd just been through, anything more didn't seem like an option. We needed to make things clear-cut and unambiguous for both of us so we knew where we stood. And the only way I knew how to do that was the same way I handled my business. We would sit down and talk about the terms of our arrangement, put everything out on the table, and make sure we were both still good.

It seemed like the right way to go. Mature. Responsible. Modern, even. Until she gave me that smile. I knew that smile. It wasn't the kind of smile any man wants to see on a woman he's interested in. That was the type of smile I saw women at the mind-numbing networking parties and mixers at conventions gave to the men around them. It was the type of smile that Katya used to give me. That was a smile that said she was going to stay quiet and not say anything about the situation, but only because she was choosing to hold back what she was really thinking. And it was the one Bridgit flashed me right before leaving my office.

Apparently, she didn't feel the same way about the conversation as I had. I wanted to touch base with her again, to spend a little more time with her and get her to talk to me, but so far it hadn't worked out. I didn't see her for the rest of the day on Monday, and before she even got to work on Tuesday, I got an urgent call from a supplier in Chicago. I had to jump the first flight I could and head out there for a couple of days. I'd been so busy since landing I hadn't even had a chance to check in at the office. I knew Gina could hold down the fort almost as well as I could. She knew everything there was to know about the company and could be trusted to make the types of decisions I would make. But it kept me away from Bridgit and not even able to check in with her.

The tension and anxiety were growing by the minute, and when I walked into my meeting Wednesday afternoon, the expression on my client's face told me he could tell something was going on.

"Everything all right?" he asked.

I loosened the button on the front of my jacket and dropped my briefcase to the table as I sat down. Not wanting to get into any conversation about my personal life, I brushed the question aside.

"These shipments were guaranteed to arrive at my office by tomorrow," I said, pulling papers out of my brief-case. "The communications are very clear, and I empha-sized the importance of them being on time. Now I've been informed the supply chain has been compromised. The products essential for my client's upcoming event are not only not arriving on time but are no longer accessible and have an indeterminate estimated delivery time."

Mr. Greene shifted uncomfortably in his seat. "This is an unfortunate situation, but I hope you understand it is one that is beyond our control."

"This is not beyond your control," I told him angrily. "My company has worked with yours several times, has it not?"

"Yes," he said, "but—"

"And each time we've worked together, it has been made expressly clear that there is a process the order goes through. There are set points of contact during that process that inform you of when products will arrive with you and then move ahead to my office. The purpose of those points of contact is to make sure you can keep your schedule under control and know what's happening along the way. This means you have been aware of a delay for several days, if not since the beginning of this order. You have had ample opportunity to alert me to the problem and find another supplier, but you chose not to. Now I'm in a situation where I am without the products I need, and I've had to come all the way here to deal with issues with your supplier and attempt to source alternatives so my client does not miss out on what they have already paid for and are relying on receiving."

"I understand this is an inconvenience for you..."

"This is more than an inconvenience. I am wasting a tremendous amount of time and energy, and now will lose money because items I've already paid for will need to be replaced. I will not allow my client to do without or to know there was a problem, which means I have to take it on myself. Now, I suggest you stop attempting to justify this situation and we move right into how this can be resolved. And you will be getting me my money back."

The anger was gone by the time I got back to the hotel, but the frustration was still lingering. It was less about the situation with the order, which I'd managed to resolve, and more about not being able to talk to Bridgit. I didn't realize how accustomed to seeing and talking to her I'd become until I went without it. Now I missed her and felt on edge not being able to communicate with her. Even though I was heading back to town the next day, I didn't want to wait to talk to her. I needed to at least try to get in touch with her that night.

After taking a shower and changing into boxers to sleep in, I dialed Bridgit. I was happy when she answered the phone.

"Hello?"

"Did I wake you?" I asked.

"Andrei?" she asked, and then there was a pause. "It's eight thirty."

"So, I guess I didn't wake you," I said.

"No. I was just finishing dinner and watching some TV. How's Chicago?" she asked.

"It hasn't been my favorite trip to the Windy City ever, but things are getting done. How is everything there? Are you surviving without me?"

Bridgit laughed but it sounded hollow.

"I don't know how," she said dramatically. "It's been so hard."

She was teasing, but the words went straight to my gut. I couldn't help it. I had to keep going.

"I can commiserate," I said.

Bridgit paused only for a second, like she was making sure she heard what she thought she did.

"Oh, really?" she asked.

"I've been hard ever since I started thinking about you."

Phone sex was definitely not my preferred type of sex, but just the thought of Bridgit made my whole body crave her. Hearing her voice made it almost unbearable. She made a little moaning sound, and my cock jumped, instantly hard as a rock and straining against the front of my boxers.

"What have you been thinking about?" she asked.

I smiled. It wasn't going to take any convincing to get Bridgit to join in on my little game. Maybe she wasn't as put off by our conversation as I thought she was.

"How much I wish you were here. I'm alone in this big hotel room, and I could really use some company," I told her.

"And if I was there? What would you do?"

I eased my boxers down off my hips and kicked them away so I could wrap my hand around my shaft.

"I'd undress you slowly, kissing every new inch of skin I uncovered. Then I'd lay you down on the bed and open your thighs so I could taste you. You're so sweet," I told her.

She whimpered again and I kept going, describing my tongue gathering her silky fluids and my fingers delving deep inside her. Bridgit groaned, and I could imagine her replicating the touch with her own hand. It turned me on even more, and I thought I'd totally lose control when she joined in, describing her mouth closing around my cock and sucking me. I stroked myself harder and faster when she told me how good it felt to have me inside her. We kept going, and by the time I couldn't take it anymore and exploded, I heard Bridgit let out a gasping cry and knew she'd come at the same moment.

Both our voices sleepy and satisfied, we promised to talk the next day and ended the conversation. I hung up feeling calmer and more relaxed than I had in days.

CHAPTER 14

BRIDGIT

Ugh, *what the fuck is wrong with me?* I chastised myself.

I had vowed to stay away from Andrei and just keep my head down until I could find something new, but the moment his voice had hit my ears last night, my hands had been in my panties. I was weak. But maybe that wasn't a bad thing.

Maybe it didn't have to be about him "keeping" me like a secret. Maybe I could get something out of it too. Maybe I could just have a little fun myself while I looked for an out. It wasn't like I didn't enjoy Andrei's company, and clearly even just his voice had me hot and dripping.

I decided to change my plans and enjoy myself a bit until I could make a change.

As I came to this conclusion, my phone rang and I learned yet another lesson in the workplace. Always look at your caller ID before answering your phone.

I fully expected to answer the phone and hear more

deliciously sexy suggestions, and Gina wasn't in earshot, so I let my voice fall low.

"Hey, there," I purred in a velvety tone. "I've been thinking about you."

"That's... nice," Steven said awkwardly.

Hearing my brother's voice was like getting a bucket of ice thrown in my face. A shudder rolled through me, and I squeezed my eyes closed.

Always check your caller ID before answering the phone. Lesson learned.

"Oh my God. I thought you were someone else," I told him. "What's up? Why are you calling me before nine in the morning?"

"I didn't realize was only allowed to call during a specific timeframe. Did I miss a memo?" he asked.

I started pulling out my paperwork for the morning and arranging my desk, propping my phone between my ear and my shoulder.

"No. I'm just surprised. I don't usually hear from you this early unless something terrible happened." I stopped and caught my phone in my hand, my eyes widened. "Oh, no. Did something terrible happen? Something terrible happened, didn't it?"

Steven chuckled. "Still haven't lost your flair for the dramatic I see. No, nothing terrible has happened. But you should know that Mom and Dad have been asking about you," he said.

"What?" I asked. I couldn't possibly have heard what I thought I did.

"They've been asking about you," he repeated. "The last couple of days, they've been asking a bunch of questions about you and trying to find out how you're doing. I wouldn't tell him anything, so they just kept trying. This morning they really started prying, like they're trying to push my buttons and get information from me. They want to know what you're doing, where you're living, how you're getting by. All those things," he said.

"What did you tell them?" I asked.

"Nothing. I promise," he said. "I wouldn't go to all this trouble to help you adjust to blow it by telling Mom and Dad how to hunt you down."

"Yeah, I know. But if they're asking you about me and they won't let it go, that means they were waiting for me to go crawling back to them," I said.

"Of course they were. You know them. They can't stand the idea they didn't get something they wanted. Especially when it was from their child. They fully expected you to go out into the world, fail miserably, and go whimpering back with your tail between your legs. Now that you haven't, they don't really know how to deal with it," he said.

"They know exactly how to deal with it. They're going to try to come confront me face-to-face. They figure if they're able to talk to me about it, they can convince me to see the error of my ways and get back in line with everything they want," I said. "And the thing is, you know it won't be long until they find me."

"So, what if they do? Are you going to let it change anything?" he asked.

"No. I don't feel any differently now than I did when it first happened. Actually, I take that back. I do feel different. I feel like I've grown and changed. I see the world in a new way, and I can handle this. I don't need their approval, and I definitely don't need their arranged marriage," I told him.

"Good," Steven said, sounding proud and relieved at the same time. "Then you tell them that. If they do show up, you make sure they understand exactly how you feel and that nothing is going to change. I'll be there for you."

"Thanks, bro. I really appreciate you letting me know... and everything else."

"No problem. Have a good day at work," he said and hung up.

"Yeah," I muttered under my breath as I set my phone back down on the desk. "That's totally going to happen now."

I was on edge the rest of the morning, and it didn't get too much better after lunch. When Andrei came in, I felt my heart leap and a bit of the stress and tension melt away just looking at him. He gave me a quick grin but then looked over at Gina and asked her to go to his office with her. I did my best to not stare through the glass at them and try to figure out what they were talking about, but my eyes kept wandering over. I wanted to know what was going on and why he wanted to talk to her first. When they were done talking, Gina came out of the office laughing to herself, and a surge of jealousy rushed through me.

I scolded myself as soon as I felt it. Nothing was going on between the two of them. They were close friends and had been for years, and Gina had already reassured me nothing like that had ever happened between them or ever would. She wasn't attracted to Andrei and was fairly certain he thought of her as a sister. She was just Gina to him. Despite all that, I still felt an uncomfortable twisting in my stomach at the smile on her face. It was ridiculous. I didn't have the right to be jealous. Andrei and I weren't in a relationship and had no commitment to each other. He didn't belong to me. Yet, I couldn't shake the feeling.

The tension stayed with me for the rest of the day, distracting me and making it harder to do what I needed to do. Andrei didn't acknowledge me anymore or ask me to come to his office. I was sure he would at least have me come in to say hello or send me a flirty text. It was almost as if I didn't exist. When the day finally dragged to an end, I couldn't wait to get home. I just wanted to get out of the office and go back to trying to figure out life after working here. But I didn't make it all the way out of the office.

"Bridgit, can you hang on for a second?" Andrei asked from the door to his office.

I looked over at Gina, who was gathering her things from her desk and preparing to leave. She was smirking and wouldn't make eye contact with me. I didn't like that. It wasn't the fun, silly feeling we'd had before. Gina scooped up her bag, grabbed her travel coffee tumbler, and headed toward the door. She threw me another smirking grin as she left, and I started feeling like I was being made fun of. There was some sort of joke going on, and I wasn't privy to it.

I walked back over to my desk, then dropped down in my chair feeling deflated and upset. It had been a really shitty day, and I really just wanted it to be over with. I waited there at my desk for a few minutes before his office door opened again and Andrei came out. As he came toward me, I noticed he was carrying a bag in his hand. It looked like a shopping bag from an expensive boutique, and the tufts of tissue paper coming out of the top instantly changed my thoughts.

Oh. Suddenly I knew what was going on. How could I forget I was an arrangement? I amused him while he was in his hotel room away from home, so now it was his turn to keep up his end. He smiled as he came up to the desk and handed me the bag.

"I saw this and thought of you," he said.

I took the bag with a bit of hesitation. I didn't know what might be inside. Taking a deep breath, I reached in and felt something soft and thick. Somewhat surprised by the feeling, I pulled and drew out a gorgeous pale pink peacoat. My breath caught in my throat, and my heart thudded in my chest. I couldn't believe what I was seeing. The coat was absolutely beautiful, but it still created a conflict inside me. I loved it and hated it in equal parts. Andrei stood there staring at me, and I knew I had to say something. There had to be some sort of reaction.

"Thank you," I finally managed. "It's lovely."

He nodded. "I'm glad you like it. "

His head ducked down, and he gave me a quick kiss. It shocked me. We had agreed very stringently to keep everything between us out of the office, yet he was the one to break that protocol. Of course, there was no one else around. No one could see us or would know what happened, so it didn't really matter. Something about it, though, stayed with me.

"Keep tomorrow night open. I want to see you," he said.

"Tomorrow night?" I asked.

"Yes," he said, nodding with a slight smile. "I missed you the last couple of days when I wasn't around, and I want to spend some time with you. You don't have plans already, do you?"

I shook my head.

"No," I told him. "I don't have any plans."

"Good. Then keep the evening open," he told me.

I nodded.

"Sure."

Andrei smiled wider and walked out of the office. I followed behind, trying my best not to feel like a paid escort.

CHAPTER 15

ANDREI

I woke up even earlier than usual on Friday. I'd always been a morning person and never had trouble getting up and going even before the sun came up. It made sure I got done what needed to be done during the day and helped me to stay at my most productive. But that morning I was wide-awake even earlier than I was accustomed to. I spent a little while stretched out in my bed, trying to will myself back to sleep to get a bit more rest before starting the day. But it was futile. My mind was already buzzing, and there was nothing I could do to make myself relax enough to go back to sleep. All I could think about was how I knew I would have Bridgit all to myself that evening.

This wasn't going to be like when we ran into each other at the bar and I was able to sit beside her. We were spending time together then, but it was in a room with a hundred or so other people and sitting at the same table with Gina and Gus. It wasn't like we really had the opportunity to enjoy each other's company or get to know each other any better. At least, not until we got back to her apartment that night. Tonight was going to be different. When I told her I wanted to see her, that's exactly what I meant. I didn't want to just go grab drinks or sit in a crowded restaurant. I wanted to spend time with her and take advantage of being alone.

I couldn't remember the last time I was so excited about something. It seemed like the day was far too long stretched in front of me, and I needed to figure out something to fill up the time or I was going to go crazy before the end of the workday came along and I finally had her all to myself.

Deciding to make some good use out of my surplus of energy, I got out of bed and reached for my phone. There was only one other person I could think of who might be awake at this hour. Or at least wouldn't be too angry to be woken up at it by me.

Gus sounded like he had been sleeping when he answered the phone, but as soon as I asked if he wanted to meet up at the gym for a few early-morning rounds of boxing, he perked up. Boxing was a favorite activity of ours since we were teenagers. There was nothing quite like getting in the ring and going a few rounds with my best friend. It worked in so many different situations. If I was angry or frustrated, I could punch harder and faster and get all the aggression and tension out. If I was happy and excited, it worked out my extra energy and kept me focused. Either way, it gave me a boost of endorphins, and it helped me feel my best.

Gus met me at the gym, and neither of us were surprised to be the first there. It wouldn't be too long before the place filled up with other guys wanting to get a workout in before the day started, but for now we had it all to ourselves.

"So, what's going on with you this morning?" he asked. "You seem to be in a particularly good mood. And considering you calling me to go boxing when it's still basically nighttime out can only mean you are very happy or severely pissed. I'm going to go with very happy considering that dumb look on your face."

"Fuck off," I joked.

I laughed as I strapped on my gloves and ducked into the ring.

"I'm seeing Bridgit tonight," I told him.

Gus looked me up and down like he was evaluating me, trying to figure out what I was thinking.

"Don't you see her every day at work?" he teased.

"I plan on seeing a lot more of her than I do at the office," I told him.

By the time we were done, and I was showering off the sweat, I felt better grounded and more prepared to face the workday ahead of me. I was still filled with excitement and anticipation and couldn't wait for the day to end so I could be with her, but at least I wasn't jumping out of my skin. I said goodbye to Gus, promising to make up for our usual lunch I had to miss while I was in Chicago, and got in my car to head to the office.

My phone rang and I glanced over at the screen. The second I saw it, all the stability and grounded feeling disappeared. The number glowing on the screen was one I hadn't seen in a long time and never wanted to see again. The name above it was one that still gave me a bad taste in my mouth.

Katya.

I would never pretend I hadn't loved Katya. Some men try to rewrite history after their divorces and pretend they never had feelings for their ex-wives, or they were somehow tricked into getting married. That's not the way it was for Katya and me. I'd loved her. I'd loved her hard and for many years. It broke me completely when she left me and said she wanted a divorce. I'd always believed marrying her was it for me. She was my fairy-tale ending, and I couldn't imagine life without her. Of course, I also couldn't imagine her cheating on me with someone I'd had in my home, someone I trusted and thought I could think of as a friend. It'd destroyed me when I found out, and I thought I would never get over it.

I still blamed my empty bed on her. The moment I found out about her affair was the moment I stopped trusting women. To make matters worse, she didn't just cheat on me with him or even leave me to start a legitimate relationship with him. Less than a week after the ink was dry on our divorce papers, Katya married him. The remarriage was so fast that for almost a year after, I encountered acquaintances who believed she and I were still married.

That was years ago, and I hadn't spoken to Katya since. The last time we'd had a conversation was the day our divorce was finalized, and she'd told me about her upcoming wedding. She said she was telling me as a courtesy so I could hear it from her rather than someone else or seeing an announcement in the papers. It didn't feel like a courtesy to me. It felt like a closing blow, like she wanted just one more way to put a nail in the coffin of the life we used to share together. Now all this time later she was suddenly showing up on my caller ID. That could only mean one thing. There was trouble in paradise.

That wasn't my problem. *She* wasn't my problem. I could have gone the rest of my life without ever having to see her name or consider speaking with her, and I didn't feel like breaking the streak that morning. Pushing the negativity out of my mind and reclaiming my good mood, I ignored the call. I wasn't going to let her put a damper on the day I was so excited about.

I made it to work with the bounce back in my step and the energy and excitement filling me more and more as I got closer to seeing Bridgit. I knew it would make it harder to wait until the end of the day once I got a glimpse of her, but I also didn't want to wait any longer to look at her. She and Gina were already working when I walked into the office, and she smiled when she glanced up at me. I winked at her, and the splash of warm color that crossed her cheeks made my belly tighten.

Throughout the rest of the day, I smiled at Bridgit every time we met eyes. It almost became a game, trying to figure out if I could give her a wink or a meaningful smile without Gina or anybody else catching on. I liked having a little secret between us. Rather than feeling lascivious or deceitful, it was fun and playful. It made it even more exciting, sexier to think about not being alone with her. As she began replying it to each wink or smile with a lick of her lips or a brush of her fingertips through her hair or over her collarbone, it was like the entire day became one long session of foreplay.

It felt like one of the longest days in the history of working. At least it was busy, and I managed to fill the time with as many meetings, phone calls, and other tasks as humanly possible to keep the time churning by. Bridgit and I both made it a point to be in the middle of different activities when the day came to an end and Gina packed up. She offered to hang around and help either one of us with what we were doing, but we both shooed her away. She eyed us with a touch of suspicion, but when neither one of us let on to anything, she finally relented and headed out of the office. It was Friday night, which meant she was probably going out for the evening.

When she was gone, Bridgit looked up at me and smiled.

"Are you ready?" she asked.

"Yes. Are you?" I asked, looking over her shoulder.

Bridgit looked around seriously, following my gaze.

"What do you mean?" she asked.

"You don't have anything with you," I said.

I was happy she waited for me so we could get our evening started right off the bat, but she didn't have an overnight bag with her.

"What would I have with me?" she asked. "Aren't we just going for drinks or dinner?"

"Actually, I have something planned for us. I thought maybe you would have brought a bag along with you."

"I'm sorry I didn't get the memo about needing luggage," she joked.

Maybe next time, I thought to myself. *If this goes well, hopefully there won't be a question next time.*

"Let's go," I said.

"So, where are we going?" Bridgit asked.

"You'll see when we get there," I told her.

We went out to the parking deck, and I helped her into the car before closing the door behind her. She kept asking questions, trying to either guess or get me to reveal my plans for the evening, but I kept it to myself until we made it to my building. We got out of the car, and the valet took over as I took Bridgit by the arm and brought her inside. We got into the elevator, and I used my key to activate the segment of the ascent that brought us to the very top floor. The doors opened and we walked out onto a short hallway with a door at the end. I guided her inside my penthouse and gestured around.

"Home sweet home," I told her.

CHAPTER 16

BRIDGIT

I didn't really know what I was expecting when it came to spending an evening with Andrei, but this definitely wasn't it. Rather than whisking me away to some exclusive destination or expensive restaurant, he brought me to his ridiculous penthouse. I suppose in a way that was a very exclusive destination, but it was nothing like I would have thought it would be. Of course, I was familiar with extravagant homes and the super luxurious lifestyle afforded by wealth and power. That was the lifestyle I used to live, and I'd spent a considerable amount of time traipsing through these types of homes. But that was something very specific that stood out about Andrei's home when compared to all the other penthouses, brownstones, and even country houses I'd visited.

There was no staff. Servants were just something I was accustomed to seeing in places like this. Even just thinking about that word now kind of made me shudder, but the reality was I was used to going to homes and encountering butlers, housekeepers, cooks, and other professional help there specifically for the purpose of seeing to the needs of the members of the households and their guests. I would be the first to admit they could become tiresome when used too much. Everyone I knew had been to a party or an event where a family was trying to throw around their wealth and increase the perception of their importance by having far too many members of their staff milling around. I really didn't need a dedicated person to fill my drink or take away my plates the second I finished eating.

I didn't think Andrei would be that way. But I did expect to see at least a few people taking care of him in the sprawling apartment. Yet when he brought me inside, I realized it was only the two of us. Which meant the incredible-smelling food coming from the kitchen wasn't made by a cook or even a private chef. He brought me home for a homemade dinner, which took my breath away.

"Wait. When did you have time to cook?" I asked.

He smiled and helped me out of my coat. "Lunchtime. I ran home to start dinner. It should be ready."

I'd never really thought of him in any sort of domestic way. Until that moment, I didn't even think I'd envisioned what his home would be like or even what he was like outside the settings I'd experienced him in. He was just my larger-than-life boss and the guy who made my knees go weak. It didn't occur to me he might putter around his beautiful home alone and know how to cook amazing meals.

He was being unbelievably sweet and attentive, and even though I still had a bit of angst over how it seemed this was all just a deal to him, I still wanted Andrei. No matter what, I was happy to be there with him that night and was looking forward to going to bed with them. Even if this was just a business transaction, I was more than enjoying my end of the deal.

After a delicious dinner, Andrei poured us glasses of an impressive vintage wine and brought me out onto the balcony that overlooked the city. It was a gorgeous view, and as he came to stand behind me, his arms wrapped around my waist, it was almost perfect. Almost. I sighed. This was the kind of moment women longed for in their relationships, but this wasn't a relationship. Knowing I couldn't talk about this with anyone or share how happy he made me feel was frustrating, and it seemed the sweeter he was, the more it irritated me.

He kissed the side of my neck and nuzzled me. I didn't want to feel the butterflies in my stomach or the way my heart pounded when he did that. I wished I could just think of him as nothing but a good time in bed and be done with it. But he was affectionate and caring and had an indescribable way of making me feel beautiful and desirable even without saying a word. It was a strange position to be in. This was the agreement we'd made, but it felt different than anything I'd ever experienced.

I turned around to him and let him kiss me. The kiss deepened and he took the glass from my hand, setting it aside so he could wrap his arms around me again and I could loop my arms around his neck. He leaned me back against the edge of the balcony, and we kissed in the soft night air. Soon the kiss deepened and became hotter, and he led me into the apartment. I let him guide me through the penthouse into the bedroom. Our kiss broke, and he scooped me into his arms to carry me over to the bed. Rather than tossing me onto it like he did at my apartment, he placed me gently into the center of the mattress. I slid toward the pillows and rested back.

I lay back on the bed, expecting him to climb on top of me, but instead he took a step back. Walking to the wall, he turned a knob and the lights dimmed. Walking back to the bed, he began to unbutton his shirt slowly, and I felt the rise of heat growing between my thighs. He was taking his time undressing, but his eyes never left mine. They stared deeply, hungrily, and I returned the gaze as best I could, but they kept wandering away to watch as his muscles moved beneath his tight white shirt. When his dress shirt was crumpled and lying on the floor, he reached for the buckle of his belt and unhooked it, then grabbed one end and ripped it from his pants. The sound was violent and intense and intoxicating, and I shivered with anticipation.

Reaching down, he unhooked the button of his pants and let them fall off his waist, kicking them off and removing his socks before stepping up so his thighs touched the edge of the bed. He reached forward and grabbed me by the ankles, pulling me toward him, and I slid easily and weightlessly across the silk sheets. I giggled as my body rested with my ass at the edge of the bed, expecting him to take out the hardened erection from his boxer briefs and to fuck me right there, but instead, he grinned and traced a finger down my chest.

When he reached my pants, I was ready to toss them off myself, but he beat me to it, hooking them and pulling them off in one motion, tossing them over his shoulder with a grunt of satisfaction. I pulled my shirt off and lay back again, reveling in his eyes tracing my body, glorifying me in his attention. Internally I was warring with myself to try to take control and get him inside of me, or to let him dominate me, and to let myself relax into his touch. Before I could make a choice, his fingers traced down my bare stomach to my panties and pulled them down and off. His eyes widened and then narrowed on my pussy, and he knelt down beside the bed.

Pulling my legs apart, he ran his tongue along my thigh, toward my core, and then stopped when he was nearly there. He blew a stream of warm air across the now slick surface, and my body writhed involuntarily as he repeated the action on the other side. I craved his attention, and he wasted no more time, letting his tongue rise up through my folds until it found the pearl in the center. Gently massaging it from under its hood, he poured attention onto my clit, letting one thick finger trace my opening and then slide easily inside. I was slick and wet and ready for him, as he let me ride the wave of an immediate and explosive orgasm through his touch. My hips bucked, and after just a few moments, I squeezed my thighs around his neck, and he pressed hard into my clit with his tongue, licking me through the pleasure.

When the wave of the climax had passed, he trailed kisses up my stomach and to the swells of my breasts. Unhooking the bra from the front clasp, he pushed it away and sank down onto them, covering one perky nipple with his mouth and then the other, leaving them wet and hard as he massaged them with his palms. Crushing a kiss into my lips, his tongue slid inside, and he ground his hard cock into my wet core. I craved the chance to pull his boxer briefs off and let him fuck me. Letting go of my breasts, he reached down and pulled them off himself and tossed them away. His hands slid up to mine and pushed them down into the bed as he climbed up, resting his knees on either side of my chest.

His enormous, thick cock filled my vision as he leaned over me, and I took him into my mouth eagerly. He took control, pushing my hands down gently but firmly into the bed as he fucked my mouth. I could feel his cock pulse on my tongue and knew the pleasure was as overwhelming for him as it was for me, but he slid out before he came and took a breath. As he rested back on his heels, I pushed my breasts together around his erection, and he groaned loudly at the invitation. Rocking back and forth between my large, heavy breasts, he let his head fall back and focus on the sensation.

Suddenly he stopped, stepping off the bed and grasping me firmly by the hips. Turning me over, he let out a sound somewhere between a groan and a grunt as I arched my hips back toward him. I was presenting myself for him, and he ran his hands over my ass in appreciation. Kneeling again, he ran his tongue through my folds and then slid inside of me. The sensation of his tongue inside me was new and exhilarating, and I gripped with the bedsheets as I let myself drop my inhibitions and just enjoy the ecstasy of his tongue. A few moments later, his tongue slid out of me, and before I could pout at the sudden loss of his attention, the head of his cock pushed against my opening, and then he sank into me.

Pulling me by my hips into him, he stretched me, filling me until he could go no farther. I cried out and had to breathe deeply before I could relax and let him press himself all the way in. He was pushed so far, I felt like it might be too much, and the pressure was enough that I gripped onto the sheets, but after a moment of waiting, letting me adjust and form around his cock like a glove, I relaxed, and he slowly began to rock in and out of me at a measured and controlled pace. The pressure lessened, and the pleasure grew beyond anything I had ever experienced. He was so deep inside me, but I only craved him more. His balls pressed into my clit with every thrust, and soon his movements grew harder and more intense. With each thrust, a yelp escaped my lips and I arched back even farther, giving him even greater access to me by pressing my cheek into the sheets and angling my ass up.

Grunts of effort and pleasure filled the air around me, and I lost myself in what seemed like a never-ending climax. Time slipped by and he increased his speed, slamming into me with wild abandon, filling his hand with my hair and pulling my head back toward him. It was rough, kinky, but it made me feel alive and sexy and desired. Adrenaline ran through my veins, and I looked back over my shoulder to meet eyes with him. Something about the way I looked at him, hunger for more burning in me, seemed to embolden him even further. His teeth gritted, and he clasped me by my waist and picked me up without sliding out of of me. He turned so that he sat on the edge of the bed, and I straddled him, facing away. My toes barely touched the ground, but it didn't matter; his grip was bouncing me easily on his cock.

I reached down and put my hands on his knees to gain some measure of support. I slid one hand between my legs and grasped his balls, massaging them as he leaned his hips off the bed so he could thrust up into me. His hands wrapped around me and pulled me back so I lay across his chest, but he was still angled so he could pound into me. One hand filled with my breast as our lips crushed into each other, and I could feel his breath beginning to hitch. A rumble began deep inside his chest, and I pulled myself off. He was unwavering, and he climbed up to me, pulling me toward him as I lay on my back. He sank into me again and thrust hard. I cried out in pleasure, an impossibly explosive climax rolling through my body as his voice rose like thunder around me. Then he locked stock-still, his cock pulsing as he came deep inside me. The feeling of his orgasm filling me with his hot, sticky seed sent me over the top, and I clutched around him, my nails digging into his back and my mouth clamping down on his shoulder. I shook as I came with him, and he pumped a few more times, letting himself empty completely. When he was fully spent, he crumpled down bedside me, and I curled into his arms, more satisfied than I had ever been and content to lie languidly there beside him as the sweat rolled down my back and he covered us with the soft silky sheets.

I lay there with Andrei until my body cooled down and I felt like I could move again. As I rolled to the side of the bed, he reached out and rested his hand on my hip.

"Where are you going?" he asked.

I turned over my shoulder to look at him and smile.

"Home," I told him. "It's getting late, and I need to get some sleep."

He walked back his fingertips, drawing me closer.

"You're right. It is late. Way too late for you to be going home. You should just stay here and sleep," he said.

I gave him a look.

"Andrei, that's not part of the arrangement," I told him.

"That's actually not a term we ever discussed," he pointed out. "So, we should. I think you should stay the night when you come over here."

I laughed and dropped over so I lay on my stomach, my chin rested on my hand on his chest.

"Just that simple, right?"

"Yes."

"And if we're at my place?" I asked.

"Then I stay there. Let's say we each reserve the option to stay the night in any given situation," he said.

"Andrei," I said again, but he looked at me with puppy dog eyes that made me both laugh and melt.

"All right," I said. "I'll stay. But I'm going to take a shower."

He grinned at me, and I climbed out of bed to go into the large en suite bathroom just off the master suite. The massive rainforest-style showerhead was glorious, and I stayed under the hot stream until it nearly ran cold. When I got out, there was a pair of boxer briefs and an old T-shirt sitting on the counter. I laughed as I stepped into the boxers, rolling down the waistband to get them to fit. The T-shirt swallowed me, but I loved the soft fabric and the fresh smell coming from it. I walked back out into the bedroom and found Andrei already asleep. I slipped under the covers, nestled down into the pillows and drifted to sleep.

CHAPTER 17

ANDREI

The first thing I thought of when I woke up the next morning was how happy I was that Bridgit had stayed with me the night before. The second thing I thought was "where the hell is she?" I reached out to my side and felt nothing but a stretch of empty mattress where I figured she would be curled up beside me. I just imagined I'd wake up with her in my arms and her head on my chest, and we'd peacefully cuddle that way for a while before we got up. It turned out, Bridgit was not a cuddler. Instead, she'd stolen one of the blankets, wrapped herself up like a burrito, and was at the very edge of the mattress.

It didn't feel like a slight. She wasn't trying to get away from me or avoid contact with me. This was apparently just the way she slept. I stared at her for a minute, laughing to myself. Even all wrapped up so I could barely see her, she was beautiful, and I enjoyed waking up with her. Having to chase her across the mattress was a small price to pay to know she would be one of the first things I saw when I opened my eyes. She was solidly asleep, and even me crawling across the bed toward her didn't seem to jostle her at all. It was still very early, and I was aware many people didn't like to wake up early on the weekends.

I decided not to wake her. She was resting so comfortably and looked so peaceful. As hard as she'd been working and with all the upheaval she'd gone through recently, I figured she deserved some good sleep when she could get it. I kissed her on the forehead and went into the bathroom to grab a shower.

As the water beat down on me, I couldn't help but think about Bridget and how much I wished she was there under the water with me. I made a mental note to get her in there as soon as I could. When I was clean, I got out, threw on some lounge pants and a T-shirt, and headed into the kitchen to make coffee. One of my favorite parts of the morning was choosing the type of coffee I'd brew for myself. Now that I'd experienced waking up with Bridgit and had plans to ensure that happened plenty more times, picking out my coffee was knocked down a few pegs on that particular list. But it was still a ritual I enjoyed. That morning called for something special, and I went for a small-batch roast that brewed up with hints of dark chocolate and cherry. It filled the space with rich aroma, and I wondered if it was going to work like those old commercials where brewing a pot of coffee magically woke up everybody in the household.

I was on my second cup of coffee when I got my answer. Rubbing sleep out of her eyes, Bridgit padded into the kitchen and locked wither gaze on the coffee maker. Her hair was wild and out of control, and she wasn't wearing any makeup, and still she took my breath away. She made a sound that was somewhere between words and grunting, and it took me a few seconds to put together she was asking for a cup of coffee. I was so comfortable with her there I'd forgotten she had never been there before and didn't know where to find things like coffee mugs. Opening a cabinet, I pulled down a second mug and filled it.

"I drink my coffee black, so I don't have any creamer. I have regular milk and sugar," I told her.

Bridgit shook her head.

"Black's fine," she said.

"It's strong," I warned her.

She took hold of the mug and downed it like it was water. A second later, the intensity of the coffee hit her, and she made a face, her body shuddering in response to the strength of the brew. I laughed and she shook her head again, sliding the mug across the island toward me with her fingertips.

"Another," she said.

I filled the mug again and handed it to her. This one she took down with a bit more caution, and by the time the mug was empty, her eyes were all the way open. I took that as a small victory, and the sloppy, still-sleepy smile she offered was even better.

"Are you hungry?" I asked.

She nodded and I grabbed an oven mitt out of a drawer so I could reach into the oven to pull out a pan of muffins. I sat it carefully on a cooling rack and nodded toward it.

"Banana walnut," I told her.

"That's my favorite," she said.

I smiled at her. "Mine, too. My mother taught me how to bake these when I was about thirteen. She thought they were incredibly exciting and subversive because they aren't Russian. They were her concession to being in America."

"How long had she been here?" she asked.

"Since before I was born," I told her. She laughed

through another sip of her coffee, and I grinned. "But she was still very old-world. She still is in a lot of ways. But she told me she and my father came here for a reason, and they wanted me to be as much American as I am Russian, maybe even more. So, she tried to make American food sometimes."

"How did that go?" Bridgit asked.

"I blocked everything out except the muffins," I joked. "Actually, it wasn't terrible. There were a few things she kind of mastered, but they were the ones you can't really mess up. Hamburgers. Spaghetti. Meatloaf."

Bridgit plucked a walnut out of the top of one of the muffins.

"Believe me when I tell you there are myriad ways to mess up meatloaf. I have probably done all of them in the last few weeks," she said.

"You've been trying to make meatloaf?" I asked.

She shrugged. "Seemed like something I should try. Since I have to cook for myself now anyway."

"I'm guessing it's been quite an adventure."

Bridgit nodded and climbed up on one of the stools at the kitchen island to watch me. I went to the refrigerator and pulled out a dozen eggs along with cream and some vegetables. She watched with admiration as I took out a cutting board and knife and chopped up onions, peppers, and mushrooms.

"Have you always done a lot of cooking?" she asked.

"As an adult, yes," I told her. "I mean, I depend on eating out probably a lot more than I should. But I also cook a lot. I know most people probably don't expect me to be good in the kitchen. But, again, that's all my mom. Ever since I was just a little boy, she drilled it into me that I needed to be able to feed myself. I was not to ever assume I would find a woman who would do all the cooking and cleaning for me. That was another part of being an American," I said with a laugh. "Banana walnut muffins and women who weren't going to cook every meal. So, I learned the basics."

"That dinner last night definitely wasn't basic," she said. "That was incredible."

"Thank you," I said. "I have a few solid impressive meals I keep tucked in my back pocket so I can trot them out in the right circumstances."

"And I'm the right circumstances?" she asked.

I leaned across the island to kiss her.

"You are the right circumstances for many, many things."

We chatted about nothing in particular as I finished cooking the omelets and slid them onto plates. I handed one to her along with a fork and set the other in front of another of the stools. She reached into the pan and took out the muffin she had plucked the walnut from. I offered her a butter knife, and she split the muffin open, releasing a puff of sweet-scented steam. Bridget scooped some butter from the butter dish and smeared it inside her muffin before setting it on the edge of her plate. She looked down at the food and let out a happy sigh.

"This looks delicious," she told me. "I have a feeling if you would keep cooking for me, I'm going to keep saying that."

"Then you're just going to have to keep coming back so I can cook for you more," I said. "Or you could just hang out here for the weekend."

It was an impulsive invitation, and I didn't know how Bridgit was going to react. It probably wouldn't have surprised me if she had immediately jumped down off the stool, went to get dressed, and headed right home. Fortunately, she didn't. Instead, she smiled and blushed. I sat down, and we ate. When we were finished, I took Bridgit by the hands and dragged her to the couch. Toppling over, I brought her down with me and pulled a blanket off the back down over top of us. I grabbed the remote control and flipped on the TV, scrolling through until I found an old comedy movie.

"How does a lazy day sound?" I asked.

Bridgit sighed and nuzzled down into the couch and up against me, draping one leg over mine and resting her head on my shoulder as her fingers traced up and down my body. Apparently, she was a cuddler in the right circumstances. I could happily put her in this position again.

"It sounds amazing," she said.

So that's exactly what we did. We stayed on the couch and watched movies, and then she noticed the retro video game consoles I had on display and asked if any of them worked. That led directly to a fairly epic Tetris competition. Finally, I grabbed her up, tossed her over my shoulder, and brought her back into the bedroom. She giggled as I carried her and let out a squeal when I twirled her around before setting her to her feet so we could crawl into bed together. I didn't want any of this to end, and I relished the idea of having a whole weekend with her in my arms, on my couch, in my bed. Everywhere and anywhere. But first, the shower.

CHAPTER 18

BRIDGIT

Our lazy day on Saturday was the closest thing to bliss I might have ever experienced. Draped across the couch in Andrei's sprawling living room, we watched movies and I introduced him to the trashy TV I loved. It was one of my guilty pleasures I never would have been able to tell my parents about. That sounded so ridiculous when I really thought about it. I was a grown woman, and before the break with them, I was so concerned about how they perceived me I resorted to clandestine watching of reality TV like I was concealing a planned overthrow of the government. It was times like that when it really occurred to me how much getting booted out of the nest was starting to feel like being set free.

I pretended to be shocked when Andrei told me he'd never seen any of the shows I mentioned, but it really wasn't that much of a surprise. He didn't strike me as the kind to pop a big bowl of popcorn and tuck into the drama of families who love to hate to love to hate each other or get emotionally invested in people baking. I was slightly more surprised he wasn't into the physical competition shows that both impressed me and made me laugh. I was impressed because I would never be able to manage any of the feats featured on those shows without snapping myself in half. I laughed because it made me feel better when the people who were capable of the feats fell over.

It wasn't noble and I wasn't proud of it, but if that was the worst of the deep dark secrets I'd carry around in my life, I could live with it. And it turned out Andrei was just as amused by the people flinging themselves into the water as I was and got particularly involved in the creation of elaborate cakes in death-defyingly short periods of time.

Watching the shows and movies was interspersed with bouts of hot, playful sex followed by naps that just built us up for the next round. It was one of those glorious days where I didn't follow the passage of time and didn't care about anything happening when or how it was supposed to. I wore little more than his underwear, ate stretched out in bed, and was schoolgirl levels of happy.

That night I slept in nothing and woke up on the very edge of the bed with Andrei wrapped around me, determined to be close even if I wasn't. He cradled me against him like he never wanted to let me go, and I let him hold me that way because I didn't want him to. We wriggled into the middle of the bed, and he reached down to pull the comforter up over our heads. I giggled when it surrounded us in a white puff liked we'd embedded ourselves in a marshmallow.

"I own the company, you know," he said. "I could cancel Monday and we could just stay here."

"I don't think you can cancel Monday," I told him.

"Sure, I can. We'll just go straight to Tuesday," he said.

"But wouldn't that mean we would still have to go to the

office at the same time, we would just call it something else?" I asked.

"Technicalities," he said and kissed me, then sighed. "I guess you do have to go home eventually, don't you?"

"I think so," I affirmed. "People would probably notice if we got to work together on Monday morning and I was wearing the same clothes I was on Friday and no makeup. That might spark some curiosity."

He nodded. "That's true. Gina is a stickler for lipstick. She'd notice that right off the bat."

I laughed and nudged him playfully. "Come on. You've been cooking so much for me. Let me make breakfast."

"Sure. I'll get your clothes washed while you do that."

It was a good thing I hadn't chosen any of the dry-clean-only clothes for work on Friday. There wasn't any official casual-Friday concept at the office, but that day I'd opted to go with the custom anyway. I'd assumed Andrei would bring me back to my place to get changed for our date and I'd end up in heels, which meant I wanted to give my feet a reprieve for at least the day part of Friday. Instead I ended up at his house in clothes that just straddled the line of what was appropriate for work. That meant they were easy to wash, and I got a bit of giddy pleasure from knowing my clothes would be tumbling around with his in the washer.

While he headed farther into the penthouse to throw the laundry in, I went into the kitchen to start breakfast. The refrigerator, pantry, and cabinets were extremely well-stocked, and soon I had eggs, bacon, toast, and hash browns cooking. I may not be able to master meatloaf, but breakfast I could handle. Andrei came into the kitchen to help me cook, but I shooed him away, wanting to make it for him. I felt like he had already done so much for me, and I wanted to do this for him.

It was late in the afternoon by the time we finished eating, and I changed out of his clothes into my own to head home. He held my hand on the center console as he drove me through the city. The natural, easy affection felt good. The whole weekend had been so nice, and I couldn't help but wonder if my initial reaction to our meeting in his office had been off base. Maybe Andrei misspoke when he talked about our relationship. Calling it an arrangement might have just been a poor choice of words because he was certainly treating me like a girlfriend. If it was nothing but the set of terms he presented, he wouldn't have objected to me leaving on Friday night. He wouldn't have spent so much time just holding me and laughing with me. It wouldn't feel like this. Would it?

Andrei was treating me like much more than just a fling, and I was quickly becoming addicted to it.

When we got to my apartment, he pulled me across the car to kiss me. His forehead rested against mine for just a second, like he was savoring the last few moments of our weekend together.

"I'll see you tomorrow morning," he said.

I nodded and got out of the car, waiting just inside my building so I could watch him drive away. As soon as he was gone, it was like all the adrenaline drained out of me and the weekend took its toll. I was suddenly exhausted, and I dragged myself into my studio so I could fall flat on my face on the bed. It was nothing like the huge pillowy bed and luxurious sheets I had enjoyed for the last two nights. But there was still something comforting about being back in my own space. It was like the first day you get back from a long vacation. As much fun as the trip was and as reluctant as you feel to leave, it's always nice to be back home.

That thought going through my mind was surprising in

its own right. I realized it was the first time I'd really thought of this place as home. Not just where I was living or my temporary apartment, but actually my home. It was funny how it took enjoying something else so much to show me how my perceptions had changed. I lay there on the bed for a while, telling myself I needed to get up but feeling too comfortable and tired to want to move. Outside the sun was dipping down, and I knew I had to get up if I was going to get anything accomplished before it was time to actually crawl into bed for the night.

I finally willed myself to get up with a promise of a tamale from the bodega down the street and opened my phone to the notes app. Poking around in the kitchenette area of my apartment, I took notes of groceries I needed. It was a fairly short list considering I still had much of what Steven had bought me before my first paycheck came. With the exception of a few fresh items, there majority of what I added to my list was to make lunches to bring to work for the week. Gina regularly invited me to go to lunch with her or asked if I wanted to order in with her, but that got expensive very quickly. Especially considering I was trying to save as much money as I could, buying lunch out on a regular basis when I could just bring it with me seemed like a waste.

When I had my list of things I needed from the store, I grabbed my purse and headed out before I could be tempted back into my bed or onto the couch. I wasn't very hungry after the massive brunch earlier but couldn't resist the delicious homemade tamales sold at the front of the bodega. Pulled out of the steamer individually and wrapped in paper, they had become a favorite treat of mine after Steven bought some as a snack the day he brought me to the apartment for the first time. I chose to remember the excitement of that new experience and think of it as, quite liter-ally, my first taste of my new life.

The tamale was enough to give me a boost to get me through my shopping, but the energy was waning by the time I got back to my apartment hauling my stuffed reusable bags. When I was feeling perkier as I wandered the bodega and ticked items off my list, I came up with all kinds of recipes and meals I was going to prepare for the week. That whole meal prep thing was still going strong, and I hadn't tried it yet. Now seemed as good a time as any. I could save money, look like I had my shit together like a real adult, and attempt to eat healthy all wrapped up in tiny plastic containers.

Only by the time I managed to make it to my kitch-enette and unpack my bags, I didn't have it in me to chop up enough vegetables for a week of meals and snacks, or boil a couple pounds of pasta to make into pasta salad. Instead, I stuffed everything into the refrigerator with the promise of getting to it after work the next day. I took a shower, changed into pajamas, and dropped into bed. I was quickly realizing a weekend of sex was enough to take it out of a person.

Setting my phone alarm to make sure I got up in time, I stuffed the phone under my pillow. As I reached to turn off the bedside lamp, somewhere in the back of my mind I registered a series of texts that had shown up on my phone. They came from an unknown number, so I didn't bother to open any of them. They must have been from someone thinking they were sending them to someone else. That would be embarrassing for them when they realized it.

Sleep took over quickly, and I sank away into dreams of Andrei.

CHAPTER 19

ANDREI

Well, that day went to shit early.

It started off great. After I dropped Bridgit off at her apartment on Sunday, I stopped by the office to check over some work and get ready for the week ahead. There was still a lot to catch up on, especially with the last-minute fixing and rearranging I had to do after the incident that led me to travel to Chicago. I wanted to stay on top of everything and keep away from any risk of getting behind. But it was difficult to concentrate. Not just because of the images of my time with Bridgit dancing in my head. Those were actually calming now. The last time I came into the office with her on my mind, I couldn't focus because I wasn't sure where we stood. We still hadn't talked about what really defined our relationship or how we were going to move forward, but I wasn't as bothered by it. I wasn't worried about putting any type of definition on it or trying to look too far ahead. Instead, I just wanted to enjoy the memories of holding her in my arms and enjoying her for two days.

The furthest ahead I needed to look was to the next time I could be with her.

Her staying with me after our dinner on Friday gave me a boost of confidence and made me feel more settled. That actually helped me focus and got my productivity rolling. What stood in my way was the repeated phone calls from my ex-wife. My phone rang and rang until my voicemail took over. There were a few seconds of silence, then it started up again. I didn't even know how she had my number. It had been years since our divorce, and I'd changed my number since then. But I shouldn't underestimate Katya. She had proven time and time again what she wanted, she got.

Eventually I turned off my phone, so I didn't have to listen to it anymore and was able to push away the negative thoughts hearing from her created. By the time I left the office, I was back to only thinking about Bridgit and looking forward to seeing her again the next day. Even though we'd only been apart for a few hours, I already missed her, and I wanted to be close to her again. I knew it was going to be more difficult to be in the office with her and not scoop her up in my arms to hold her or sneak a kiss or two. We'd agreed to keep everything out of work, but with the way I was feeling, I might have to figure out a way to get creative and be able to touch her during the day.

I was still riding high on the time I spent with her and knowing I was just a few minutes away from seeing her smile and hearing her voice when I got to work Monday morning. And that's where all the good feelings ended and everything else went straight to hell.

Pulling into the parking deck, I went to my usual spot and saw the one next to it was already occupied by a Lexus. It was a new model, but the license plate would have told me everything I needed to know about the owner even if it was all I saw. It was the same one I'd seen every day throughout my marriage and watched disappear into the distance just moments after I found out that marriage was over. Seeing that would have put me on edge enough. I definitely didn't need to see the woman it was attached to standing beside the car.

And yet, there she was. Years after the last time we'd come face-to-face, but looking just as unpleasant as when we signed the final papers, there was my ex-wife, showing back up in my life at the time when I wanted to see her less than I ever had.

I was tempted to drive around to the other side of the parking deck and try to avoid her, but I knew that would be useless. She would just follow me or show up inside. I needed to just deal with her and whatever had possessed her to resurface in my life so I could put it behind me again. Parking my car, I got out and looked over at her. Katya was exactly the way I remembered her. Perfectly dressed, flawlessly groomed, and looking pissed as hell. The last time I saw her, that anger came from me refusing to give in to her demands and not handing over the money or the vacation house she wanted.

"Why are you ignoring my calls?" she demanded before I even had a chance to close my door.

"Why are you at my office?" I asked in response.

"Don't act like a child. I've been calling you for days. If you answered your phone, maybe I wouldn't have to show up here like this," she said.

I got my briefcase from the back seat of the car and walked past her car on the way to the staircase leading into the office. It wasn't going to make much of a difference. She was going to force me to listen to her one way or the other. I might as well go inside where I could at least be comfortable rather than having to deal with her out here in the parking deck. Just like I expected her to, she fell right into step behind me.

As she followed me, Katya ranted at me in rapid-fire Russian. Most of it just washed over me without me bothering to pay attention to what she was saying. The few words that did slip through were essentially her evaluation of how selfish, arrogant, and spoiled I was. Not anything I hadn't heard from her during our divorce proceedings. She continued to rant all the way up the stairs and into the office. Gina looked up at the sound of her voice, and I saw my assistant's eyes narrow when they fell on Katya. I held up my hand to silence my ex-wife.

"Gina, hold my calls, please. It appears I'll be busy for a while," I said.

Not taking her glare away from Katya, Gina nodded. I continued toward the office with Katya right behind me, seeming not to notice the other woman, just like always. I hazarded a quick glance toward Bridgit's desk, wondering how she was reacting to Katya and the upheaval already begun first thing in the morning. It was a relief to see the desk empty. It wasn't quite the start of the day yet, so I had no reason to be worried about her being late. If there was ever a morning for her to skate in right under the wire, this was a good one. This was something she shouldn't have to witness. Hell, I didn't want to witness it and I was right in the middle of it.

I walked into my office and closed the door behind me. As soon as the door closed, she flopped herself down in the chair at my desk.

"Make yourself at home," I muttered.

"Don't you have someone who can get me a coffee or

something?" she asked, sighing as if she was withering away.

"No," I told her flatly.

She looked horrified I would dare not to coddle her.

"What about that woman you just told to hold your calls. Isn't she your assistant?" she asked.

"Yes, Katya. That's Gina, *my* assistant. Just like she has been since we were married," I told her. "And it's her job to be my assistant, not yours. And by the way, she doesn't even get my coffee. If you are in such need of caffeine, maybe you should go to a coffee shop rather than intruding on my work."

Katya immediately shifted gears, letting her eyelashes droop and sniffling. It was a move I'd become accustomed to during our marriage. Even when things were good between us, it was one of her habits that drove me insane. When she was in a tense situation or was trying to manipulate someone, she would jump from emotion to emotion trying to find the one that was most effective. She started this confrontation with anger hoping it would make me feel bad for ignoring her. Now that she knew it hadn't, she was trying her hand at sad and fragile.

"I knew you would be surprised to see me after all this time, Andrei, but I didn't think you would be so cruel. Especially while I'm going through this," she said.

"I have no idea what you're going through," I pointed out. "We haven't spoken in a very long time."

She wasted no time on filling me in. "He cheated on me! Cheated!" she exclaimed.

"Peter?" I asked.

"Of course, Peter. Who else would I be talking about?" she asked, seeming to forget she had moved on to her sad phase. She quickly shifted back, giving another sniffle and blinking away invisible tears. "My husband cheated on me with his secretary. It's been going on for months."

"I can imagine how unpleasant that is for you," I said without emotion.

She glared at me for a few seconds like she was trying to gauge my emotion, then continued.

"We are divorcing. It's already started, and my whole life is upside-down. Now I need a place to stay as I absolutely cannot stay at the home we made together and he defiled," she said.

I stared at her, blinking a few times as I waited for her to finish, but she didn't.

"Would you like a hotel recommendation?" I asked.

"A hotel? He cheated on me and you think I should have to stuff myself in a little hotel room and go through this alone?" she gasped. "I want to stay with you."

It was a good thing Gina wasn't the kind of assistant to bring coffee to me in my office because I would have just spit it all over. She must have lost her ever-loving mind. This irony was unreal.

"You have got to be kidding me," I said.

"Why?" she asked, genuinely looking confused. "You have that big penthouse all to yourself. And we have so much history, Drei."

"No," I said matter-of-factly.

"But no one knows me like you do. I need to be with someone familiar right now," she tried.

"No."

"I can't get through this by myself."

"Katy, no. You can't come home with me," I said firmly.

And I was done. She kept talking, eventually slipping back into Russian, but I ignored her until she finally got up and left in a huff. It wouldn't be the end of it, but at least it was over for now. I had reached my quota of being able to deal with her for the morning and needed some time to rebuild my tolerance.

The conversation with Katya kept me from noticing Bridgit come in for the day, but when I went to the break-room, I saw her standing at the coffeepot. I had to restrain myself from walking over and scooping her up. Especially after having to deal with Satan in Gucci heels, all I wanted was to have her in my arms. One of the guys from the warehouse came in and reminded me why I needed to stick to my own rules. I had to do my best to ignore Katya, resist Bridgit, and just focus on work.

CHAPTER 20

BRIDGIT

Monday and Tuesday were weird days. That was really the only way to put it.

Just when I thought I'd gotten into a groove and understood what was going on around me, I got thrown for a loop again. The extra hours of sleep Sunday night did me good, and I woke up Monday morning feeling full of energy and ready to face a new week of work. I was excited to see Andrei even if I wasn't able to acknowledge anything or get close to him. It felt like it was going to be a good day, and maybe I could feel like a high schoolgirl later and smuggle him over to my place for some alone time. But then I got to work and almost instantly realized it wasn't going to be that simple.

There was a strange tension in the air when I walked through the door into the open office space where Gina and I worked. Everything seemed strangely quiet, like nobody wanted to say anything. I felt awkward even just crossing to my desk and making noise by putting my tablet down. I glanced over at Gina, but she didn't look up at me with her usual morning smile. I wondered if I might have done something wrong or caused yet another problem. I didn't think I did. I was catching on better, and it had been a few days since I'd screwed up anything particularly badly.

I looked over at Andrei's office and saw he was having a meeting with someone. It was a woman, which wasn't all that unusual considering many of the clients he worked with were women. But her posture seemed off, like she was upset and worked up about something. I couldn't really see his expression from where I was, and I wished the glass wasn't so good at insulating sound. Something was happening in there, and I wanted to know what it was. I was tempted to ask Gina, but she was hunched over her desk in the middle of something and was giving off the vibe of not wanting to be interrupted. I'd have to just wait and see if someone offered me the information.

I delved into work, and several minutes later the door to the office burst open and the woman stalked out. Her face was tense and furious, and she stomped out without even acknowledging Gina or me. I waited for Andrei to come out and say something to either of us, but he stayed in his office. After a few minutes, I needed a break from the strange atmosphere. I got up and went into the breakroom to get a cup of coffee. I was waiting for it to brew when Andrei walked in. He hesitated slightly when he noticed me but didn't say anything. Our eyes met for only a brief moment before Jared from the warehouse came in and greeted both of us boisterously.

Andrei grunted at him and turned on his heel to stomp away. The encounter left my heart pounding and the back of my neck stinging with heat. I took my coffee back to my desk and looked over at Gina again. It was her turn now to be looking into Andrei's office like she was trying to figure out what was going on. She watched him storm back to his desk and drop down in his chair, then immediately hop up and stomp out onto the platform overlooking the warehouse. Without saying anything, she got up and went into the breakroom, briefly leaving me completely alone in the silence. When she came back, she was carrying a large mug of very strong-smelling coffee in each hand. Masterful balancing let her open the glass office door, and she set the mugs down on the desk.

I saw her look over at the platform, and her mouth moved like she was calling out to him. He shook his head and continued to lean on the railing, staring down at the warehouse. She gestured to the coffee, and he nodded but didn't look at her. Finally, Gina grabbed up one of the mugs again and stomped back out to her desk. She sat down hard in her chair and took a swig of the coffee.

"Is everything all right?" I asked.

"Fine," she said.

I took that as a clear invitation to close my mouth and stay out of it. The last thing I needed was to rock the boat. Gina loosened up slightly by lunchtime, but Andrei's foul mood continued throughout the day. He barely came out of his office, and when he did it was only to accept a delivery of food he'd ordered in for lunch, then closed himself right back up in his office. That immediately struck me. He never ordered himself lunch without letting Gina and me know he was and offering to order for us as well. This time he didn't even acknowledge either of us.

I took my bagged lunch outside again, retreating back to the corner beside the loading dock. After the first time I ate out there, I'd prepared for the potential of a future backlot picnic by bringing a blanket along with me and stuffing it under my desk. I brought it with me now and spread it out to make the concrete curb a bit more comfortable. Spreading the plastic storage containers of my haphazardly prepped food around me, I tried to think only about the beautiful weather and enjoying my lunch. Instead, I couldn't help but wish Andrei would come out and find me again. I wanted to know what was going on, to see him smile at me and know everything was all right.

But he never came. I took as long as I could to eat my lunch, then had to shake out the blanket and head back inside. The rest of the day was quiet and uncomfortable, and Andrei stayed cloistered in his office even when the day ended, and Gina and I left. I didn't hear from him that night.

The next morning, I entered the office building cautiously optimistic. Maybe it was just a case of the Mondays that infected the office and wreaked havoc, and now everything would be back to normal. Not so much. If anything, Andrei's mood was worse on Tuesday than it had been on Monday. He stomped around and barked orders at Gina. At one point he crossed to my desk only to drop a file folder in the middle, shoot me a fleeting look, and walked away. I left work that day feeling off-balance and somewhat sick to my stomach. I hated the harshness that seemed to have developed and the sense that I was missing something, like something had happened but I didn't know, and no one thought to tell me. It felt like being on the outside again, and I couldn't stand that.

Those feelings melted over into Wednesday, and by the middle of the afternoon, we were all snapping at each other. Andrei came out into the main office with his eyes wide and his teeth set.

"What is this?" he demanded, holding up a stack of papers. "What the hell is this?"

"What are you talking about?" Gina asked.

"These invoices. They're bullshit. I told you these three orders had to be changed and that the client wanted to cancel the first and double the second. So, why don't the invoices show that? I've dealt with enough incompetence from the suppliers recently, I need things to actually be done correctly around here," he said.

Gina slammed her hands on the top of the desk and pushed herself up from her chair. She leaned toward him, glaring through flashing dark eyes.

"If you would look carefully enough at them, you'd see those are the copies of the original invoices with notes added to the bottom to reflect the changes. There are then reference numbers for you to find the new invoices. Just like every other time some supplier screws something up or a client decides to pussyfoot around and demand special attention, I kept invoices from every step of the way to ensure proper record keeping," she said.

Andrei squared off against her, looking down at the papers and then back at her.

"They need to be filed more effectively, because it's confusing as hell this way. If this company is going to continue to grow and thrive, things have to be done properly."

"You mean like using the organizational scheme you came up with?" Gina fired back.

His nostrils flared. "Just make sure it's done correctly."

He turned back toward his office, but Gina wasn't going to let him get away with that. She finally snapped.

"Drei, I love you like a brother, but if you don't calm down and stop talking out of your ass like that, I'll walk," she said. "Katya coming here was a shit move, but that doesn't mean you get to act like this."

When Andrei didn't turn back to look at her, Gina threw up her hands and stormed away. I watched her go, feeling shaken and blindsided. Who the hell was Katya and why would her showing up here put him a foul enough mood to last three days? The door slammed and he turned slowly to me. I crossed my arms over my chest, glaring at him through narrowed eyes. I was one hundred percent with Gina on this.

He at least had the decency to look guilty. Without saying anything, he went back into his office, leaving me shaking my head as I tried to process what was going on. A few minutes after I sat back down at my desk, Gina came in smelling strongly of smoke. That was a bad sign. She already told me she'd quit smoking a year before, so if she was slipping back into the habit, it meant the situation really was bad.

"I'm sorry about all that," she finally said.

I shook my head and shrugged.

"You didn't do anything wrong," I told her. "Who's Katya?"

"Andrei's psycho bitch of an ex-wife," she told me.

I felt like I'd been punched in the gut. Why didn't Andrei tell me he'd been married?"

"Oh, so that was who came storming through here on Monday?"

She nodded, her face almost contorting in a visceral reaction to the mention of the woman.

"Yeah. Katya," she said the name like it tasted bad on her tongue. " A real gem that one. She's been gone for years and then just showed up." She shook her head. "Anyway. It doesn't have anything to do with work. He needs to get himself together."

We went back to work, but there was still a heaviness in the air. About an hour later, a courier appeared at the door.

"Can I help you?" Gina asked.

"Yes," he said. "I have a delivery for Gina and Bridgit?"

"I'll take it," she said.

He handed her a large box, and from my angle I could see flowers sticking up over the edge. Gina thanked him and brought the box over to me. Two vases of flowers sat inside, one purple and one pink. Nestled between them was a bottle of whiskey and what looked like a couple dozen tacos from a fantastic restaurant just down the street. I had to smile. As a peace offering, I figured we'd take it.

CHAPTER 21

ANDREI

I didn't hear from Gina or Bridget after the showdown in the office. I didn't know if that was a good thing or a bad thing. It could mean they'd decided to just gloss over it, and everything was going to go back to normal. It could also mean they were stewing in their anger and disgust toward me and I was going to deal with the aftermath for the foreseeable future. There are few things as unpleasant as facing down a cultivated grudge against you for days on end and not know when it's going to be over. Multiply that by two women encouraging each other along, and work had the potential of being pretty much hell.

But there wasn't much more I could do about it at that point. After Gina bit my head off, chewed it up, and spit it back at my feet, I went back to my office to think about what happened. Of course, I was completely on my own side at first. She was overreacting and throwing a temper tantrum. Then I thought about the way Bridgit had looked at me and the way Gina stormed out of the office, and fairly quickly I wasn't on my side anymore. I'd been an absolute dick the whole week, and neither of the women in the office deserved it. It wasn't their fault Katya showed back up without warning and fell right back into her pattern of making my life miserable.

Yet, I managed to take it out on both of them, and it eventually pushed them over the edge. I couldn't blame them. The groveling gift I ordered for them was meant as an olive branch, hoping to show them I was sorry and to smooth things over. Flowers because every woman deserves flowers. Tacos because it was late in the day and they should have something tasty to fuel them through the work they were going to be doing after I slipped away so I didn't have to face them for the rest of the day. And whiskey because they had already had to face me for the week. As soon as it arrived, I slipped out through the warehouse and went home to contemplate my life and its direction.

Actually, I went home to be pissed off at myself, my life, and its direction. The last thing I needed right now was for my ex-wife to wander back into my life. Things were just getting good with Bridget. Even if we didn't have anything specifically laid out, any agreement or obligation, I was enjoying my time with her and looking forward to much more. Katya coming back in such a mind-blowingly ridiculous way was an inconvenience and aggravation at best but could be so much worse.

All I could think about was Bridgit and how I wanted to find solace in her right now. I wanted to disappear into the world we created when we were together and not have to think about things like suppliers getting things wrong and ex-wives coming to fuck up my life.

That was the thought on my mind as I headed into the office the next morning. I could only hope I wasn't going into a war zone. It didn't occur to me until I was starting into the building that they might be upset I'd left before saying anything to them the day before. I let the gift do the talking for me when maybe I should have gone in and apologized in person. After all, they were completely right. I was acting like a fool; it wasn't their fault, and I should have acknowledged it sooner.

As soon as I got into the main part of the office, I saw my worries were all for nothing. Not only did it seem they didn't mind me not apologizing in person, but they had clearly thoroughly enjoyed the gift I left for them. The remains of the early dinner were still scattered throughout the space, and I couldn't help but wish I'd been a fly on the wall as they enjoyed it. It would have been fun to see what happened between them receiving the offering and finally heading home for the night.

The whiskey bottle sat on the edge of Gina's desk, half-empty. It wasn't a small bottle, and the whiskey inside was far from weak. Taking down that much of it would have probably loosened some lips and created some silly behavior I wish I could have witnessed. Hopefully Bridgit was able to contain herself enough not to reveal what happened between us to Gina while she was in her impaired state. Of course, with that much whiskey gone, there was no way it was only Bridgit drinking it. That meant Gina wasn't all there either by the end of the evening, and even if Bridgit had given her full details of our encounter, she likely didn't remember any of them. Or I would do my best to convince her she didn't actually remember it.

I looked around for the aftermath of the tacos and found it on the table positioned in the small waiting area off to one side. Though I'd designed it with the intention of having clients come to the office for meetings, in practice that rarely happened. Most of the time if I was going to meet with a client, I arranged for a meeting outside the office or in one of the conference rooms on the bottom floor of the building. That meant the waiting area usually sat empty. Except for the night before when it apparently became the setting for their impromptu dinner. The bag was missing, but all the crumpled wrappers had been formed into a smiley face in the middle of the table.

I didn't know if that was something that happened over the course of the meal because of the abundance of wrappers and little else to do with them, or if it was a message to me. I chose to take it as a message to me, an acceptance of the apology without any of the awkward talking. I laughed and took out my phone, needing to have evidence of this even when it was gone. That way if the women forgot what they did, I could show them. That and it would just be fun to bring it up with Gina down the line. Snapping a picture of the wrapper smiley face, I tucked my phone away and cleaned up the mess.

There didn't seem to be much hope the two would be in on time. This little party probably left them fairly incapacitated, and I wouldn't have been surprised to find them curled up asleep under their desks. Since they weren't there, I figured they would be in late. That was fine. I wasn't going to call or bother them. They'd be in when they got in, and we'd move forward from there.

As it turned out, my estimation was far off. I was just changing the trash bag after filling it with the wrappers when I heard their voices coming down the hallway from the elevator. I looked up as Bridgit and Gina rolled into the office together, chatting happily. They were obviously both wearing Bridgit's clothes, which made me laugh. Evidently, they'd managed to make it to her apartment, but Gina didn't get any further than that. When she heard my laugh, Gina's eyes snapped over to me. She squinted and stuck her tongue out at me, then swept past over to her desk.

I laughed again and shook my head as she plopped down into her seat and busied herself with the work waiting for her. The clothes didn't fit her well and were definitely not her style. Messy hair and makeup appropriate for Bridgit's skin tone and coloration rather than hers completed the awkward side effect of the whiskey. I looked over at Bridgit as she crossed the office to her desk. She took out a plastic food keeper, tucked her bag away, and grabbed her coffee cup. Flashing me a grin, she headed toward the lounge. I followed her and watched her go to work making coffee. As it brewed, she went to the refrigerator and put her lunch away for later. When the coffee was finished, she poured herself a cup, augmented it heavily with cream and sugar, and flashed me another smile, lifting her eyebrows at me as she headed out of the lounge and back to her desk. It wasn't words, but I would take what I could get.

Gina passed by me as I headed for the office, probably lured toward the breakroom by the smell of the coffee brewing. That was one thing I could always rely on about my assistant. Pickle her in alcohol, put her in different clothes, it didn't matter. She would never get through the morning without her coffee. We met eyes as she walked by, and I tried to gauge if she might have heard about what happened between Bridgit and me. She gave me another narrow-eyed glare, this time without the protruding tongue, but didn't say anything. I gave her a grin and made my way to my office.

I sat down behind my desk and looked at the work still spread across it from the day before. I didn't even realize how much I'd let my emotions about Katya showing up get in the way of my work. Now with the clear perspectives of morning, I could see what a mess everything I did before actually was. This was going to take some serious damage control and intervention to try to prevent anything major from happening. I let out a long breath and picked up my phone, dialing the number of the first client whose name I saw on the papers scattered across my desk.

It was just after noon when I stopped working long enough to get a phone call. Seeing Gus's name across the screen reminded me of our rescheduled lunch from the day before. It had been too much of a shit day for me to take the time to go to eat, breaking our tradition and leaving me in even a worse mood. We'd agreed to meet up today at our usual place, and I was already late. I promised him I was on my way, told him to order what he thought I'd want, and headed out. As I left the office, I called out to Bridgit and Gina that I'd be back.

I was already out in the parking deck before I thought I should have clarified where I was going. Maybe they would think I was off to see Katya or that something was wrong. Grabbing up my phone, I texted Gina, casually telling her if any clients or suppliers called to take the message and let them know I'd call the back when I got back from lunch with Gus. As I tucked my phone away, I wondered if I was being petty, covering my ass too much when I really shouldn't have to answer to them. But at that point I felt like I'd dodged a bullet with neither of them trying to stage an intervention with me over the whole incident earlier in the week, so I wasn't going to rock the boat. If that meant a bit more accountability for a while, I'd do it.

It felt good to unload everything on Gus, even if my best friend wasn't the most helpful person in the world when it came to Katya. Mostly it was a bunch of grumbled profanity and shaking his head in disbelief. Even years later he held a tremendous amount of distaste and hard feelings for my ex-wife. He was there for me through the whole separation and divorce and kept me from going totally off the rails when she got remarried. He saw me at my absolute lowest and knew how much the woman hurt me. That had affected him, and he still carried that anger and dislike for her. Maybe even hatred. But despite him not being able to really give me much insight or advice, it was nice to just be able to vent and not have to justify myself or my feelings.

After lunch I went back to the office and delved back into the long list of phone calls and untangling everything I did over the last few days. It was a relief to find out I hadn't completely screwed anything up in my snit, and by the end of the day, I was back on track. That made me even more determined not to deal with Katya and her drama. I shouldn't have to. We were divorced for a reason, and I was far from forgetting what it was.

CHAPTER 22

BRIDGIT

Friday couldn't have come soon enough, and I was excited when Gina swaggered up to me in the middle of the afternoon and handed over my paycheck. It was only my second one, but I enjoyed the rhythm of it. It was fun knowing every two weeks I'd have that moment, that recognition of everything I'd done. It was honestly the first time in my life I was really held accountable for anything. I did well in school, but the grades didn't really matter much. It wasn't like they ever felt like an actual acknowledgement of the effort I put into the work. The teachers at my exclusive private schools knew the power my father wielded and wouldn't do anything to possibly upset him. Even when I knew I earned the good grades and recognition, I didn't feel satisfied.

The paychecks did it for me. I earned them. I put the effort in, and there was no reason for anybody to give me the recognition for any other reason. I loved that about it. Gina might have given me the position out of friendship with my brother and a bit of sympathy for me, but she didn't keep me around or pay me because of it. The check was for a tiny fraction of what my father used to toss my way as pocket money when I went out shopping, but if I messed up, I wouldn't get the check, and that made the amount seem vastly more impactful.

But this paycheck meant more. My second paycheck marked two weeks since the first night Andrei and I had spent together after going to the bar. I felt the need for a new tradition and celebrating every check with a few drinks and him felt like a good one.

Andrei was busy all afternoon, and he was still hunched over his desk buried neck-deep in a job he was trying to pull to a close when I left for the evening. I headed to the bar and slid onto one of the stools before taking out my phone and texting him to come meet me when he was done. I liked the idea of going back to where it all started. The thought of both of us needing a drink after a fraught week was just a bonus.

For a second, I considered inviting Gina. Our friend-ship had continued to grow much closer, and I really enjoyed spending time with her. After the blowup with Andrei in the middle of the week, everything seemed totally out of whack. The chaos was unnerving, especially for me. It seemed like those two had been through a lot in their years of friendship and were probably not unaccustomed to the occasional tiff. But I didn't have that history with either one of them. What I did have was a sense of reliance on the office and the people I worked with to create stability in my life. The tension and arguing felt like all that was going up in flames in front of me. Quite literally when Gina came back into the office reeking of smoke and looking like she was having briefly homicidal thoughts.

But getting the gift from Andrei put things back in

order. He disappeared sometime after the fight and before we got the delivery, but that just left us to enjoy it, which we definitely did. Work fell by the wayside as we dug into the decadent street-style tacos and took back shots of the whiskey. We probably could have tried to be a little classy about it and poured out servings into coffee mugs, but we didn't bother. Instead, we kicked off our shoes, sprawled out on the couches positioned around the table in the small waiting area, and passed the bottle back and forth as we talked.

The intention had only been to take a break and relax for a bit, to let off some steam after the week of pressure building up. But that plan went to hell somewhere around the third trading of the bottle, and before we knew it, the tacos were gone, we were both swimmy, and it was hours past when we'd usually leave the office. There was no point in either of us trying to get back home on our own. It was safer for us to just pour ourselves into the back of a rideshare and crash at my place. The alcohol blurred most of what we talked about, but I know that night cemented our friendship.

Having her come to the bar would be fun. After all, she was the one who'd introduced me to the bar to celebrate my first check. It seemed appropriate for her to come along this week, too. But she'd already mentioned going out with some other friends for a birthday, and I didn't want to put her in the awkward position of asking her to choose. That didn't disappoint me too much. I didn't like the idea of having to hold back from Andrei at the bar. If it was just the two of us, I wouldn't have to.

I ordered a drink and relaxed, enjoying the music and the atmosphere. Andrei didn't respond to my text, but as I started on my second drink, I saw him walk in. He paused just inside the door, and his lips turned up in a smile. That look all but made me swoon. It was a good thing I was sitting so I could at least maintain the semblance of having myself under control.

Andrei started toward me, and I ordered him a drink before he got to me. The bartender set it down as he stepped up beside me, and Andrei gave me an impressed look.

"You pay attention," he said.

"Of course I do," I told him.

Andrei picked up the drink and took my hand, leading me away from the bar and to the same booth in the back. We slid into the same side of the table, and his hand ran along the small of my back, his fingertip briefly dipping beneath the waistband of my pants to touch my skin. I leaned sideways toward him, brushing my face against the curve of his neck as I pretended to reach for a napkin. We tried to carry on a conversation, but the longer we sat there, the harder it was to resist touching each other. We were getting friendlier than was really good for us considering the public setting, pressing closer together and nuzzling against each other. It took everything in me to stop from kissing him, but soon I couldn't take it anymore.

Getting out of the booth, I took his hand and led him up to the bar. I tossed money onto it and all but dragged Andrei outside and to my apartment. The only thing on my mind was getting him naked.

We crashed through the door and into the living room, our mouths crushing against one another and our tongues dancing. We rolled across the wall, hands searching for buttons and zippers, his breath heavy on my neck when his mouth wasn't against mine. His cologne filled my nose and made me think of bourbon and leather, and I closed my eyes to drink it in. One hand slid up my shirt and pressed against my left breast, and I let out a moan directly into his ear. My voice had an effect on him, as he immediately responded, both in his own voice and with his body, pressing me against the wall, his hard cock pushing against my stomach through the layers of clothes.

I slid my hand over the curve of his erection, straining against the zipper of his pants, and rubbed. As I did, he stepped back and tore at his shirt, opening it without bothering with a few of the buttons and tossing it away from him. The soft cotton t-shirt underneath formed tightly over his muscular chest, a dark tuft of hair poking from the v-neck. My knees weakened as he reached for the bottom of it and pulled it off over his head, and I leapt into another kiss, my fingers encircling his cock and stroking it through his pants.

It was my turn now to take off my own shirt, and as I did, he unzipped his pants and let them fall. As they pooled at his feet, he swept them away, and I reached behind me to unhook my bra. He took another step back now, dropping his boxers and letting his hard, massive cock spring out of them. I took my time unhooking the strap and felt a flush of blood run up my chest as he wrapped his own fingers around his cock and stroked it as I let my breasts tumble out. My nipples were perky and pointed, and he reached out with his free hand to fill it with one of my heavy breasts.

The moan escaped my lips without bothering to pass through my brain, a primal, sensual sound that came from my body responding to his touch. I quickly unzipped the skirt and let it fall away, and his hand left my breast to wrap around my wrist. I hesitated and searched his hungry eyes as he guided my hand into my own panties. Stroking himself, he instructed me to touch myself wordlessly, and I followed his lead. I leaned back against the wall, letting my hips push out as I rubbed my clit in slow circles. His mouth wrapped around one breast, his hand the other, and his tongue played languidly with my nipple. Moving across my chest, trailing his tongue along, he switched and took my other breast in his mouth, using his free hand to mimic the motion of his tongue with his thumb.

When my nipples were hard and wet, he stood up straight and placed a hand on my shoulder, gently guiding me to my knees. I knelt in front of him, resting my ass on my heels as he positioned himself in front of me. I reached up with my free hand to run it down his chest to the base of his cock, and his reached down to lift my chin. My rubbing was getting faster now as the head brushed my lips. He continued to stroke himself as I let my tongue unfurl. I opened my mouth wide, and he slid his thick rod between my lips. I took all of him I dared and wrapped my hand around what was left. I stroked him into me for a few moments before he reached down with both hands, filling them with my hair before resting them on the sides and back of my head.

He thrust into me, slowly, and I let his cock reach the back of my throat. I nearly choked at how deep it was but held myself together as my fingers played on my clit and the oncoming storm of an orgasm began to form. He guided me faster, thrusting until I took over, bobbing on his cock while I stroked him into me. I squirmed as the orgasm was right at the edge of overflowing, and I let go of his cock to cry out. As I did, he lifted me easily, turning me and pressing my chest into the wall. There was no wasted movement, no hesitation as he pulled my panties away and slammed his cock into me from behind. Clasping onto my hips with his strong hands, he repeated the movement, his long, thick erection stretching me, filling me in more ways than I had ever thought possible. My body couldn't hold on any longer, and I cried out, my hands pressing against the wall and pushing myself back into his rocking hips. He began to gain speed, fucking me hard and fast, and I lost myself in the pleasure. My voice was a chorus of groans and moans and yelps as he hammered into me with an animalistic desire to bring me to the brink of madness.

I shook violently as the climax peaked, and I collapsed into the wall. He slowed down behind me and pulled out. He turned me to face him, and there was a grin stretched across his face, sweat forming on his brow. Putting his hands below my ass, he lifted me, and I wrapped my thighs around him as he carried me across the room to the bed. He laid me down gently and climbed on top, and I felt the weight and dominance of him hovering over me. His cock brushed through the folds of my wet pussy, and I moaned again. He guided his cock through them and to my clit, where he rubbed the head against it for a moment before moving it back down to my opening.

I wrapped my legs around him again as he sank into me, and now that my body was prepared for him, he went deeper, and I bit down into his shoulder as he blurred the line between pain and ecstasy. Sitting up on his knees, he pulled my legs up and over his shoulders before leaning down over me again. I was folded up below him, and his arms steadied him on either side of me as he was impossibly deep inside my body. His hips reared back and then thrust into me again, and I howled with delight. His groans grew deeper as he concentrated on fucking me from this position, my hips high off the bed as he held me in place.

He leaned down for a kiss, and I tasted the sweat off his upper lip. It was warm and salty, and something about it brought me back to yet another climax. I reached down to clasp my fingers on his ass as he pounded into me, his groans growing louder and staccato. I matched them, letting myself go completely into the moment, and my toes curled as a wave crashed down around me. As it did, he suddenly went still, his veins pumping on his neck as he came hard. We locked into another kiss as he emptied himself fully deep in my womb and pumped a few more times before collapsing beside me, where I curled up in his arms.

My bed was far too small for both of us, but Andrei crashed on it anyway. We curled up tightly around each other, and he quickly fell asleep. I stayed awake a little longer, just enjoying the way it felt to be in his arms with the warmth of his skin against mine. In those blissful moments, I accepted that I was wrong about him. He wasn't trying to have an arrangement or some sort of reciprocal agreement. It was only his wording, the businessman coming out in him, that made it sound like he wanted something somehow both cold and lascivious at the same time. He really did want to enjoy being with me the way I enjoyed being with him.

With that thought, I let myself fall asleep. I woke up to him getting dressed, and I rolled over to my side to watch him. It was a habit now, and I was more than happy to keep it going. I relished those last glimpses of his body and being able to cling to them until the next time I got to reveal them. Andrei buckled his pants, then sat down on the edge of the bed and reached over to rub my hip.

"Do you really have to leave already?" I asked.

"Why don't you come back to my place with me?" he asked.

"Your place?"

"Yeah. Come spend the rest of the weekend with me."

I tilted my head to the side, twisting up my lips like I was thinking about the offer and weighing my options.

"Well... the bed and shower are better there," I said.

He laughed and gave me a playful smack on the butt.

"Come on. Get some stuff packed and we'll go," he told me.

I got out of bed and put together a bag with what I'd need for the weekend. As soon as I was packed, he took my bag and we headed out. Another couple of days hidden away from the rest of the world with Andrei seemed like a great idea.

Right up until the moment we got to his penthouse and found his ex-wife there, complete with luggage and a huge smile.

CHAPTER 23

ANDREI

I wish I could say I couldn't believe what I was seeing when I walked into my penthouse and saw Katya walk out of the kitchen with a drink in her hand. Unfortunately, I more than believed it. As much as I would have hoped I'd made it clear to her I didn't want anything to do with her and was definitely not interested in being the soft place she landed after getting kicked in the ass by a taste of her own medicine, I knew her better than that. Telling her she wasn't welcome to come to my place and stay with me wouldn't deter her. If anything, it would make her more determined to dig her heels into the ground and get what she wanted. She believed what she wanted was all that mattered in the world, and if someone disagreed with her, it was only because they hadn't seen the light yet. They just needed some convincing.

I probably knew that better than anyone. I was on the receiving end of plenty of her 'convincing' in the years we'd spent together. Showing up at my house was a clear message I had no choice but to help her. She would do anything it took to wedge herself back into my life, including getting in the way of Bridget and me. To her, I was in a perpetual holding pattern. She drifted off into her own life when it was convenient for her, but now that that was over, she wanted me to fall back on. I was her property, and she would use me any way she saw fit. The thought disgusted me, and rage rushed up inside me as soon as soon as I saw her.

Bridgit and I were wrapped up in each other, laughing and happy as we kissed and tumbled through the door into the penthouse. I had every intention of stripping off her clothes right there and starting a naked tour of the every room of the house, but before I could even fully process the pile of luggage sitting in the middle of the living room, Katya walked into view. She stepped into the room like she belonged there, casually sipping a drink and staring at us with a smug smile on her lips.

"Took you long enough to get home."

Before I could say or do anything, Bridgit pulled away from me and took off back through the door. I reached for her, trying to grab her and stop her, but she slipped away from me.

"Bridgit, stop," I called as I ran after her. "Let me talk to you."

"Leave me alone," she said just before stepping into the elevator and smashing the button to close the door behind her.

I wanted to chase after her, but there was no way I was leaving my ex-wife in my apartment alone. I stomped back and slammed the door hard behind me. Katya was laughing, shaking her head as she continued to drink.

"Really, Andrei?" she asked. "Wasn't that your secretary?"

"What the fuck are you doing here, Katya?" I demanded.

"Wait, let me make sure I've got this straight. You're not only robbing the cradle, but the girl you're sleeping with—who is about half your age, if that—is your secretary. Just how many clichés are you going to try to fit into this fling?" she asked, laughing again.

Strangling someone was something I'd never even considered in my life, but if there was ever something that was going to inspire that thought, this was it. In that moment she wasn't the woman I was once married to, or even a person. She was an infuriating annoyance I wanted to throttle and toss out the window to be swept away by the street cleaners. I wasn't proud of my reaction to her, but her condescending words were enough to push me over the edge.

"What are you doing here?" I repeated through gritted teeth.

She knocked back the rest of the drink and glared at me, the humor gone from her expression just that fast.

"I told you, Andrei. My husband and I are getting a divorce, and I need somewhere to stay."

"And I told you I couldn't give a shit about what was going on between you and your husband, and that you aren't welcome here. How did you even get in, anyway?" I asked.

"The doorman," Katya said matter-of-factly. "He was more than happy to help your wife surprise you. The superintendent, too. It's amazing what a little flirting and flashing a ring will get you." She looked at her hand and made a face at the ring. "Maybe I'll get it reset so I can still wear it."

"You are not my wife," I said. "Far from it."

I took out my phone and dialed Bridgit, but she didn't answer.

"Don't be that way," Katya said. "Things were so good between us. Don't you remember? They can be like that again."

"No. No, they can't. In order for them to be like that again, I would have to have any interest at all in having you around," I pointed out to her. Another call to Bridgit went unanswered, and I let out an aggravated growl. "You need to leave."

"I'm not going anywhere. I told you, I can't go back to my house, and I need somewhere to stay. You have this big penthouse all to yourself."

"It wasn't going to be to myself this weekend. I'm supposed to be here with Bridgit."

Katya rolled her eyes and tossed herself down onto the couch. I made another call, but Bridgit still didn't answer, and all I wanted to do was hit something. It was obvious Katya wasn't going anywhere without some more stringent convincing, and I couldn't stand to be in the same room with her anymore. It was well before ten o'clock in the morning, but my ex-turned-squatter was already at least one drink in, so I wasn't going to let the time stop me. I poured myself a glass of vodka and brought it with me into my bedroom. For good measure, I locked the door behind me. There was no telling what Katya was going to try to do, and I just wanted her out of my face.

After leaving a voicemail for Bridgit, I called my parents. I didn't want it to seem like I was crying to them, but I needed to cut this situation off at the pass before Katya made it any worse. My mother and father were going to hear she was at my apartment, even if I did manage to kick her out sometime soon. I didn't want them to get the wrong idea or for her to be able to get to them and convince them something else was happening before I got a chance to explain it to them. They prescribed to Gus's perception of my ex, hating her as much as I did. Possibly even more since she was responsible for hurting their only child.

Despite despising her and the way she left me, my mother tried to stay calm during the conversation. She listened to me explain everything that happened over the last few days and reassured me as much as she could.

"Would you like me to come talk to her?" she asked.

"I don't know," I admitted. "I don't know if she's going to listen to anybody at this point. You know Katya. Once she has something in her mind, she's not going to let it go for anybody."

"Don't worry. I'll come and talk some sense into her. She's worried right now and not thinking clearly. She just needs to hear it from another woman, and it will become clearer to her," Mom offered.

"Thank you," I said. "I'm going to call her husband and see if I can get him to handle the situation. At this point, I've only heard her side of the story. It's entirely possible she completely blew the entire thing out of proportion, and if he just talked to her, it could resolve everything."

I got off the phone with no more hope than I had going into the conversation. There was no chance Katya's husband was the victim of some sort of vast mistake or misunderstanding. I knew both of them well enough to know he was not only the type of man to cheat on his wife, but that she wasn't the type of woman to come to conclusions like that if there wasn't very strong evidence. She thought far too highly of herself to suspect a man would choose another woman over her. The only way she would ever come to terms with her husband having an affair was if she had absolute, conclusive evidence of it. But I couldn't exactly tell my mother I was planning on calling another man to tell him to bring his cheating ass to my house and fix the mistake his wandering dick caused.

I didn't have Katya's husband's phone number in my phone. The only reason I had hers was because I didn't want to be caught off guard if she called me, much like I was even though I saw her name on the screen. I could have done some research to find it, but I didn't feel like putting that much energy into the situation. Instead, I took a deep breath and called Gus. He wasn't friends with Peter, but the Russian community was small enough there was a good chance he knew how to find his contact information quickly. Just as I hoped, he made a few nasty comments, gave me the number, and offered to come up with an alibi for me if at all necessary. I thanked my best friend and ended the call so I could dial the number he found for me. It was times like this I was glad the community was so small.

I went into the call planning to show restraint and respect. He was the man who my wife cheated on me with and married when I could still smell her perfume in the house, but that was a long time ago. This wasn't about the end of my marriage to Katya. It was about his and him dealing with his own problems. I took a moment to concoct what I was going to say to him, settling on explaining the situation in a calm, steady tone and asking him to come talk to Katya so we could get past this.

By the time the phone rang ten times without being answered, my patience and dedication to remaining calm had run thin, and then when I heard the philandering husband's chirpy voice on the voicemail, I didn't have any restraint left. All my intentions of respect and calm turned into me shouting into the phone.

"She's your problem. Come get her."

I was pretty sure nothing was going to come of that. Peter was free from her. Why would he willingly feed himself back to her?

Tossing my phone onto my nightstand, I rolled over onto my stomach to hold my pillow to my face and scream into it. When all the screaming energy in me was depleted, I flopped down and lay there. That's where I still was twenty minutes later when I heard the door to the penthouse open followed by angry screaming in Russian. I jumped up and rushed out of my bedroom and into the living room. My mother was standing inches away from Katya, face red with anger, her hands flying around as she laid into her. Apparently, her calm voice on the phone was a front, and she was using the extra key I gave her for emergencies to its full benefit.

CHAPTER 24

BRIDGIT

I was proud of myself for managing to make it all the way back to my apartment before I let the tears fall from my eyes. There was so much anger, such humiliation and betrayal, I was able to hold them back as I found my way through the city away from the shiny glamour of Andrei's world and into my own tiny studio. But as soon as the door closed behind me, the stinging in my eyes turned into an uncontrollable deluge, and I collapsed onto the couch. I couldn't even bear the thought of lying on my bed. I hadn't bothered to change the sheets before packing up and leaving for my weekend at the penthouse, intending to toss them in the wash when I got home on Sunday night. If I lay on them now, I'd be able to smell him and remember being there in his arms not two hours before. There was no way I'd be able to handle that.

I covered my head with my arms and sobbed until there was nothing left in me, then sagged on the pillow at the end of the couch and stared into the distance. It felt like I'd just been hit by a truck. I didn't know exactly what was going on between Andrei and his ex-wife. He'd never told me the whole story. In fact, when we were at the bar and he started to apologize for the way he acted, he only briefly mentioned her before shaking his head and stopping. It was as if he didn't want to open up that can of worms again, figuring the tacos and whiskey were enough to bring it all to a close.

I didn't think too much of it at the time. Everyone I'd ever known who was divorced got prickly when it came to talking about their ex-spouses, especially when there was a new crop of drama surrounding them. It would make sense he wouldn't want to bring her into any time we were spending together and would rather just pretend she didn't exist. After all, it was her showing back up that sent him on his tailspin. At least, that's what I thought.

Now, I had no idea what was going on or what I was supposed to think. Seeing her in his home completely blind-sided me. I thought I was going to go spend another wonderful weekend wrapped up in Andrei, only to find the woman not only in his apartment, but obviously planning to stay for a while. She looked totally comfortable there and didn't seem even slightly out of place or ashamed to be there. The only thing I could think was that meant he had given her permission to be there, or she was already there regularly enough it didn't seem like a big deal.

That made me feel sick to my stomach. Whatever was happening between Andrei and me, one thing was for abso-lute certain. There was no way I was going to be a side piece. I just wasn't going to do it. I left the only life I knew so I wouldn't have to be in a loveless marriage. If I had stayed, I would have been expected to behave like all the other wives, to be perfectly fine with my husband sleeping with whoever he wanted at any given time. That was simply understood in our circles. The vast majority of couples married for business purposes, and as long as the business was good, the marriage was considered good. What the husband did when his wife was looking the other way and hosting civilized afternoon teas and ladies' luncheons was never mentioned.

That wasn't something I could ever do. As much as it shattered me to think about Andrei suddenly being gone from my life, his supposedly ex-wife had clearly staked her claim and made it very obvious he was still her territory.

When I managed to gather the strength, I pulled myself up and went to the kitchen to make a cup of coffee. I hadn't had any yet that morning, and Lord knew I needed it, even if all I really wanted to do was cover my head with a blanket and go to sleep for an hour or thirty. I was sitting at the patio table that made up my makeshift dining room with a cup of coffee and untouched cheap pastry when the door opened, and Steven came in. He looked at me with concern in his eyes and came over to the table.

"Are you okay?" he asked.

I shook my head. "Not really."

"Before you tell me what's going on, have you been getting random texts?" he asked.

"Random texts?"

"Yeah. From a number you don't recognize?"

I slid off the chair and went over to my phone where I'd left it on the coffee table after listening to the third voice-mail from Andrei and sobbing even harder.

"Now that you mention it, I feel like I did notice a couple messages, but I figured they were just from a wrong number, so I ignored them. I heard my phone a few times today, but with everything that's been going on with Andrei, I didn't really pay attention," I told him.

"What do you mean what's going on with Andrei?" he asked.

I let out a sigh and sagged on the couch again. Pulling my legs up to my chest, I dropped my head onto the back of the couch and looked over at him.

"Would it be enough to tell you he broke my heart, and I'll give you more details later when I can deal with it?" I asked.

Steven's face morphed from shocked to pissed before he nodded. "Okay for now, but we *are* going to talk about that. Those texts are from Mom."

"What?" I asked sharply, my head snapping up from the back of the couch.

My brother nodded. "I just found out somehow she got your number and has been trying to get in touch with you. Look at them."

I snatched up my phone and scrolled through the messages. They were all essentially the same thing, telling me it was Mom and I needed to call her, or we needed to talk.

"You have got to be fucking kidding me," I said as I read them. "How did she find my damn number?"

"That kind of money gets you just about anything you want. You know that," he said. "But you know she's not just going to let up. If she wants to talk to you, she's just going to keep hounding you until you agree."

"This is seriously the last thing I need right now. I'm already dealing with enough. After the epic mess that was my Saturday morning, I really don't want to talk to Mom," I said.

I let out another sigh and dropped my head back again, squeezing my eyes closed against a new rush of tears threatening to fall and a deafening rush of thoughts going through my head.

"What do you want to do?" Steven asked.

I shook my head, then opened my eyes and looked at him.

"Can you help me get out of the city? I need to not be here right now. I need a break," I told him.

Steven didn't hesitate. He nodded and pulled out his phone, texting as he talked.

"Get your stuff packed," he said. "I know exactly where you can go. Bring clothes and everything you'll need for as long as you want to stay away."

"Conveniently, most of my stuff is already packed," I said bitterly, gesturing toward the bag I'd packed for when I thought I'd be bunking at Andrei's house. "I'll grab a few more things."

When I was ready, we piled into Steven's car and set out on a long drive into upstate New York. We finally pulled up in front of an adorable cabin tucked away in the foliage like a storybook. I climbed out of the car and put my hand over my eyes to block the sunlight as I looked at the cabin.

"Do you like it?" he asked.

"Birthday gift from Mom and Dad?" I asked, only half-joking.

Steven let out a short laugh and shook his head.

"No. It belongs to a college buddy of mine. He almost never makes it up here anymore, and he said I could use it whenever I wanted. No one will find you here," he said.

He put a code into a lockbox on the side of the front door and withdrew a key to let us in. The cabin was cozy and welcoming inside, but still had the air of luxury I would expect from one of Steven's friends.

"This is perfect," I told him, looking around, then turning back to him. "I just need to figure out what I'm going to do next. Steven, I can't work with Andrei anymore. I know you got me the job, and I appreciate it so much, but..."

Steven held up a hand to stop me.

"I understand. I don't care about the job. I wouldn't want you to work with him anymore, anyway. I have half a mind to kick his ass for whatever he's done to hurt you."

I smiled and shook my head. "Thank you for that, but it's not even worth it. I promise you I am going to start looking for a new job ASAP."

He shook his head. "Don't even worry about that right now. Stay here and decompress as long as you need to. I'll order you some groceries for delivery, and if you need anything else, let me know. I'm really sorry, but I have to get back to the city. I wish I could stay here with you longer."

I shook my head.

"It's fine," I said. "You've already done so much for me. I don't want you to keep putting your life on hold to save me."

"Well, I will if you need me to. Just remember that," he told me. Steven reached in his pocket and pulled out his wallet. He separated a stack of cash and set it on the table. "Just in case."

I hugged him tight.

"Thank you. For everything."

He left and I immediately pulled the battery out of my phone, curled up on a massive recliner, and allowed myself to cry.

CHAPTER 25

ANDREI

By Monday, I was ready to cut my losses, run for whatever border I could get to fastest, and start a new life under an assumed identity. It was a touch melodramatic, but considering how the weekend unfolded, it seemed appropriate. Katya showing up and Bridgit storming away turned out to be the peak of the weekend. Everything went downhill from there, starting with my mother showing up.

When she burst into the apartment screaming and flailing, it was instant chaos. The penthouse filled with the women shouting in Russian, getting progressively louder until I was sure my neighbors on the floors below would be able to hear and call the police. That would just put the cherry on top of the whole incident. The SWAT team swarming the apartment to rescue the women who were clearly in distress would be fantastic for my mental state. Especially considering I was sure they would totally miss the fact that *I* was the one actually in distress and they were the ones causing it.

But the conversation took a strange, sharp turn I didn't see coming. As Mom screamed at her, finally letting out all the anger from our divorce, Katya defended herself. She got louder until her voice was above my mother's and forced her to stop and listen to what happened to her. It couldn't possibly work. Pouring out her whining because her husband cheated on her on the mother of the man who she cheated and divorced had to backfire. Right?

Apparently fucking not.

Somehow my ex-wife managed to convince my mother to not only listen to her bleeding-heart story, but to sympathize with her. I stood there in absolute shock as the screaming match turned into a shouted argument and then into a loud conversation and then into the two women sitting on my couch talking about everything.

"Can I get you two some coffee or something?" I asked sarcastically.

"That would be very nice," Mom said.

"I would prefer tea," Katya said. "Something without caffeine. I've been having such a hard time sleeping."

Mom reached over and rubbed her back, nodding with understanding.

"Of course you have. Anyone who has gone through what you are would be." She looked over at me. "Go on, Andrei. Bring us some cookies as well."

"Oh, I'm not hungry," Katya said.

"You need to try to eat something. You are nothing more than skin and bones. I know this is hard, but you have to take care of yourself," Mom told her.

My eyes rolled so hard into the back of my head I nearly tipped myself over backward. I had no interest in serving them, but I had to get away from the messed-up lovefest happening on my couch. By the time I got back with a tray laden with coffee, tea, and a plate of cookies, the two women were sitting even closer together and nodding as they talked quietly.

I set the tray down on the table in front of them and gave a dramatic sweeping gesture toward it. Mom stood up and stepped up to me.

"I have to go, son," she said.

"You seriously just asked me to make you coffee," I pointed out.

"No, thank you. I need to get home to your father. Now, you be a good boy and take care of Katya," she said.

I blinked a few times, waiting for the punchline, but she started toward the door.

"Excuse me?" I asked, following her. "Did you just tell me to take care of Katya? I sincerely hope you are using that as a euphemism and are going home to Dad so you can't testify at the trial."

"Don't talk like that," she said. "You're going to let Katya stay here until she gets on her feet."

She patted my cheek and walked out of the apartment, leaving me so shocked I couldn't even begin to process a logical thought. As soon as she was gone, a thousand responses flashed into my mind, but it was too late. I had literally been so blown away by what just happened I didn't even have the presence of mind to argue with her.

What in the living fuck just happened?

I turned around and found Katya still sitting on the couch, sipping the tea and nibbling on the edge of a cookie. She gave me a smug look, and I forced myself to walk past her and go into my room. Now was not the time for me to tell her what I was thinking or how I actually felt about the situation. There had been enough screaming in the apartment for that day, and I just needed to get this figured out, one step at a time.

That started with getting in touch with Bridgit. If I had to tolerate Katya for a couple days, fine. It was far from ideal, but I dealt with obnoxious clients and suppliers on a regular basis. I could shut her out and not engage with her any more than I absolutely had to so I could just get through and move on. What was important was talking to Bridgit and making sure she understood what was going on. As long as I had her in my corner, I could deal with this situation.

But no matter how many times I called her, she wouldn't answer. The whole thing went up in flames hours before, but it didn't seem she had calmed down at all. I left voicemails until the box said it was full, then kept calling at regular intervals until the phone stopped ringing. There was nothing left to do but ride it out.

The next day I went by Bridgit's apartment to talk to her. If she wasn't going to answer my calls, I'd just show up and force her to confront me. Even if she wanted to yell at me or demand an explanation, as long as she was talking to me, that's all I cared about. In fact, I hoped she demanded an explanation. If she didn't, I was going to give her one, anyway. She deserved to know what was going on and why everything was as much of a mess as it was.

It wasn't my intention to hide my marriage from her. It's not like I lied to her about it or went out of my way to not tell her about my past. I just never brought it up and she never asked about it. There was never a time where it fit into the conversation and made sense to suddenly blurt out. I didn't want to talk to her about Katya or get into everything that happened, so I just never did. But now I realized that was a mistake. This was part of my life I couldn't ignore, and I had to confront the reality of it. If Bridgit was going to be a part of my life, she needed to know.

But when I got to her apartment, she didn't answer. I peered in the windows I could access and saw it was dark inside. She wasn't there. That ended my ability to try to get in touch with her. No phone and her not being home meant I'd run out of options. The only choice was to deal with Katya in my apartment making herself at home despite my resistance for one more day until I could talk to Bridgit on Monday.

Only, Bridgit wasn't at her desk Monday. I got to the office hours earlier than I needed to just to give myself an escape from the penthouse and my ex-wife but kept looking out through the glass of my office so I could see when she arrived. Gina got there and settled in for work, but there was no sign of Bridgit. I finally went into the breakroom to get another cup of coffee, and when I got out, her desk was no longer empty. A tall, dark-haired man was standing there, and my stomach sank. The resemblance between him and Bridgit was unmistakable other than the color of their hair, and it only took a few seconds for me to remember I'd met him before several years ago.

I walked up to the desk, and he glared at me, his eyes dark and flashing with anger. Gina was watching us both with trepidation.

"Can I help you?" I asked.

"I'm Steven Holliday. I worked with you a few years ago. I'm also Bridgit's older brother."

"Is she all right?" I asked.

He drew in a breath, squaring his shoulders and puffing out his chest like he was keeping himself calm through a question I didn't have the right to ask.

"She left and won't be coming back. I'm just here to get her things," he said.

I waited for more, for him to lay into me or even to hit me. Even though I probably deserved both, he didn't do either, which told me Bridgit must not have told him everything that happened. I couldn't imagine a brother not reacting extremely aggressively when he heard a story like what was going on between Bridgit and me.

"Is there anything I can do?" I asked.

"You can leave her the fuck alone."

Steven collected everything from Bridgit's desk and walked up to Gina.

"You have everything?" my assistant asked, sounding sad.

"I'm pretty sure I do. If you find anything else that's hers, just hang on to it and we'll figure out a way to get it back to her. I'm really sorry it didn't work out," Steven said.

"It's not your fault," Gina reassured him. "But I'm sorry, too. I will really miss her. Tell her I'm thinking about her."

They were talking like I wasn't even there, like I didn't know I was the cause of all this. I walked around her desk and sat down hard on what was her seat, wondering how the hell my life had gone sideways so damn fast. In literally a matter of minutes, I went from feeling on top of the world to everything in a tattered heap around me.

CHAPTER 26

BRIDGIT

As lovely as the upstate cabin was, I would be lying if I said I settled right in and got comfortable immediately. It was a major departure from my tiny studio, which I thought I would absolutely love. Instead, it felt strange and unnerving at first. I was very aware of being a visitor, and not the type of visitor I was accustomed to being in places like this. The cabin was very much like places my family was invited to visit during the summer or over holiday weekends. It was different then. We were being hosted and spent our time pampered and relaxing.

This wasn't that. There was no host here to welcome me. No smiling family who looked like they should be etched on a postcard or even heavily tanned bachelor who tried to seem twenty even when he was pushing fifty. The kitchen wasn't brimming with food prepared by a private chef or delivered by a service, and no matter how much I hoped, when I put my dirty clothes outside the door in the morning, they didn't show up clean and folded on the end of my bed when I went back in at night.

But it wasn't those indulgences that set it apart the most. It was the feeling of hiding. I wasn't a guest here, I was a visitor, a temporary intruder who was using the space not for comfort and relaxation, but to try to escape from the awful situation back at home. For the second time in less than six months, I had run away from my life. Only this time, it didn't feel like there was another one waiting for me. When I left my parents' house and embarked on my own for the first time, there was a lot of fear and uncertainty, but also a sense of relief and almost adventure. I was taking control of my life and had hope I'd figure out a way to land on my feet. Or at least to skate by until my parents came to their senses.

This time, that feeling wasn't there. I didn't run from a life I didn't want or try to escape a situation that personally harmed me. And I didn't have the hope of something better waiting for me. I left because of hurt and embarrassment, anger, and not wanting to tumble down that slippery slope toward being used again. Ahead of me was nothing. I didn't know what I was supposed to do next or even what I wanted to do. I liked the office. I liked Gina. But every time Andrei came back into my mind, it reminded me of why I had leave in the first place.

I couldn't stay in the cabin forever. It was on loan from Steven's friend, so at some point I was going to have to leave it and figure out where I was going to go and what I was going to do next. But not now. For now, I was going to keep my head firmly in the sand and ignore everything.

Saturday was spent mostly crying and staring into the distance wondering what had happened to throw my life for a curve so suddenly. When I woke up Sunday, all my tears were gone, and I had to scrape myself together to accept the grocery delivery Steven sent for me and start trying to settle into the cabin. No matter how long I ended up staying there, it was my temporary home, so I might as well get comfortable in it. That started to happen right around the middle of Monday when I prepared my first meal after surviving the last few days on snacks and far too much sweet tea. It was the only thing that sounded good. But Monday I looked out the window at the beautiful surroundings and let out a sigh. I felt almost at home.

By Tuesday morning I was rethinking the sweet tea. It seemed I'd gotten way too much of it in my system, and my body was rejecting the influx of sugar. I felt sick to my stomach as soon as I woke up, and it got more intense when I got out of bed. Just the thought of eating anything made my stomach flip over, and I steered clear of the kitchen. The feeling settled down after a while, and I was finally able to eat some crackers without feeling too bad. When the feeling came back the next morning, my thoughts turned away from overdoing it on the sweet tea and to the possibility I was actually sick.

That was the last thing I needed right now. I hated being sick and was a self-admitted pansy when it came to even a slight bug. Ending up with some sort of stomach flu while I was alone in a secluded cabin did not sound like my idea of fun. But I didn't know the nearby town well enough to find a doctor there, so I figured I would give myself just a little more time to see if I got over it on my own.

Thursday it was still there, and by Friday, I knew I needed to see someone. As much as I would have liked to pretend I was a survivalist out in the field able to take care of myself in any circumstances that might happen, the continued nausea coupled with a total lack of appetite that left me feeling tired and weak worried me. I popped the battery back into my phone and scrolled through listings for the town to find a clinic that accepted walk-in patients.

Steven and a friend of his had brought my car to me on Wednesday so I was able to drive to the town, though in retrospect, I probably shouldn't have. I was dizzy and woozy as I drove along the narrow road, hoping the entire time I would be able to get there without being involved in any sort of accident. When I finally got to the clinic, I wasn't looking forward to a long wait to be seen and was relieved to see the waiting room completely empty. As soon as I filled out the paperwork at the registration desk, a nurse called me back and led me to an examination room.

She asked what brought me in, and I described my symptoms, being sure to include I was going through an emotionally difficult time. I didn't want to sound overly dramatic about everything, but I knew the upheaval in my life might have contributed at least some to my change in appetite and difficulty sleeping. She nodded and went through her list of usual questions, before landing on one I hadn't even considered.

"Could you be pregnant?" she asked. The question hit me, and my heart jumped so hard I couldn't respond. The nurse was staring down at the tablet in her hand and looked up when I didn't answer. "Could you be pregnant?" she repeated.

"Um," I said, trying to buy myself time as I struggled not to throw up.

Now that she said it, it hit me. I knew I could be.

"When was your last period?" she asked.

I thought about it, counting back and trying to piece it together. With as much stress and turmoil as I was dealing with, I might have gotten off with my tracking.

"Over a month ago," I admitted.

"And have you been sexually active in that time?" she asked.

"Yes," I told her, reality starting to settle in and panic starting to creep up through me.

The nurse lowered the tablet and looked directly at me. The expression on her face said she knew she had to walk me through this step by step.

"And did you use protection? Were you on birth control?" she asked.

I shook my head.

"No. On both accounts. I hadn't been in a relationship in a long time, so I didn't feel the need to be on any sort of birth control, and the encounter was... unexpected. I didn't have any condoms in my apartment."

I waited for the judgment, for the nurse to cluck her tongue at me and start lecturing me on how I should have thought ahead and been more responsible. But that didn't come. Instead, she nodded.

"I'll be right back."

She left me alone in the room, a million thoughts going through my head, and a few seconds later returned with a cart of medical supplies. She took my hand and pricked my finger, gathering some blood to use for a test. Spots started dancing in front of my eyes, and I tried to hang on to my consciousness, but there was nothing I could do. Darkness closed in around the outer edges of my vision, and everything went black.

I had no idea how long I'd been out when I started waking up again. At first, I was only aware of the sound of a machine beeping and muffled voices. The more I concentrated on them, the more aware of my surroundings I became. Little by little I realized something was in my arm, and I was stretched out with a blanket draped over me. As I opened my eyes, I became aware of someone sitting beside me. The first thing I saw was the IV taped to the inside of my elbow, pumping fluids into my vein. Then I lifted my eyes and found my brother sitting in a chair with his arms crossed angrily over his chest and his eyes burning into me.

"Steven?" I asked.

The nurse came into the room just at that moment and offered me a hint of a smile.

"You're awake," she said, coming to the side of the bed and starting through the rotation of checking my vital signs. "How are you feeling?"

"All right, I guess. How long have I been out?" I asked.

"About an hour. When you passed out, we called the emergency contact you put on your registration forms. We thought you would appreciate having someone with you when you woke up," she told me.

I nodded, even though the way Steven was looking at me was far from comforting and reassuring. He looked furious and still hadn't said a single word.

"Thanks. How is... everything?" I asked.

"Well," the nurse said, looking at her tablet. "You are definitely dehydrated, which is why we have you hooked up to the IV. It's just some fluids to help get you back to a good place. You're also a few pounds shy of where you should be for your height and body type, so you'll need to be really conscious of your nutrition moving forward. Especially with the baby."

Steven's eyes snapped to the nurse and then back to me. He still didn't say anything, but I could see the disappointment, anger, and worry in his eyes. This was far from what he wanted from me, but I knew a lot of the negative emotions were directed at Andrei rather than just me. The nurse disconnected my IV and gave me a thick stack of papers, instructing me to get in touch with the OB/GYN soon to make an appointment. Since it seemed I was still very early in my pregnancy I wouldn't need regular appointments for a little while, but it was important to start my prenatal care as soon as possible to ensure the baby stayed safe and I was keeping myself healthy.

The baby.

I listened to all of it with my head spinning and my heart pounding. By the time they discharged me and I started getting dressed, I felt like I might faint again. But I had absolutely no interest in staying there in the doctor's office any longer, so I fought to keep it together and managed to make it outside to the car. Steven demanded I let him drive me back to the cabin, saying he would go back for his car later when I rested up.

"How did you get here so fast?" I asked.

"I happened to already be on my way to the cabin when they called," he told me. "I have more clothes for you and picked up some extra food. Seems you're definitely going to need it now."

"Steven, I want to tell you everything," I told him. "You should know what's going on."

He didn't respond, so I jumped right into the story, starting from the very beginning and telling him all that happened. I spared him most of the details but ensured he got the general idea of how I got to this place. It was an awkward conversation, but at least it gave him an idea of why I was in such an emotional place even before finding out about the baby. By the time I finished, we were back at the cabin and sitting inside.

He got to his feet and paced back and forth in front of me, sighing as he seemed to try to think through everything as calmly as he could. Finally, he looked at me again.

"I've talked to my buddy, and he said you can use the cabin for as long as you need. He'll let me know if he needs it, but he rarely uses it. That gives you somewhere to be, and you don't have to go back until you're ready. You'll be safe, no one will know where you are, and you'll be able to think about everything and decide what you're going to do. I'll do all I can to take care of you," he promised.

I wanted it to make me feel better, but I was too deep in my confused, overwhelmed thoughts to feel much of anything.

CHAPTER 27

ANDREI

No one would ever be able to say I didn't try. They just also wouldn't be able to say I didn't try for longer than a week. That's exactly the amount of time I was able to tolerate living under the same roof as my ex-wife again.

I was in no mood to socialize with her when I got home from the office Monday after finding out Bridgit was gone and had no intention of coming back. In fact, it was knowing she was at my penthouse that kept me from leaving the office as soon as Bridgit's brother left with her things. I wanted to just go home, lock myself away, and wallow in my own misery for a while. It wasn't the most mature or responsible reaction, but I truly didn't care. She was the only thing I wanted, the only person I could see actually being able to get me through the whole situation with Katya. But it wasn't just that. Even if my ex hadn't shown back up, I would still want to be with her, and the thought of her being gone left a massive gap in my life.

It was difficult to think about not seeing her in the office when I went to work in the morning, or to be able to look through the glass wall of my office just to see her working at her desk or chatting with Gina. In only the month she'd been working with me, I'd become so accustomed to Bridgit being a part of my office and my world. Her absence would be dearly noticed and already hurt. It made me not want to focus on anything, to not think about anything or talk to anyone. All I wanted was to be alone and deal with my emotions on my own.

But the thought of spending even a second longer in Katya's proximity than was absolutely necessary kept me right in place in the office until an hour after Gina left. She peeked in at me partway through the day and stared at me with expectation. I knew she was waiting for me to tell her what happened, to give her some sort of insight into why Bridgit was suddenly gone. But there was nothing I could say to her. She knew Katya was back in town, and that was as much as I had to go on. I was hoping Bridget would get in touch with her and let her know what was happening. But neither of us had anything to offer the other, and she walked away without saying anything.

As I made my way back to my penthouse, I held out hope my ex-wife would stay out of my way when I got there. Surely, she had some semblance of tact, some awareness of how ridiculous these circumstances were. She had to know the vast majority of people would just kick her out on her ass without a single second thought, and she was lucky as hell to be where she was. But apparently, I gave her far too much credit. When I got home, she was in the kitchen wearing nothing more than lounge shorts that barely cover her butt cheeks and a tank top that scooped low over her ample cleavage.

"Welcome home," she said with a grin as she came toward me when I walked into the penthouse.

She reached out for me, and I ducked out of the way just before she latched on.

"What are you doing?" I asked, surveying the epic disaster of my kitchen.

"I'm welcoming you home after a long day of work, of course," she said.

The irony of that didn't escape me. Even when we were married, she made a special effort to welcome me home after work only a handful of times beyond our first two years of marriage. Evidently all it took was a divorce, several years apart, and a dose of reality from a cheating husband to convince her to give me so much as a cursory hello when I came in. Not that I even wanted that. I would have preferred to come inside and find her cloistered away in the guest room at the opposite end of the apartment.

"I mean in here," I said. "This place is a disaster."

She waved her hand like she was trying to brush away the observation and gave me a dismissive look.

"It's not that bad. Besides, your housekeeper will take care of it. I'm assuming she comes in tomorrow morning? I was expecting her today, but it occurred to me it was only just you here before now, so she doesn't need to come every day," she said.

I rolled my eyes as I reached into the refrigerator for a bottle of beer.

"Or maybe she doesn't come every day because she doesn't exist," I pointed out.

"No housekeeper?" she asked as if she couldn't possibly fathom the reality.

"You were the one who insisted on having one when we were married because you didn't want to do the cleaning, and you didn't want me doing it because you said I already spent too much time working as it was," I told her.

I started for my bedroom, deciding to leave her to deal with the aftermath of her culinary experiment on her own.

"Where are you going?" she whined after me. "Aren't you going to have dinner?"

"Not whatever you cooked. If I get hungry, I'll order something," I called back.

She made an angry sound not unlike a small child having a temper tantrum, and I heard her stomp her foot just as I stepped into my room and shut the door behind me. The week didn't get any better from there. Katya drove me crazy every minute, trying to flirt with me and fighting with me in equal measure. It took until Tuesday for her soon-to-be second ex-husband to start calling back. She refused to speak to him, so he called me. When I left him the voice-mail, I didn't think it all the way through, not expecting him to use my phone number to start calling me at all hours of the day and night. He alternated back and forth between calling us, even when I silenced my own ringer, then resorted to blocking his number, and Katya just let the phone ring.

By Friday I was completely done. But I couldn't just cast her out into the street as much as I would have liked to do it. I made an unspoken agreement with my mother as soon as I didn't argue with her about my ex-wife staying with me, and at forty I still hadn't gotten to an age where I was willing to go against her.

That didn't mean I actually had to spend any time with my ex. So, before going into work Friday morning, I contacted my Realtor and had him find me a small apartment for rent nearby. I packed up what I thought I would need for the weekend and left Katya there at the penthouse. The apartment was small and sparse, but I was willing to deal with just about anything to get away from her even for a short time.

That night I called up Gus and had him meet me at the bar. It wasn't easy to be in such close proximity to Bridgit's studio, knowing that she wasn't there, but I needed the time with my best friend. In all honesty, I needed the vodka, too. He sat across from me at the booth, listening to me ramble on about Bridget and come up with various different scenarios and stories to explain why she went away the way she did. He sipped at his own drink, nodding and making acknowledging sounds when he could wedge himself into my tirade. He had been a saint since the morning Katya appeared and listened to me lament Bridgit running away several times since then.

"You already know how I feel about all this," Gus said when I was finished and took a breath to drain my glass. "This isn't really your fault, and as much as you want to blame yourself for it entirely, that's not the case. Bridgit didn't even give you the chance to explain what was going on. If she had, you could have worked it out."

I knew he was right. If she had just talked to me, I could have explained the whole issue with Katya and convinced her not to just leave. Maybe we could have even tucked ourselves away in her studio together for the weekend rather than my penthouse. As long as I was with her, I didn't care where I was. But she hadn't given me the benefit of the doubt, and instead chose to just disappear without saying anything. I didn't tell Gus about my thoughts, but I couldn't help but privately wonder if there was more to it than just seeing Katya.

The beginning of an answer to that question came Monday morning when I went to work after spending my weekend tucked away in the small apartment. It was infinitely better than hiding in my bedroom in my own house, and even with the drastically reduced space and amenities, I was more comfortable than I'd been all week. But it didn't take long for that improved feeling to disappear. I'd only been at work for an hour or so when two very well-dressed older people walked through the door into the office. Gina immediately got up and stepped toward them, intercepting them from coming right to me where I was walking back to my office with another cup of coffee.

"Can I help you?" she asked.

"Yes," the man said flatly. "We need to speak with Andrei Petrov."

"Is he expecting you?" Gina asked.

"No," the woman said. "But we need to speak with him."

"I'm sorry, you're going to have to make an appointment. Mr. Petrov is very busy and cannot accommodate people simply walking into his office demanding his time," Gina said, obviously not giving two shits about how important these two clearly thought they were and losing her patience with them by the breath.

"Excuse me, young lady," the man said, and that was the moment I decided to intervene.

Gina was an amazing assistant and could usually deal with a lot, but after everything going to hell over the last couple of weeks, she was a touch on edge. I could handle this more quickly and smoothly.

"It's all right, Gina," I said, stepping up to them. "I'm Andrei Petrov. How can I help you?"

I didn't bother to extend my hand, and neither of them gave me the courtesy, either.

"Mr. Petrov, can we speak?" the man asked.

His eyes flicked over to Gina and back to me in that way

influential people often thought was subtle but was glaringly obvious. I wasn't going to humor him.

"I have a few minutes. Go on," I said.

He looked exasperated but didn't push.

"We are Bridgit Holliday's parents," he said, not bothering to give me names. "I believe you are familiar with her."

"She worked here recently, yes," I told them, my stomach clenching in anger. I could see now why Bridgit had run from their arrogance.

They exchanged glances, and I saw their expressions shift, suddenly taking on worried looks that didn't seem entirely genuine.

"We are so very worried about her. I don't know what she told you of her life before she came to work here, but she is a very troubled girl going through a difficult time. She's in a state of rebellion right now, and we're afraid her actions are going to threaten her safety and her future. Surely you can understand our concern. Your children must be around her age," he said.

I bristled, drawing myself up and squaring my shoulders to him.

"I don't have children," I said.

No matter how upset I was with Bridgit for leaving me, I wasn't going to throw her to the wolves. From everything she told me about these people, they weren't to be trusted, and she wanted nothing to do with them. If they couldn't get in touch with her, that was by design, and I wasn't going to be the one to force her back into their clutches.

"Oh, well I'm sure you can still understand our worry. She left home without notifying us of where she was going or what she was doing. We've been trying to get in touch with her for months now to no avail. We have reason to believe she's participating in unsavory activities not befitting her raising," her mother said, adding a few layers to the sob story.

"From what I know, Bridgit is a grown woman who doesn't have to be accountable to anyone," I pointed out. "She is well beyond the age necessary to live on her own, and she's not obligated to make an accounting of her actions to you."

"We are her parents," Mr. Holliday said with an edge of offense in his voice.

"I understand that, but she is an adult, and if she doesn't want her whereabouts or actions known, that's not anyone else's business."

"We're worried about her," Mrs. Holliday insisted again as if that would make a difference. "You must know where she is."

"I don't. I haven't seen her in over a week. She only worked here for a short time, and moved on," I told them, leaving out the part where she'd disappeared and sent her brother to get her things.

"But..."

"Listen Mr. and Mrs. Holliday, I told you everything I know. Now, like my assistant told you, I'm very busy and I have to go back to work now. You can see yourselves out."

They both looked startled by my rudeness, but there was nothing else for them to say. They made their way out, and as soon as they were gone, Gina came up to me and gave me a hug. She didn't know all the details of what happened, either, but she knew enough to understand that was hard for me. The gesture was nice, but I hated her pity, even if I deserved it.

CHAPTER 28

BRIDGIT

It would be a lie to act like I immediately jumped right into the maternal instincts and got the hang of pregnancy as soon as I got back from the clinic. In truth, the news didn't even fully settle in until the next day, and it was Monday before I felt like I really understood what was going on and had come to terms with it. I happened to see a note on some of the papers the nurse gave me suggesting eating crackers while still in bed in the morning to help curb the effects of the morning sickness and tried it that morning. It really did make a difference, and I felt like I could get up and get around the house for the first couple of hours of the day without feeling like throwing up was imminent.

That got me on the path of taking better care of myself. I hadn't realized my weight had slipped so much in the days after seeing Andrei's ex-wife in his penthouse. The stress and sadness had taken away my appetite, and I hadn't bothered to think about eating. But now that I realized I needed to get my weight up for not just myself but also a baby who was depending on me, I had to pay better attention to how I was taking care of myself. Not that I really had the option of forgetting. Ever since I fainted and he was called as my emergency contact, Steven was checking in with me multiple times a day to ensure I was drinking enough water and eating regularly.

Several grocery deliveries had already shown up at the cabin along with a massive water cooler like the ones usually accompanied by stacks of tiny paper cone cups. It seemed a little excessive, but he was determined I was going to remember to eat, drink, and take the vitamins he also had delivered. I hadn't even had an appointment with an OB yet, and I felt like I was already way ahead of the game. Uncle Steven was on the case, and he wasn't going to let me slide at all.

It wasn't always easy. Even with the crackers, there were times when the thought of food made me want to run for the hills, or at least the nearest bathroom. I learned to find foods that didn't have a strong smell but gave me a boost of nutrition when those times came up. It took a few days, but I was getting into the groove of it.

As I started to feel better, I also started exploring the small town more. I discovered I didn't actually need to drive into town but could take a different access road that gave me a pleasant walk down to the shops and restaurants that lined the picturesque streets. It was nice to get out and enjoy some fresh air away from the city smells. Every day I made my way down there and explored the town, getting to know it a little more. I had no idea how long I was going to be staying in the cabin, but for as long as I did, it was home, and this was my neighborhood. Getting to know it would at least draw me out of my shell and stop me from becoming a hermit in the cabin. It would also help distract me from all the feelings I had and the questions coursing through my mind. I'd have to deal with them eventually, but for now I just needed to focus on my well-being for the baby's sake.

It was a Wednesday morning when a stroll along a quiet stretch led me to stumble on a small shop with a hand-written HELP WANTED sign taped in the window. I peered beyond it through the glass of the window and saw it was an adorable little art store. Steven had promised to take care of everything for me throughout my pregnancy and was seeing to my every need, so I didn't have to worry about anything. But that just put me right back into the position I was in when he first got me the job through Gina, and I didn't want to be there again. Even more now that I wasn't just thinking about myself.

I was only a few weeks into my pregnancy, but I already knew that I had to get my shit together in order to be a single mom. The rest of these months were going to go by faster than I was probably prepared for, and I needed to be ready to stand on my own two feet and provide for not only myself, but my child. It was just the two of us, and whether that ever changed or not, I needed to feel like I wasn't just moping around waiting to be rescued. I needed to be able to do this on my own.

Drawing in a resolute breath, I walked into the shop to talk to the owner.

I walked out two hours later with a new job and a possible new friend. It turned out I didn't need to talk to the owner of the shop, but rather the manager who took care of everything while the owners spent most of their time in Florida. They retired there a few years back and returned for visits occasionally, but for the most part left everything in the hands of the competent manager who had been with them for many years. Her name was Rhea, and the wrinkles around her eyes from her bubbly, laugh-filled personality pegged her at being around Andrei's age. She was thrilled when I said I was interested in the job, though that was tempered slightly when she clarified the position wasn't exactly a high-powered full-time one.

Reassuring her I was only in the market for something that would earn me a little money and help ease me back into the market brought back all the brightness and spirit. There was only one more bit of news I needed to share with her, and it was as much in the spirit of full disclosure as it was to give me practice saying it. I hadn't told anyone about the baby yet. Steven was the only one who knew, and technically I hadn't even told him. The nurse did. This would be a good chance for me to get used to saying the words to someone who didn't really have a stake in the game. If she was upset about it, the only real issue I would face is her rescinding the job, and then I wouldn't be any worse off than I already was.

So, I took a breath and told her.

"I'm pregnant," I said.

Rhea looked me up and down, focusing on my stomach behind my flowing sundress.

"Where?" she asked.

I laughed. "It's very early. I only just found out. But I am."

"Well, congratulations," she said. "Babies are wonderful. And don't you worry. From the looks of it and if you just found out, you have lots of time before you have to worry about it getting in the way of anything you'd be doing around here. We'll figure it out when you're ready to pop."

I laughed when she said that, but as I walked away, the thought settled into me that I didn't even know if I'd still be there at the cabin when that time came. It was so hard to think about anything in the future, particularly that far.

Right now, I had to focus on just one thing, one step, one day at a time. If I could get that down, I'd move on to the next.

The walk took it out of me, and by the time I got back to the cabin, I was more than ready to kick off my shoes and relax for a little while. I was pleasantly surprised to find I was hungry and cautiously started nibbling my way through some of the food filling the cabin kitchen. I brought a plate into the living room and stretched out on the couch to call Steven.

"Are you okay?" he asked by way of answering the call.

"I really hope that isn't the way you intend on answering every phone call from me for the next eight months, because it's going to get really obnoxious, really fast," I said.

"I'm sorry. I'm just jumpy and worried about you. What's up?" Steven asked.

I laughed at his attempt to sound casual and pulled a blanket down over my legs as I rested my head on a throw pillow.

"I got a job," I announced.

"Why did you do that?" he asked. "I told you I could take care of everything. You need to be resting."

"I don't need to spend my entire pregnancy resting. This isn't medieval times. You know how much I appreciate everything you've done for me and everything you're doing for me. I'm not saying I'm pushing you away or that I don't still need you, because I definitely do. But I want to be independent. I need to take care of myself and this baby. It's not like I'm going to be laying brick or anything. I'm just going to be working the register at a little art shop. The manager there is really nice, and I need a friend after everything. Being away from Gina has made this even harder. I'm really happy. Can't you be happy for me, too?"

"Of course I'm happy for you. If you want to have a job, then I think it's great. And it's great for you to have a new friend, too."

He drew in a breath, and I had the slightly sinking feeling there was something else coming.

"What is it?" I asked.

"You mentioned Gina. I was going to call you later to tell you..."

"What's wrong? Is she all right?"

"Yes, she's fine. I didn't know if I should tell you this."

"Tell me what?" I asked, starting to feel nervous.

"I talked to her a few days ago," he said.

I let out a breath.

"Please don't tell me she told you Andrei is moping around and I need to talk to him," I groaned.

"You might not want to talk to him, but Mom and Dad did."

"What?" I asked.

"They found out where you worked and went by the office to talk to Andrei. Gina says he didn't tell them anything, but they are sniffing around and tried to really push him to give them more information," Steven said.

"Why won't they just leave me alone?" I asked.

"It's going to be fine," he told me. "They still don't know where you are, and no one is going to tell them."

There was a long pause, and I felt my eyes closing under the weight of the exhaustion and the new stress.

"If you have something else you need to say, you better hurry up and say it, because I'm about to fall asleep," I told him.

"You should talk to Andrei."

"That's not going to happen," I countered.

"Fine. But you know as well as I do you should. Just think about calling him. He really should know about the baby."

I let out an exasperated breath. "Fine, I'll think about it."

"All right. You rest. Congratulations on your new job."

CHAPTER 29

ANDREI

"Looks like you're done with your work for the day," Gus said as he came into my office.

My eyes scanned the desk in front of me and the papers I'd organized to file away. My email inbox was nearly empty with most of the emails I'd received that day answered and dealt with, and the only ones lingering there waiting for response were from clients or suppliers.

"Yeah," I said. "I had a pretty productive day, I guess."

"Then why are you still sitting at the desk like you're getting ready to do something else?" he asked.

"Because I'm trying to figure out something else to do. It's still early," I told him.

He scoffed. "It's also Friday."

"Did they change the number of hours on Fridays and I missed the memo somewhere along the lines?" I asked.

"No, but why would you want to stay at work later?"

I stared at him for a few seconds before extending my hand across the desk to him.

"Hi. I'm Andrei Petrov. It's nice to meet you."

Gus laughed and rolled his eyes.

"All right. Fair enough. But you're spending more and more time here every day. Gina says you're already here well before she gets here every day, and you stay here after she's gone for the night. She came back the other day four hours after she left because she'd forgotten something, and you were still here. At some point you're either going to need to move in and just be here twenty-four hours a day or take a break."

"Let me think about that," I said.

He stood up and walked around behind my chair. Grabbing it by the top, he yanked me backward and started wheeling me toward the door to the office.

"I guess we'll do it this way."

"What are you doing?" I asked, gripping the armrests beside me.

"We'll call it an intervention. You're getting out of this funk you've been in for the last few weeks and coming back into the land of the living. We're going out tonight," he announced.

"I can walk on my own," I told him.

"Will you walk out of the office and go with me? If you say no, I will take that as a challenge and wheel your ass to the bar in this chair," he warned.

"I don't want to go to the bar," I said. "Not tonight."

He twisted me around in the chair so he could look at me.

"Not that bar. Different one. I want to bring you to this place I found across town. It's owned by a couple fellow first-generation Russian Americans. They just moved to the area from Chicago and bought this place. I've been there a couple times, and it's really great. You'll like the guys who own it, and I think it will be good for you to be away from everything. At least for a while," he told me.

I knew what he meant was he thought it would be good for me to be away from things that reminded me of Bridgit for a while, he just didn't want to say it. His new method of dealing with the situation was just avoiding talking about her every opportunity he could. It was like he figured the fewer times he put her name out into the universe, the less I'd think about her and eventually she would just cease to exist in my mind. Of course, that wasn't going to happen. The distance between us wasn't making me think about her less. If anything, she came to mind more every day that passed without even hearing her voice. But I was willing to try to move forward. If even for one night.

The bar had a totally different atmosphere than the one I'd gone to with Bridgit. Gus brought me to two men sitting at a table and introduced me to them. These were the owners, brothers who had just relocated from Chicago to follow their father's dream after he had died only a few months before. A young waitress introduced as his daughter brought us all vodka, and Gus and I sat down at the table.

There weren't very many other people there, so we were able to settle into our conversation. In a flow of Russian and English that went back and forth as naturally as if it were one language, the brothers told us about their lives and their move to New York. It was comforting and familiar to hear other people speaking my language and sharing experiences and thoughts that so closely mirrored my own. I found myself relaxing somewhat and enjoyed talking to them, but it didn't take away the thoughts going through my mind. Gus's plan for bringing me here was to help me get over missing Bridgit, but it wasn't working.

We'd been sitting at the bar for a couple of hours, and

the crowds had thickened when I noticed Gus glancing up over my head like he was looking at somebody. His lips turned up in a smile, and he raised his eyebrows at me. My heart jumped in my chest. All I could think was Bridgit was there. Somehow, she'd found me and was standing right behind me. I turned around and couldn't help the wave of disappointment when it wasn't her.

The woman standing a few feet away was pretty, and she looked more than interested in getting my attention. She leaned close to the women she was with to whisper something, picked up her drink, and came toward me. Her walk was practiced and deliberate. Her hips swayed and rolled with each step, aided by the towering spike heels on her shoes and the tight grip of her dress around her.

"Hi, there," she said when she got to the edge of the table.

"Hello," I said.

"Looks like you gentlemen have been waiting a long time for your wives to get here," she said.

She mentioned both of us, but her eyes didn't leave me. Gus immediately clapped his hand on my shoulder and gave me a playful shake.

"Not this guy. He's not married," he offered.

"Thank you, Gus," I said.

She licked her bottom lip, her eyes traveling up and down me like she was a lion sizing up her prey. It wasn't even close to appealing. I knew there were plenty of men at the bar, probably sitting right there at the table with me, who were drooling over this girl and would have very happily scooped her up right then. They were welcome to her. I had no interest.

"Now, that's hard to believe," she said. "How could a

man like you not have had a woman get her claws in him a long time ago?"

"She did," I said. "I didn't particularly like it, and that's why we're divorced."

My blunt tone made her smile falter slightly, but she cocked her hip and kept trying. I had to give it to her, she was persistent. That didn't make it any more likely I was going to be interested in giving her the attention she so obviously craved.

"Too bad for her," she said. "Sounds like you could use some fun. Why don't you come dance with me?"

She reached her hand toward me, but I didn't move.

"Thank you for the offer, but I think I'll stay here with my friend," I told her.

Those definitely weren't words she had ever heard said to her. She looked at me like she thought I was joking or was going to instantly change my mind. When I didn't, she nodded and walked back to the table with her friends.

"What the hell was that?" Gus asked.

I took the last swig of my vodka and set the glass down.

"I'm going to head home," I told him. I looked at my new friends and shook their hands. "Thank you. I'll see you again soon."

Gus got up from his seat and followed me to the door.

"What do you mean you're going to head home? We've only been here two hours."

"I know. And I really appreciate you bringing me here and everything you're trying to do. I'm just not ready for all this yet," I told him.

"That woman was hot as hell," he said. "And she was practically handing over the keys to her panties. You didn't even need to try. She was a sure thing."

"I know."

"So, what happened?" he asked.

He followed me out of the bar and out onto the sidewalk.

"Like I said, I'm just not ready for any of that. I'm not interested. But she's still in there. Maybe you should try."

I laughed as his head snapped back to the door, and he nodded. We said good night, and he went back inside. Part of me felt guilty for leaving so early and for dismissing the woman the way I did. I didn't even give her a chance to tell me her name. But I didn't need to know it. Nothing would have made me want to leave with her. All I could think when I looked at her was that she wasn't Bridgit.

I was halfway in love with her. Maybe even more than halfway. But she'd run away, and I still felt like I didn't know why. It was far too early for me to be thinking about trying with anyone else. I might not ever try again. Not when I'd had my heart ripped out by not one, but two women already.

My rideshare got to me within minutes, and I directed the driver to my new, smaller apartment. Flopping down on the couch, I turned on the TV and looked for something to numb my brain. The combination of more glasses of vodka than I could remember and late-night TV lulled me nearly to sleep, and I was barely conscious when my phone alerted me to a new text. It was Gina, just checking in. She tried to make it seem casual and like it didn't mean anything, but she'd been doing it more and more often recently. I knew she wanted to make sure I was getting through everything all right, but I hated how it felt every time she did it.

I didn't want to feel like she was mothering me, even though I probably needed it. Between Bridgit and Katya, I'd been drinking a lot more recently, and she didn't want to see that cause me to slip into a dark or dangerous place. I hadn't let it affect my work yet, and I wasn't planning on letting it. I wouldn't let it go that far. After reassuring Gina I was safe and secure and wouldn't be drinking any more for the night, I turned off the TV and headed into the cramped bedroom to try to get some sleep.

Yanking off my clothes, I slipped under the covers and tried to sleep. The stress and anxiety kept me from relaxing and I briefly considered jerking off just to help ease the feelings and get me to sleep. But I couldn't bring myself to do it. Even that wasn't right. There was no way I'd be able to touch myself and not think of her, and that would only make it worse. I flipped over onto my stomach, buried my head in the pillow, and willed myself to sleep.

CHAPTER 30

BRIDGIT

The days in between Rhea hiring me and actually getting started were even more difficult than waiting to start at the office. At least then I knew I had Steven's sway giving me some security in the position. Gina had hired me as a favor, and I was fairly certain she wouldn't just withdraw the offer at the last minute, if for no other reason than she wouldn't want to upset him. I didn't have that same feeling with this job. For better or for worse, I got it all by myself. For better, it meant I was finally taking steps to truly be independent and make choices for my own life. For worse, it meant I didn't have the feeling of a safety net beneath me giving me at least a little bit of security. Through the days that passed, I had the lingering feeling that at any moment Rhea would call me and say she made a mistake and was going to go with someone more qualified.

Like someone who had ever worked in a retail establishment. Or knew something about art.

But when Monday morning came and I woke up without a missed called or text, it seemed everything was actually going to work out. I packed lunch and decided to drive to the shop in case I was tired after work. Rhea was standing outside, unlocking the door, when I parked in the small lot and walked around to her. She was trying to juggle two cups of coffee and an artist portfolio, making it hard for her to negotiate the key into the lock.

"Here, let me help you," I said.

"Thanks." She held out one of the coffees, and I took it from her. "That one is yours. I got you decaf."

"Thank you." I took a sip and let out a sigh. "That is so delicious."

"It's a local roaster. He has a shop down the street and sells bags of his beans."

We got inside and she brought me to the small breakroom in the back. She gestured to a cubby where I could put my bag and the refrigerator where I put my lunch. She went to a row of hooks on the wall and took down a white apron with bright blue writing. I put it on and secured the ties around my waist. The thought went through my mind that those ties would help me track how my belly was growing. When we were ready, she brought me up to the front of the shop and behind the cash register.

"I've never actually worked one of these," I admitted.

"That's all right. It's not too hard to learn. I'll help you with it," Rhea said. She went through the process of ringing up sales a few times and then let me try it. "Do you feel like you have it?"

I nodded. "I think so. My last job didn't get off to the smoothest start."

As soon as the words were out of my mouth, I couldn't believe I said them. That wasn't the way I was going to impress my new boss. At the same time, she probably needed to be prepared in case this didn't go as well as my hopeful vision had it going. I waited for her reaction. Maybe this would be the moment when Rhea would rethink hiring someone who wandered in off the street on a whim.

But she didn't seem at all bothered by the declaration. If anything, she smiled at me wider, amused by what I told her more than anything.

"It's going to be fine," she said. "I promise. There's nothing high-pressure about working here. You're not going to be reporting to the CEO anytime soon. You'll pick it up. Besides, the register isn't the only thing that needs to be done around here. I'm not going to chain you to the counter and make you only ring up customers. Come on with me and I'll show you around the shop and tell you the other things we do during the day."

I liked the way she said "we." It made me feel instantly welcome, like I was really part of the team, even if that team was only two people, rather than being an extra tacked on because she needed more help. Just like when that feeling started settling in at the office, it made me want to work even harder, to really push myself and do the very best I possibly could.

I paid close attention as Rhea showed me around the shop, pointing out the various departments and telling me about the products in each. In addition to running the register, I'd be responsible for helping keep the shelves stocked, organizing products, and helping customers find what they needed. Eventually I'd get accustomed to everything and learn more about it so I could give recommendations to people who came in unsure of what exactly they were looking for.

Even though the shop was small, there was a truly amazing variety of supplies available. It was a bit overwhelming at first, and I knew it was going to take me some time to even know where everything was much less know what they were and what they did. After she showed me everything and answered my questions, Rhea cut me loose to explore on my own. The shop was empty for the first half hour it was open, and then a trickle of customers started coming in.

It seemed most of them were regulars, and Rhea was familiar enough with them to ask about their projects and give them recommendations before they even asked for them. I hoped to eventually get to be a part of that. It would be nice to have the people smile at me when they came through the door and to talk to them about their lives. The interactions felt so genuine and warm, and I wanted to experience that.

When lunchtime came along, I ate in the breakroom but didn't take all the time I had for my break. Grabbing an apple from the extra food I brought, I nibbled on it as I continued to walk around the shop trying to memorize where everything was. The afternoon brought a new wave of customers, and I got a chance to try my hand at pointing out some products and even managed to ring up three without making a mistake. It was a minor accomplishment to say the least, but still left me feeling good. I ended the day tired and glad I drove rather than facing the walk back to the cabin. The weather was nice and there was still enough light, but I was worn out and just wanted to get to the couch and rest.

It turned out I wasn't the only one who had sights on the cabin's comfortable living room. Steven's car was parked out front, and as soon as I walked in, I could smell he was cooking. I also noticed the windows were standing open, and when I walked into the kitchen, I found my brother waving a hand towel toward one of the windows like he was trying to get smoke out of the house, but there was no smoke.

"What are you doing?" I asked.

He jumped, startled by my sudden arrival, and turned around to face me.

"Trying to get the smell out of the house," he admitted. "I didn't think about it until after I started cooking and didn't want you to come home and get sick."

"Thank you. That's really nice of you," I said. "But I'm actually doing okay today. This morning was a little rough, but I've been browsing around on some of those expectant mother forums and got a few tips for how to feel less sick during the day. Apparently, the goal is not to let my stomach get empty. As long as I eat something every now and then, I'll feel better. What are you cooking?"

He grinned and displayed a plate with a golden-brown grilled cheese sandwich on it.

"I have soup warming, too," he announced.

"Elegant," I told him, then noticed bags of more groceries on the table. I started going through them and putting everything away. "When I get my first paycheck, I'm going to start buying my own stuff." I let out a sigh. "I feel like we've already had this conversation."

Steven laughed. "We have. But you don't need to do that."

"Yes, I do. You can't just keep paying for everything for me. The least I can do is buy my own food. Especially considering your friend won't even take rent for the cabin," I said.

"Nope. And that's not going to change," he said.

"You really aren't going to tell me who owns it? Not even a name?" I asked.

He shook his head as he served up the food.

"No need to. All that matters is you have access to it for as long as you want it. You don't need to worry about anything else."

We carried our food into the living room and sat on opposite ends of the couch to eat. He asked about my first day of work, and I told him.

"It was really good. I didn't really know what to expect, but Rhea, the woman who hired me, is great. She's so nice and has been running the store for years and years. The owners retired to Florida and still come back to visit every now and then, but she's the one who actually does all the day-to-day stuff. The customers are really nice, too. I didn't think an art shop would be so busy, but there weren't many times when there wasn't anyone in there."

"That's good. It will keep you busy," he said.

"That's definitely what I need right now. How about you? What's going on back home?" I asked.

We talked about everything we could think of that wasn't our parents or Andrei. Those were things we should probably be talking about, but I was more than happy to just put it aside and pretend it didn't exist for just a little while. It was such a good day starting my new job and finally feeling like I was getting a handle of life again. I didn't want to spoil it with one of the unpleasant conversations.

I especially didn't want to drift into talking about Andrei. Steven had made his opinion very clear, and I knew he wanted me to talk to my old boss. That's how I forced myself to see him. I couldn't think of him as anything else. Even as Steven was trying to convince me to tell him about the baby and figure out what I was going to do next, I wouldn't let myself think that way. It helped me not to feel the pain when I thought about him and kept the guilt at bay. I needed to think only about myself and my baby. What was going on with Andrei and his ex couldn't be a factor in my life right now.

And I also couldn't let Steven get any idea of how much I was actually hurting. He was already so angry at Andrei. He was upset about the entire situation and wanted to go after him, but I made him promise not to. It was a strange position for him to be in, wanting both to advocate for and punish Andrei. For right now, I needed him to do neither. I just wanted my brother to be there for me and to accept the decision I made and the ones I would keep making. All I could think about was one day at a time right now.

CHAPTER 31

My plan to temporarily move out of the penthouse and stay in the small apartment so I could be away from Katya had proven very successful. For the first several days, I arrived at the apartment building each day with a bit of trepidation. I wouldn't put anything past her, and I fully expected one of those evenings to get back and find she had not only discovered where I was staying, but had convinced yet another doorman to help her commit breaking and entering. But it didn't happen. Whether it was because I covered up my tracks well enough to prevent her from tracing me or she was simply satisfied to have taken over my home and have it to herself was kind of up in the air. Either way, she was out of my hair, and that's really all that mattered.

Not that I really believed it was going to last forever. Just like us staying away from each other during our divorce hadn't worked out the way I thought it would, I had no expectation, and she was just going to accept me doing everything I could to avoid her, then suddenly decide she was over her major decline and ready to embark on her own life again. At some point she was going to show back up, which was why I wasn't surprised when I showed up at work and found her waiting for me.

Just like the first time she came out of the woodwork, her Lexus was parked in the spot next to my reserved place in the parking deck when I got to work in the morning. I immediately noticed she didn't look anywhere near as infuriated as she did that first morning. In fact, she leaned back against her car in a casual way and gave me a smile that was almost friendly when I climbed out of my car.

"Been spending extra time with your secretary?" she asked.

The tone in the question told me she didn't actually mean it as insulting as it came out. It was a genuine question, her attempt at being cordial with me. It also meant she wasn't paying attention at all because she didn't know Bridgit was gone.

"No," I told her.

That was all I needed to say. She didn't deserve any explanation or justification of anything I did. If it wasn't for her, Bridgit would be here with me. I would have been spending my time with her and not tucked away in a small, inconvenient apartment that had the only a benefit of keeping me from possibly committing murder. There was a time when Katya getting angry at me didn't really bother me so much. In fact, I almost enjoyed it. This was early in our marriage, before I realized her temper tantrums were going to get more intense and more frequent, and that eventually she would destroy me with an affair. In those early arguments, I was able to appreciate how gorgeous she was in her fits of anger, how impassioned she could get.

Those feelings were long gone now. At this point I was

so tired of her, nothing could have made me want to be in the same city with her, much less in such close proximity. I just wanted her to tell me why she was there and get it done with so I could go to work. The fact that she didn't look angry or even upset was somehow more unnerving to me. That meant she was likely about to go into full manipulation mode, and I simply didn't have the time or patience to deal with that. I was braced for a sob story and ready to shoot her down, so when she started talking, I was thrown for a loop.

"Peter came back," she said simply.

"He came back?" I asked. "Are you sure he actually went somewhere? Maybe he's just avoiding you, too."

I walked past her toward the stairs, and she fell right into step behind me just like I expected.

"Your delightful quips aside, I meant he came back to me," she said.

This time, I didn't continue. She'd already taken over my penthouse and somehow brought my mother's sympathies over to the dark side. The fewer of my spaces I allowed her to infiltrate, the better. I stopped and turned to face her.

"Seriously?" I asked.

A smug, self-congratulatory smile crossed her lips, and she cocked her hip to the side as she brought her long artificial nails up to examine them.

"He finally saw the light and realized he just couldn't possibly live without me," she said.

"I thought he's the one who cheated on you," I pointed out.

That brought her smile down a notch, but she maintained the arrogance.

"And he realized what a horrible mistake that was. In the time we've been apart, he's realized just how lost he is without me and that he can't stand the thought of going even another day without me. He came crawling to me, pouring his heart out, apologizing and swearing everything is going to be different."

"Different?" I asked.

I wanted to ask if she meant he was going to keep his dick to himself but thought that might be unnecessarily petty. There was no need to keep the conversation going any longer than it needed to, and that might just stoke the flames.

"He promised me the home in London I've been wanting," she announced. "I've been asking for one since we first got married, and he has always withheld it from me. But he's changed his mind. He's already booked the tickets for us to go look for exactly what I want. My biggest specification is that he buys me a house he didn't sleep with our cleaning lady in, so that shouldn't be too difficult to achieve in London."

It was probably meant as a joke, but it fell flat and awkward.

"I would hope not," I said. "Does this mean you'll be leaving my penthouse?"

"I already have. Peter sent a car for everything earlier, but I wanted to tell you in person," she said. I nearly sang Hallelujah but forced myself to keep it together. Katya didn't deserve the satisfaction of eliciting emotion in me. "And speaking of cleaning ladies, I hired you one for the day. She's there now getting your penthouse back in order. By the time you get home, it will be like I was never there."

"Just how I like it," I told her.

She nodded and I was expecting her to make a snide remark. Instead, she stepped up to me and gave me a quick peck on the cheek.

"You're a good man, Andrei," she said.

I wasn't sure I really believed that. If I was a good man, why did women keep leaving me? But I gave her a nod and watched her walk back to her car and get in. I didn't expect an apology for ruining my day or even invading my penthouse, and she didn't give me one. All that mattered was she was gone. Katya gave me a little wave and drove away.

Gina must have noticed the happier look on my face when I came into the office because she lifted her eyebrows at me.

"You look like you're in a good mood this morning. Well, maybe not a good mood, but a better one than you have been recently."

"Katya is gone," I tell her with a grand sweep of my hand.

Gina gasped and stood up, coming around the desk to hug me.

"Ding, dong, the witch is dead!" she said.

"She just moved out," I clarified. "She's not dead."

"I can take care of that for you," she said, leaning back from the hug.

We laughed and I headed for coffee. When I came back in, I noticed she was going through what looked like personnel files.

"What are you doing?" I asked.

"Looking at the applications and resumes for the people who applied for the secretary position," she explained.

"Why would you do that?" I asked.

She let out a sigh and stared at me.

"For the same reason I looked at them the first time. We need a secretary around here, Andrei. I am not enjoying being back to having to take care of everything. We're getting ready to go into event season, and that's going to mean even more work. I can't do it all. We need to hire somebody," she told me.

"Not one of them," I told her.

"Why not?"

"Because if they're still available after all this time, that doesn't bode well for their skill and competence," I pointed out.

Gina opened her mouth like she was going to say something, then changed her mind and closed it.

"Okay. We'll find someone else," she said, closing the files and setting them aside.

I could only imagine whatever she planned on saying, it had to do with Bridgit.

That evening I was so happy to go back home to my penthouse. A little voice in the back of my mind told me to be cautious, to prepare myself just in case this was an elaborate plan on Katya's part, and she was actually waiting inside to try to lure me into her web. I tried to push it away and be happy just to be back in the building I loved. When I opened the door and only darkness and a fresh, cool smell greeted me, the relief was almost visceral. I turned on the lights and walked around, admiring the work of the housekeeper. There was truly no sign Katya was even there. I needed to find out who did the cleaning and give her a big bonus. This was amazing.

Loosening my tie, I pulled out my phone and called Gina. I gave her the address of the small apartment and asked her to arrange for it to get taken care of for me. I'd need someone to go in and collect my belongings, have the apartment cleaned, and alert the landlord to me no longer being in residence there. He'd granted me a month-to-month lease so it wouldn't be an issue to leave. She agreed and I went into my bedroom, falling face-first onto the bed.

I lay there breathing deeply, glad the bed didn't smell like Katya or Bridgit.

Having my ex-wife gone felt like a major weight off my shoulders. I went to work the next day more energized and focused, ready to tackle what was ahead of me. Everything wasn't quite back to the way I wanted it to be, but not having Katya to contend with was a considerable step forward. For the next several days I was able to dig deep into work and get a solid amount done, finally catching up to my usual productivity and getting back ahead at the margin I preferred. But that didn't mean I was completely out of the woods when it came to women driving me insane.

"Can't you at least put out another advertisement?" Gina asked two days after our first conversation. "Just start getting feelers out there and we'll try to find someone."

I didn't answer her, and she waited another day before coming at me again with another plea to look for a secretary. I still wouldn't agree to starting to search again, and she decided to take another tactic. Rather than actively asking me to hire another secretary, she started complaining about the amount of work she was doing and making it plainly obvious how much smoother things would be if she had someone to help her. This made me ignore her just for the humor of it, but after two weeks of dealing with her grumping, I decided she was probably right. There was a reason we had hired Bridgit to begin with, and that was because we had too much work for the two of us to manage completely on our own.

"All right," I told her when she let out a sigh that would have a good place in any production of *Streetcar* and draped herself over a stack of files. "We'll look for another secretary. But look for an older man. Possibly gay if you can manage it."

Gina laughed but nodded.

"I'll figure out a way to have that in the job listing," she said. "I've already been working on the ad."

"Tell me how it goes," I said and headed for my office, feeling like I was taking steps toward finally having closure.

At least, that's what I was going to tell myself.

CHAPTER 32

BRIDGIT

"Are you going to find out what the baby is?" Rhea asked.

I looked over at her from where I was unpacking a shipping box of acrylic paint and organizing the bottles on a shelf.

"I don't know," I told her. "I haven't really thought about it."

She gave me an incredulous look.

"You haven't thought about it? Not even once? You have a human being growing inside you right now and you're trying to tell me there hasn't been a single moment in the last four months when you have tried to envision your child? One time when you haven't imagined having a tea party with your little girl or digging in the sand with a little boy?" she asked.

"Maybe my little boy would want to have tea parties," I pointed out.

"True. That is absolutely valid. But does that mean you think it's a boy?"

She gave me a knowing smile, a glint in her eyes that said she knew she was cornering me into making the admission. I laughed and went back to stocking the shelf.

"All right. You got me. Yes, I have a feeling it's a boy. It's just a feeling. I could be completely wrong. But there's just something that tells me I'm having a son."

Rhea sighed and shook her head back and forth, her eyes widened.

"Wow. That is just so... beautiful," she said. "You have this incredible connection to a person who hasn't even walked on the earth yet. There is a person forming inside you right now who will one day talk and laugh and play and find someone to love. And you have this mystical link to him."

"It's not all that mystical. It's just hard not to feel connected to someone when you are literally physically attached to them," I told her.

She thought about this, shrugged one shoulder, and went back to the inventory of brushes she was putting into place. In the two months since I'd started working in the art shop, Rhea and I had become the best of friends. We were close enough to hang out on the days when the shop was closed, and she'd even come to my first ultrasound with me when I was too nervous to go by myself and Steven couldn't come. I was so happy to have her in my life and felt fortunate to have stumbled on this job and our friendship.

The door to the shop opened and we both looked up, expecting a customer. The people standing there looked somewhat familiar, but I was sure they hadn't come into the shop with me there before. Rhea let out a happy sound and rushed toward them, gathering first the woman in a tight hug, then the man.

"It's so good to see you!" she gushed. "What a surprise. Bridgit, come here."

I got up and wiped my hands on my apron as I made my way to the front of the store.

"Hello," I said to the older couple.

Now that I was closer, I realized I recognized them from the pictures pinned up on the bulletin board in the back room. I knew who they were before Rhea even introduced them.

"Bridgit, this is Candace and Roger Hastings. They own the shop." She gestured at me. "This is Bridgit. I hired her a couple months back to help out around here. You'll love her. She is amazing."

I blushed and glanced away before looking back at them. They each shook my hand.

"It's nice to meet you, Bridgit," Roger said. "It's good to hear Rhea found someone to help her."

"It's particularly good to hear it's been busy enough around here for her to need someone to help her," Candace added.

"I've been telling you for years, people love this place. We are never bored," Rhea said. "But enough about us. What about the two of you? What are you doing here? You didn't even tell me you were coming."

The way she said it made me briefly afraid Rhea had revealed some sort of surprise inspection and we were about to have everything we'd done for the last two months scrutinized. But she didn't look nervous, and the older couple exchanged secretive glances.

"Well, if we had told you, it wouldn't have been much of a surprise," Candace says. "There's something we want to talk to you about."

"Sure. Bridgit, can you keep an eye on the shop?"

Rhea asked.

"Of course," I told her.

The three went into the tiny office at the back of the shop, and I wandered around trying not to feel nervous. It was my experience people didn't get brought into back offices for good conversations. Of course, my experience wasn't really so much my experience as it was watching movies, but that was all I had to go on right then. Fortunately, I didn't have to mill around on my own for long. Two customers came in and by the time I finished helping them, the office door opened, and Rhea, Candace, and Roger were walking out.

I noticed Rhea wiping her eyes, which didn't seem like a great sign, but there was also a smile on her face, which was more encouraging. They walked up to the front of the store, and each hugged her tightly.

"We'll be in touch tomorrow with the papers," Roger said, then looked over at me. "Bridgit, it was very nice to meet you."

"Nice to meet you, too," I said.

His wife waved at me as they headed out of the shop, and I waved until they'd disappeared past the large window, then turned to Rhea.

"You will not believe what just happened," she said.

"What is going on?" I asked.

"They're selling me the shop!"

"What? Are you serious?" I asked, stunned by the revelation.

"Yes! And for an absolutely ridiculous price. Like a fraction of what it's worth ridiculous," she said.

Her eyes were wild as they flashed around the shop, taking it all in with an expression that said she couldn't believe what was happening, that it was actually hers.

"Congratulations! That's amazing!" I said.

I rushed to hug her, filled with so much excitement and happiness for her I didn't even know how to express it. In the time we'd worked together, one thing I'd learned about Rhea for sure was how much she loved the shop. She totally devoted herself to it and put everything into how she ran it. She loved it like it was hers but was always held back by knowing the way the couple wanted it run. Now that was gone, and she could do everything she ever hoped for it and know its success was all hers.

"We have to celebrate," she said. "Let's close down and go do something."

"Close down in the middle of a Monday?" I asked.

"I'm the owner now, I can do anything I want!" she said.

"Yeah, you can," I laughed.

We went to the breakroom to hang up our aprons and get our things. As we left, Rhea locked the door, then gently rested her hand on it, looking into the window with a smile of sheer contentment and happiness. Then she turned to me with a broader grin.

"So, what do you want to do?" she asked.

"It's your celebration," I told her. "You decide."

"Well, your baby is a buzzkill and can't drink, much like my last five years of sobriety, so going to a bar and getting blitzed is out," she said, making me laugh. "But I know of another place we can go and knock back a few."

She started down the sidewalk, and I followed after her curiously. A few blocks later, we arrived at an adorable bakery. I recognized the name from boxes Rhea occasionally brought in full of treats for us on early inventory mornings or when there was a particularly difficult day. We went inside, and she ordered a pot of Earl Grey tea and an assortment of cupcakes. As we indulged in the delicious cakes, we talked about what wanted to keep the same about the shop and what she planned on changing. There wasn't much she really wanted to change, but the ideas she had were exciting. I was so happy to be able to be there with her to celebrate and looked forward to seeing what she made of the shop now that it was hers.

After a long bath and sipping a cup of the tea blend I bought from the bakery on the porch of the cabin, I sank into bed. As I turned off the light, I realized I was smiling. For the first time in a long time, I was truly happy. This wasn't where I ever thought I would be in my life. I never would have imagined I would find myself single, pregnant, and living in a small tourist town far away from everything I'd ever known. And yet, I had fallen in love with it. I loved the slow pace and the people. I loved the quiet and the beautiful surroundings. The thought had been drifting through my head for several days, but that night it really sank in and became a permanent plan. This was where I wanted to be. If it was at all possible, if I could find a way to work it out with Steven's mysterious friend, I wanted to stay in the cabin.

If someone had told me a year ago I would be happy working at a tiny art shop and living in a cabin in the woods of upstate New York, it would sound like they were talking about a different person. That didn't even begin to sound like me or the type of life I ever would have wanted. Yet, here I was, looking forward to raising my little bean and living that quiet life together. I could only hope it was a life I'd be able to keep.

Those peaceful, contented thoughts brought me into a comfortable sleep that night and gave me wonderful dreams, but they didn't last long. The next morning it was all shattered.

Rhea was already hard at work implementing the changes she envisioned when I got to the shop on Tuesday. Before I had even gotten my apron tied, the strings slightly shorter now with the swell of my belly, she was rattling off her ideas for in-shop classes and workshops, art kits customers could buy to try out new ideas, and holiday decorations and events for Halloween and Christmas. It was all coming at me so fast I could barely process it, so all I could do was nod and occasionally throw in a word or two. I was so excited for her I didn't want to lessen her enthusiasm or make it seem like I wasn't encouraging her, so I just kept listening to her as I made my way around the shop doing my morning duties.

She hadn't even slowed down to take a breath when the door opened. Rhea was in the back of the store, so I came around the end of the aisle where I was standing to greet the customer. As soon as I saw them standing there, my smile melted, and my stomach dropped so hard I nearly clutched it. Clark had just walked in, a very pretty blonde draped on his arm and clutching the front of his shirt with one manicured hand like she was too delicate to stand on her own. She smiled as she looked around, but he was staring only at me.

Our eyes locked and I couldn't move. Everything froze and I could hear the blood rushing in my ears. I didn't know what to do or say. There was no way I could duck out of the way and hope he didn't see me at this point. He was not only fully aware I was there, but he saw me in my full aproned glory. Which meant he was going to be able to tell everyone back home exactly where I was.

My only relief came when he looked at the girl.

"Let's go. We don't need to shop here. There are places around here that are actually on our level," he muttered.

The snide comment didn't bother me. All I cared about was they were leaving, and when the door closed behind them, I sagged against the display shelves. It took everything I had in me to not slide down and just sit directly on the floor. Instead, I managed to make my way over to the counter and drop down hard on the stool behind it. My hands were shaking, and spots danced in front of my eyes as I took out my phone to call my brother.

CHAPTER 33

ANDREI

Just like every other employee I selected when I started my company, my team in the warehouse was carefully chosen to ensure they would follow the policies and procedures designed to keep my company running smoothly. I never wanted to expand the team too much, adding on extra people that might make day-to-day work more confusing. As the company got more successful and expanded, I had to occasionally add a new member to the team. Just before bringing in those hires, there were often days when the workload was too much, especially if a member of the warehouse team happened to be out sick or was otherwise wasn't up to their usual productivity. When those days happened, I would go down onto the floor and help the team get over the hump.

It was one of those days that Thursday morning. I was down on the line with the guys, hauling boxes from the conveyor belts and ensuring the orders were organized properly. The system moved quickly, and if we didn't pay attention and keep up with it, everything could get completely out of control. Boxes going to the wrong clients, counts from the suppliers coming up wrong, and the supply chain breaking down so I couldn't fulfill my orders could be disastrous.

Which was why I wasn't really paying attention when I heard the knocking sound somewhere above me. It went on for several seconds before one of the guys beside me nudged me and pointed up at the glass wall beside the catwalk from my office. Gina stood there, pounding on the glass with her fist and angrily holding up my cell phone that I'd left on my desk in my office rather than bringing down to the floor with me. I could only imagine she wasn't pleased I was down there and was going to rag on me for needing to hire another employee for the warehouse. She wasn't wrong. The increase in work recently meant there were more days of too busy than there was just a usual workflow, and eventually my team was going to get so exhausted they wouldn't be able to handle it effectively and efficiently.

I waved and nodded, then checked with the guys around me to make sure they had everything under control. When they reassured me they were on top of it, I headed to the door to the stairs that led me up to my office. If Gina was trying that hard to get me back upstairs, it probably meant I'd gotten a series of calls that only I could handle, and she was tired of telling them I'd get back to them. But when I walked into my office, I realized that wasn't the case.

It had been months, almost three in fact, since I saw Bridgit or her brother. Neither of them had contacted me at all since the day I saw Steven at her desk getting the last of her things. I didn't know if he had been communicating with Gina, though I assumed he had, but that didn't take the edge off the shock when I walked off the catwalk into my office and saw Steven standing out in the office area between Gina's desk and the desk that was once Bridgit's, but now belonged to our new secretary.

I stopped in my tracks and stared at him, trying to figure out why he was there. He'd taken everything that belonged to Bridgit, and there was nothing else that my company owed her or needed from her. I was sure his parents told him about their visit and that I had nothing to tell them. From what Bridgit had told me about her relationship with her parents and the way her brother had to rescue her from their clutches, I didn't think he would have any problem with me talking to them the way I did, or not giving them any information.

Even if he did have a problem with it, or think I knew more than I told them, that was months ago. It didn't make sense he would be coming to confront me about it now. I finally got my head about me and walked out of my office, unrolling the sleeves of my shirt from where I'd tucked them at my elbows while I worked down on the floor. I searched Steven's posture and what I could see of his expression as I approached him. He looked pissed and nervous in turns, making it even harder to figure out what he might be thinking or why he might be there.

"Hi, Steven," I said.

He whipped around to face me.

"You still want to find her?" he asked with no preamble, not even a gossamer attempt at cordial exchange.

Despite the bluntness of the question, I didn't have to stop and think about my answer. It was immediately clear as soon as he asked it. I nodded.

"Yes," I told him.

It wasn't the same type of compulsion I would have felt if he'd asked me that question just days after Bridgit disappeared. As the days turned to weeks turned to months without her, I forced my heart to listen to my brain and push aside the feelings that were growing there. I had to remind myself of who I was before she came into my office, the way I had lived and thought before I ever saw her. That man wouldn't have been wrapped up in some silly fixation. He never would have even begun to think it could be more than the instant attraction and chemistry between us. It wasn't easy to believe. It wasn't something I even wanted to believe. It was what I had to convince myself out of in order to push ahead and be able to envision a life without her.

But that didn't mean I didn't still want to know what happened to her. There wasn't a day that went by that I didn't wonder where she went and why and wished I could just know she was all right. I might no longer be halfway in love with her the way I thought I might be, but I really wanted closure. I would really like to feel as if that part of my life had come to an end in a way I could accept, and I could forge ahead without lingering questions and worry. If nothing else, I wanted the chance to know why she'd left without even giving me a chance to explain. Even if she already knew she was ready to move on. Even if she had already come up with the plan of disappearing to stay a step ahead of her parents, I felt like I deserved the chance to tell her what happened and get an explanation of my own.

Steven nodded.

"Can you come with me?" he asked.

"Where are we going?" I asked.

"Upstate," he said. "She needs you. Right now. This has gone on long enough."

I nodded, a sudden anxious feeling in my gut. She needed me? What did that mean exactly?

"Sure. Gina, I need you to take care of the office for me while I'm gone. Handle everything you can, and if there are questions or concerns you can't do on your own, just take notes and I'll get back to them as soon as I can. I'm sorry to do this to you. I'll make it up to you somehow," I said.

"Don't worry about me. I can take care of this place. I've been halfway taking care of it by myself for the last few months, anyway. You go do what you need to do," Gina told me.

There was a message in those words. She didn't just mean I needed to go talk to Bridgit and find out why she left. She was telling me to do much more.

Getting everything I needed out of my office, I followed Steven to the parking deck. He was parked just a few spots down from my car, and he gestured for me to go with him, but I shook my head. I preferred to drive on my own. That was one thing I rarely compromised on. Unless it was a hired driver, I avoided getting into the car with other people. That was giving up far more control than I was willing to. I still barely knew Steven, and in this type of heated situation, I wasn't willing to just get in the car with him and let him be in absolute control of where I went and how long I was gone. I wasn't going to be at his mercy.

Instead, I called over to him that I would follow him and got in my car. Steven spun out of the parking deck with a screech of his tires and blasted out onto the street. We made our way through the city in close proximity to each other because of the traffic, but as soon as we were out of the tight streets and thick congestion, Steven took off. I followed after him as best I could, wondering exactly what was going that would make the seemingly calm, controlled man speed like this.

The longer he sped and the more speed he picked up, the more concerned I got. This couldn't just be that he thought we needed to talk or that he was done listening to her talk about me. That would be a phone call, maybe a talk through Gina. That didn't warrant death-defying driving away from the city.

We drove for a long time before he finally turned off the main road and slowed down as we followed a narrow drive. He ended up parking in a small gravel parking area in front of a cute little cabin in the woods. I tried to figure out where we were and why he would bring me out here as Steven climbed out of his car beside me. Figuring the chances of him just coming up to me and explaining it all were fairly slim, I followed suit and got out of the car. My legs and back were stiff from the long drive and tension of not knowing what was happening, so I bent and stretched to loosen them up.

I had my hands on my lower back and was arching back to open up my hips when the door to the cabin opened. I nearly choked when Bridgit stepped out and I noticed her belly. It was small, but the way she ran her hands over the rounded slope made it unmistakable. She was pregnant.

Her expression was frightened and nauseated, and I had so many questions. My mind spun and my heart trembled, and I knew in that moment as I stood in front of her, just steps from gathering her into my arms, that I hadn't gotten over her. Not even a little bit. I didn't want closure and to move on. All I wanted was her and I was going to fight for her, no matter what it took.

"Come in," she said, looking first at me, then to her brother.

Steven walked toward the cabin without hesitation, and I followed behind him. We walked into the quaint, cozy space, and Bridgit gestured to the living room where a tray of tea and cookies waited for us. She sat down on the couch, and I sat on the other end, wanting to be close to her, but not knowing the boundaries yet. This wasn't the time to be forceful with her or to make any assumptions. I needed to give her the space to tell me what was going on and how she was feeling before I laid anything out for her.

Bridgit took a deep breath. It was time to get it all out.

CHAPTER 34

BRIDGIT

I couldn't believe Andrei was actually there. He was actually in the cabin, sitting on my couch, holding one of the lemon cookies I'd baked like it was a prop. When Steven told me he was done and going to get Andrei so we could have the talk that was long overdue for both of us, I didn't actually believe him. That seemed so outlandish, so excessive considering how well I had adapted to my new life. I managed to stop him the first time he threatened it. I told my brother I appreciated his protectiveness and how concerned he was about every-thing working out in my life, but that I needed to do this the way that was right for me.

In my mind, there was no way I could balance every-thing, all the pressures around me. I couldn't keep my parents out of my hair, avoid Clark and the mess he'd created of my life, and also stay in touch with Andrei. It just wasn't going to happen. I needed to be satisfied with what I had, be grateful for the happiness I'd found, and focus on building the life I needed to for myself and my little bean.

Keeping us away from my parents and their world was my top priority, and that's the way it needed to be.

Steven begrudgingly agreed at that point. He didn't think it was right, and he made sure I knew that, but he wasn't going to force anything, either. But then Clark had appeared at the art shop. The second I called Steven and told him what was happening, he went right back to insisting I talk to Andrei. He had the exact same understanding of the situation I did. If Clark found me, that meant it was only a matter of time, probably a short time, before he spread it around to everyone and their mother. Including ours. That was going to make things much more difficult and complicated for me, and I needed to just take the plunge of calling Andrei. I told him I needed more time, that I needed to wrap my head around everything, and he refused. Steven said if I didn't call Andrei by the next day, he was going to go to the office and get him. I didn't believe him.

I'd been wrong. I didn't really have much of a choice. He called me from the road when they were half an hour away, giving me just enough time to make myself presentable, steep some tea, and bake a tray of the cookies I kept prepped in the freezer for just such an occasion. Well, maybe not exactly *this* sort of an occasion. That was the kind of thing I did now that I lived in the cabin and was preparing to welcome a baby. He or she deserved the kind of mother who baked cookies and was wearing lipstick when visitors came to the house.

This was good practice.

It was also terrifying.

I took a sip of the sweet peppermint tea to buy myself a few more seconds. Lowering the cup to my lap, I took a breath, looked at Andrei, and started my story.

"I assume by now you know the basics of what's been going on in my life. But you don't know all of it. My parents deciding to marry me off to Clark wasn't a spur-of-the-moment decision. It was something they were building up to my entire life. I was raised in a lot of privilege and indulgence, but both of those things came with the price tag of obedience and being seen as a commodity. I was expected to look a certain way and act a certain way at all times in order to seem like the ideal representation of my parents. If I was out of line or didn't live up to my pedigree, as they like to think of it, it was a reflection on them, and they wouldn't tolerate it. As much as I would like to think they love me in whatever way they are capable, I didn't grow up with the type of warm and fuzzy relationship with my mother and father other people do," I told him.

"I had no idea how much she went through," Steven added.

I shook my head.

"He didn't. Mom and Dad did a really good job at keeping the two of us apart most of the time, so we didn't really know what was going on with the other one. He didn't know everything they said to me and what I went through. It meant I always thought he was on their side and against me. Not necessarily in a bad way, if that makes sense. Just that I was different from them, and if I disagreed with something, it was a problem with me. I did everything I could to fall into line and do what was expected of me. Right up until they told me they chose a husband for me."

"Did you even know him?" Andrei asked.

I nodded.

"Yes. We weren't close friends or anything, but we knew of each other basically our whole lives. It wasn't all that much of a surprise when my mother and father told me they wanted me to marry him. I had known for a while my father wanted to make a business deal with Clark's family, and offering up an attractive marriage between the families was a good way to cement that," I explained to him.

"It's hard to believe things like that still happen," he said.

"Not for us," Steven told him. "Unfortunately, it's more common than anyone would want to think. People get married because they look good together, both physically and on paper. There are couples who love each other, sure, but it's not every couple, and it's far from shocking when you find out people who were never even linked to each other are suddenly planning a wedding right around the time there are rumblings of new business connections."

"Even with that, though, I didn't think they were going to be as forceful as they were. I thought they would probably suggest men to me, or even make it clear which they wanted me to be with. That's not all that unusual. But it didn't ever cross my mind they would demand it of me, basically tell me there was nothing I could do, and I had no choice. When I argued with them, they softened only a little. They asked me to spend some time with him, to see how I felt about him. Clark was already interested in me, and maybe I'd find a spark with him. They were optimistic, so I agreed to it."

"From what I understood, they were dating," Steven said. "My parents told me they reintroduced them as adults and were encouraging the relationship, but I didn't realize how forceful they were being until later."

"The problem was, they said we were dating, but we were never allowed to be alone together. That would be too risky. That would give us a chance to talk and possibly decide we really didn't like each other or combine forces and decide to refuse to go along with what they said. By this point, they'd already started planning the wedding. I have no doubt they would have just brought me to the church in the morning and pushed me down the aisle if they had to."

"What happened?" Andrei asked.

"Even after spending time with him, I was sure it wasn't what I wanted. We were allowed to have one short date alone together, and he essentially told me he wasn't looking for a monogamous marriage, but he would make sure I was well taken care of and he promised he would be discreet so I wasn't embarrassed."

"How kind of him," Andrei said sarcastically.

"That's when I started figuring out what was going on," Steven said. "I'll admit I was in support of the marriage at first. I thought it would be good for her to have a solid, successful husband, and of course, it would be good for the business. But then she told me what happened the next time they were alone together."

My brother and I met eyes, and he gave me a sympathetic look. I offered as much of a smile as I could but was shaking. Steven reached over to take my hand and squeezed it.

"Deep breath, sis. You can do this. Just keep going," he said.

I nodded and kept going.

"The next time we were alone together, he tried to get me to sleep with him. He said he hadn't been with anybody since our parents started trying to get us together, and he thought it would be nice to have an arrangement. I refused him and he got rough. I got away from him and told my parents what happened, but they didn't care."

"They didn't believe you?" Andrei asked.

"It's not that they didn't believe me. It's that they didn't care. They essentially told me it must have been a misunderstanding, and they were sure Clark wouldn't act like that again. He was a good man, they said, but sometimes their heads got the best of men. I needed to give him another chance. That wasn't something I could do. That was the moment I really saw my future. I wasn't just going to be in a loveless sham of a marriage, I could also be in danger. I wasn't willing to do either one of them. So, I ran."

"When I found out what actually happened, I pushed back against our parents. I knew I needed to help her, so I got her an apartment, made sure she had money, and linked her up with Gina for the secretary position," Steven explained.

"That's how I met you," I continued. "And I thought things were good. I didn't have any expectations. I didn't even want any. Even after we started hooking up, I just wanted to enjoy our connection. But then you called me into your office and said you wanted an arrangement. Your wording immediately brought me back to Clark and made me feel like I was just another deal to close. It hurt and upset me, but then I decided it was different, because you were an arrangement I chose for myself, if that makes sense. Then I got to the point where I didn't believe it anymore. I didn't really think you wanted something more." I looked Andrei in the eye. "I thought I might love you. Right up until your ex-wife showed up."

He let out a groan and inched toward me.

"Bridgit," he started, but I shook my head.

"Let me finish," I said, and he fell silent. "When I saw Katya in your penthouse, it broke me. It made me feel like I was never going to get out from under her. She obviously still had a hold on you, and it really seemed like the two of you still had something going on, or that you had picked up again. Why else would she be looking so comfortable in your apartment? Then that day I found out my parents had started figuring out what was going on with me. My mother somehow got my phone number and had been texting me. I couldn't take it, so I left."

"I brought her here," Steven said. "I thought it would be comfortable for her and she would be able to kind of figure herself out."

"Well, I did figure myself out," I continued. "I figured out I'm pregnant. I didn't know when I left the city. It wasn't until I'd been feeling sick for a few days here that I went to the doctor and they told me. I knew you were the father. You were the only option. But I couldn't bring myself to go back if Katya was still there. I wasn't going to be the pathetic other woman who showed up pregnant when your glamorous wife was keeping your bed warm. I've spent my whole life depending on other people and not taking care of myself, and I decided I couldn't do that anymore. I needed to be on my own and take care of myself. I wasn't going to let my parents get me back in their grasp, and I wasn't going to go crying to you. But then Clark showed up."

"Clark showed up here?" Andrei asked.

I nodded. "At the shop where I've been working. He walked in with some woman and looked right at me. There was no way he didn't see me or didn't realize it was me. Him knowing where I am means I don't have long before my parents show up. I'll be surprised if they don't show up today. They're going to try to drag me home, but I won't go."

My voice was firm and resolute. I wasn't leaving, and

there wasn't nothing they could do to make me. I watched as Andrei's face went through a series of emotions. I figured he deserved them, but I wasn't backing down on anything I said. This was the choice I made, and I wasn't deviating from it.

CHAPTER 35

ANDREI

I sat there staring at Bridgit, letting myself process everything I'd just heard rather than saying anything right off the bat. There was a lot to try to work through, so much to untangle and analyze. But I was mostly stuck on the revelation of her pregnancy. I kept letting my eyes drift down to the swell of her belly and the way her hand rested on it. By now she was nearly five months along by my calculation. Five months of a baby growing inside her, becoming a tiny person still waiting to be born. It was mind-blowing, and I struggled to really think about anything else.

But then my thoughts suddenly snapped to what she told me about her parents. Looking at her sitting there, tenderly stroking and occasionally cradling her belly, made me think about her mother and how she felt when she was pregnant with Bridgit. She must have thought about her future child, and if she found out she was having a daughter before she was born, there had to have been times when she envisioned the life she was going to have with her little girl. I tried to imagine what she thought about and how she could have gone from an expectant mother to a woman willing to trade her daughter over for a boost in business.

Could it really be possible she'd never felt a true motherly link to her baby? Could she have always seen Bridgit as some sort of investment, like a piece of livestock she was raising to eventually barter with? Just the thought infuriated me. I couldn't wrap my head around any mother thinking about her child that way, any father agreeing and going along with it. Or even the other way around. She mentioned her father was the one who wanted the business connection with Clark's family. Maybe he was the one who'd looked at his baby girl and saw a bargaining chip he would one day be able to include as a bonus perk during negotiations, and it was her mother who'd agreed to let it happen.

Either way, it was revolting. They were supposed to protect her, to cherish her and make sure she had the best life she possibly could. Not only did they completely fail in that, but they'd hurt Bridgit. My Bridgit. I was furious, and every bit of protective instinct I ever felt for her surged back stronger than ever.

Bridgit and Steven sat silently, staring at me and searching my face as if they were waiting for something. I knew they were expecting me to say something, possibly to explode or just scream at them. But I was doing my best to be level-headed and stay calm. After everything she had gone through and was still going through, the last thing Bridgit needed was someone else being angry and causing stress in her life. No matter what I was feeling at that moment, all that mattered was making her feel at ease and helping her get through this. I moved slightly closer to her on the couch.

"First, I want to explain what happened. Katya was only at my apartment that day because she decided she needed somewhere to stay. Remember that day when I got so angry and Gina threatened to quit?" I asked.

"And you sent us tacos and whiskey?" she asked. "Yes."

"Well, the reason I was so angry that week was because Katya showed up out of nowhere, calling me and wanting to see me. I didn't even answer the phone, so she showed up at the office."

"I remember that, too," Bridgit told me.

I nodded, trying not to let her words cut into me so deeply.

"She told me she was getting a divorce and needed somewhere to stay. I flat out told her I didn't care and that she wasn't allowed to come stay at my place, then I sent her away. She didn't want to take that for face value and went anyway. I was just as surprised as you were when we got there and she was inside. Yes, she stayed at my place, but absolutely nothing happened between us. The only reason I let her stay there at all was because my mother felt bad for her and told me to let her stay. The vast majority of the time I was even still there, I spent in my bedroom."

"What do you mean the time you were even still there?" Bridgit asked.

"I didn't want to be near her, so I rented a little apartment," I answered.

She looked like she might laugh, but she fought it and nodded, gesturing at me to keep going.

"All right. Go on," she said.

"Like I said, nothing happened between us. Nothing at all. And now she is back with her husband. Probably in London by now. He crawled back to her—literally, apparently—and offered to buy her back. I was more than happy to have her on her way. We were married a long time ago. She cheated on me. I divorced her. She married him. He cheated on her. I wasn't about to let that cycle keep going. Besides, there's been something else on my mind."

I was about to say something about her and about our baby when the sound of gravel outside stopped me. Bridgit froze, her eyes widening, then snapping to her brother. He pointed at me.

"You stay with her. Keep her right here. I'm going to head them off. It's time this is over," he said and stormed toward the door to the cabin.

I moved across the couch, so I sat right beside her. She was shaking, and I took the teacup from her hands before she could drop it or spill the tea on her lap. Placing it on the table in front of her, I wrapped my arm around her shoulders and held her against me. It felt good to have her close to me again, to feel her warmth and how comfortably and easily she fit against me. She drew in a trembling breath, pressing her hands to the sides of her belly and staring down at it. I could only imagine the thoughts going through her head as she thought about the baby and the family she escaped.

"It's going to be all right," I murmured to her, trying to comfort her.

Her eyes, filled with tears, lifted to me and searched mine.

"Is it?" she asked.

"Yes."

"How do you know? I thought I could do this on my own, but... "

"Hey," I said, holding her closer as a wave of tears rocked her body and made her shake harder. "Listen to me. We have things to talk about, sure. But we're going to. And we're going to figure all this out. You aren't alone, and you don't have to even think about trying to do anything on your own. I'm not going to let them hurt you, okay? Whatever it is they are thinking or are going to try to do, it's not going to happen. They aren't going to get to you or to my baby. They would have to get through me first, and I didn't grow up pampered and wealthy. They haven't dealt with the likes of me."

Bridgit managed a slight laugh, but I was completely serious. There was nothing that was going to let them get to either of them. I would do anything to protect Bridgit and the baby she was carrying. She sensed my sincerity and nodded, and I felt the shaking of her shoulders start to lessen.

Voices erupted outside, and even though we couldn't hear the words clearly, the arguing made Bridgit lean into me, tucking her head against me like she just wanted to hide away from it. I held her closer and rested my head on hers so she would feel surrounded by me. Part of me wanted to take her away somewhere else where she wouldn't be able to hear what was going on, but Steven asked us to stay right there. Besides, I didn't know the cabin well. It was possible there wasn't anywhere else I could bring her that would be any more sheltered.

Instead, I held her right up until the screaming outside stopped and Steven came back into the cabin alone. Just after he stepped inside, a car door slammed outside and tires ground against the gravel as they peeled out of the parking area and headed back for the road. Steven let out a sigh and crossed to the chair where he'd been sitting. He slumped down into it and stared into nothingness ahead of him for a few seconds before turning to Bridgit.

"So, I'm pretty sure I just went through my initiation, but is there like a secret handshake I should know for the

Excommunicated Club? Are there dues? What night do we meet?"

Bridgit looked up at me, then back at her brother. I didn't know what she was going to do. Obviously, Steven had managed to stop her parents from storming into the cabin and demanding she go back to the city with them. But he got himself cut off and tossed out of their lives in the process. She slid out of my grasp and moved across the couch cushions toward her brother. Reaching her hand out, she rested it on Steven's. Staring seriously into his eyes, she gave a single nod.

"I'm still working on it. No. Tuesdays. Welcome," she said.

There was a tense, silent moment before she finally started to laugh. Steven looked at me, and I stared back at him. A laugh bubbled up in my throat, and I saw his mouth twitching. Soon enough we were all laughing.

CHAPTER 36

BRIDGIT

It had already been a long day, and it wasn't over yet. The sun was still high in the sky, and there was plenty of day left. A little voice in the back of my mind said that meant there was plenty of opportunity for something else to go terribly wrong, but I cut it off and forced the thought out of my mind. I just didn't want to think about it anymore. In a strange way, there was a tremendous sense of relief and almost happiness after the epic explosion that was the beginning of the day. As hard as it was to sit there and tell Andrei everything that happened, and as terrifying and painful as it was for my parents to show up, at least it was over.

Both of those confrontations were situations I knew had to happen eventually. I tried to pretend I could avoid them, like I could just keep going with my life and not have either of them cross my path ever again. But that wasn't realistic. At some point I was going to have to talk to the father of my child and let him know about his baby. Even more than that, I was going to have to clear the air and get both sides of the story out in the open so he and I didn't go the rest of our lives wondering how everything broke down so quickly. When it came to my parents, I knew I couldn't keep avoiding them forever. They were going to find me, and it was going to be a showdown.

Now both those things were done. In all honesty, they probably went better than I could have hoped. Andrei listened to everything I had to say to him and was receptive to it all. And his explanation was far more palatable than any I could have come up with on my own. Steven had been there for me to buffer my parents and keep them away from me. I felt bad about how it went down, but at least now I could commiserate with him and we could go through this new chapter of our lives together. Despite them having as positive of outcomes as I could have possibly imagined, they were a lot, and when the adrenaline and humor of the funny moment passed, I realized how exhausted I was.

Just then, almost as though she could sense something going on, Rhea suddenly called me. I'd told her everything the day before after Clark showed up at the art shop, and she immediately told me to go home and take care of myself, that I could take Thursday off and just try to figure things out. I knew she was there for me, that I could tell her anything and she wouldn't judge me. It was invaluable and I nearly crumbled into tears when she said she was just checking in and wanted to tell me I was fine to take Friday off as well.

"Thank you," I told her. "I'm so grateful I found you."

"I'm grateful for you, too," she told me, and I knew she was being sincere.

"I'll see you soon. There's more to tell you," I said.

"Oooo," she said playfully. "I look forward to it. Do you need anything?"

I looked at Andrei and then my brother and shook my head even though she couldn't see me.

"No," I said. "I have everything I need."

"Good."

I got off the phone and sighed, standing up from the couch. Both men jumped up along with me, their hands raising slightly from their sides as if they were sure I was going to topple over at any second.

"Today completely took it out of me. I'm going to take a nap. If you stay, I'll cook dinner when I wake up," I said.

They both nodded and I made my way into my bedroom, closing the door behind me and standing there for a moment just to enjoy the quiet peacefulness of the space. I slipped between the sheets, pulled my sleep mask down over my eyes, and relaxed. Out in the front of the cabin, both of the men in my life were being left to their own devices. I knew they were going to be talking about this whole mess while I napped, but I was past the point of caring. It wasn't like I could really hide anything anymore. Everything was splayed out for the world to see now. I might as well let two of the people closest to me know it all and talk about it for themselves.

I didn't know exactly how long it had been since I fell asleep, but when I woke up it was already dark outside. The nap had been deep and restorative, leaving me feeling refreshed and with my mind clearer than it had been in a long time. As I set up, my nose caught a whiff of delicious-smelling food. I breathed it in deeply, memories filling me before I even realized what they were. Those were smells I knew but wasn't exactly sure why. It wasn't until I walked out of my bedroom and into the kitchen that it occurred to me those smells reminded me of Andrei. They were the smells that came with him when he got back from his lunches with his friend Gus, and that wafted out of the occasional plastic container of leftovers he handed over to Gina after dinner with his parents like he was sharing the spoils.

Steven stood next to a table overflowing with platters of food. Some of it I recognized as things he'd prepared for me the weekend I spent at his house, but the others were unfamiliar. As soon as he saw me come into the room, Steven grabbed a towel off the counter and started waving it frantically over the food. I laughed.

"It's all right, Steven. I appreciate the gesture, but I'm in my second trimester now. The morning sickness is gone for the most part," I told him.

"Force of habit," he said, tossing the towel aside.

"What is all this?" I asked Andrei as he stirred something bubbling away on the stove. "I said I was going to make dinner when I got up."

"It's just some of my favorite things," he said. "Steven and I were getting hungry. Besides, your kitchen is stocked with everything I needed, and you deserve a night off cooking. I've been out of the loop for a few months now. Let me take care of you for a night."

My heart warmed, and I smiled at him.

"Thank you," I said. "It smells incredible. I look forward to seeing if this baby likes it."

"Of course he will. He'll be just like his Papa," he said affectionately, resting one hand on my belly and rubbing it gently.

"He?" I asked softly.

Andrei shrugged. "I just have this feeling. Does that bother you?"

I shook my head. "No. I have that feeling, too."

Our eyes met and he smiled at me. Every thought I ever

had of not needing Andrei in my life or being satisfied with just being here and living my life disappeared in that moment. I knew this was the life I wanted, but I wanted him to be a part of it alongside me.

When he finished cooking, we sat around the table and dug into the amazing spread of food. He described each dish as I served a scoop onto each of our plates. After we'd tasted everything and gathered more of our favorites, we settled in for our feast.

"So, what now?" Steven asked.

"Rhea said I can take tomorrow off, too, but then I'll have to go back to work." I looked at Andrei. "You should come see it. I think you would like it."

Andrei looked over at Steven. "She's going back to work?"

I narrowed my eyes. "Why are you asking him? Of course I'm going back to work. I love my job, and since my gravy train is all dried up, I've got to do something."

"That was uncalled for," Steven said, but there was levity in his voice that told me he wasn't actually upset with me.

"How are you going to handle being cut off?" Andrei asked. "Your sister seemed to manage it because you helped her."

I made a face at him, but I couldn't really argue with him.

"He'll manage it," I said. "He's going to be better off than I ever was. He might not have the hookup with our parents anymore, but I know for a fact he's been squirreling money away. Am I right?"

Steven nodded. "Some." I eyed him and he smiled. "All right, more than some. I wanted to do some investing."

"It's also how he's been taking care of me without our parents noticing," I pointed out.

"I should be set for at least a little while," my brother said. "I can't imagine I'm still going to have my position with my father's company, so I guess I'll have to take a cue from my sister and get a job."

"Oh, the horror," I teased.

Our dinner took nearly two hours, and for another hour after that, we continued talking until Steven announced he needed to head back to the city. I offered to let him sleep on the couch, but he refused, saying he wanted to start getting some stuff in order. He had smuggled me so many of my belongings he was pretty good at it, which was a plus since he would need to start sneaking his own things out of his apartment at our parents' estate.

When he left, Andrei and I curled up on the couch and casually chatted, catching up on each other's lives and all we'd missed with each other over the last several months. I told him how much I loved the town and the cabin, and how happy I'd been. He wrapped his arms around me and brought me to cuddle on his chest.

"I can definitely understand why you don't want to leave," he said. "I promise we'll figure it out."

Smiling, I nuzzled closer to him. It was definitely the best part of the night.

CHAPTER 37

ANDREI

Something I learned as I got older was no matter how young you feel and how good a shape you keep yourself in, your body will figure out ways to remind you of your age. That's the first thing that came to mind when I opened my eyes the next morning and felt how stiff and painful my neck was. It was doing everything it could to remind me that I'd slept crunched up on the couch in the living room of the cabin. Holding Bridgit in my arms the night before while we talked was wonderful. I couldn't get enough of the way she felt or smelled, and I constantly put my hand on her belly to try to connect with my little baby growing inside. Even though we weren't talking about anything serious, not even skirting on the issues we really should be talking about, it was my favorite part of the day.

It also meant we spent hours there, and by the time she was tired enough to go to bed, I didn't want to drive home. I made sure I had my own car so I could leave whenever I wanted to, not realizing that would mean I didn't want to leave at all. I was happy when Bridgit said she was tired and wanted to go to bed, but some of the enthusiasm disappeared when she announced without hesitation that she didn't feel ready for us to share a bed again. She didn't offer any sort of alternative, leaving it up to me to decide what I wanted to do. But I still didn't want to go anywhere. I didn't want to be far away from her anymore. That's how I ended up camped out on the couch with a pillow and a blanket.

In retrospect, it didn't really surprise me that Bridgit didn't want to immediately jump back in to sharing a bed and living so familiarly with each other. I would have to earn back her trust and create that connection again. Even though nothing happened between me and Katya, Bridgit had been worried and scared. Possibly even more than those, she'd been humiliated and forced herself to change how she saw our entire relationship. So, that's what I had to do. Whatever it took, I would earn that trust back and get us back to the level where we were, and even beyond.

Stretching my neck and trying to loosen my back, I got up off the couch and folded the blanket. I headed into the kitchen and scoured the cabinets for the coffee I'd noticed the night before while I prepared dinner. The label on the bag had excited me when I first saw it. I'd heard of the roaster, knowing it was a well-respected local place known for their unique blends. I was excited to try the coffee but was admittedly disappointed when I found the bag and discovered the beans inside would produce decaf. I should have expected that. Bridgit wouldn't be drinking fully caffeinated coffee while pregnant, and beans like these had to be ground and consumed within a fairly short time of buying them. That meant she hadn't gotten the coffee when she first moved into the cabin before she knew about the baby.

I wasn't particularly looking forward to not getting my

morning jolt, but I figured I could be supportive in drinking the decaf with Bridgit. At least for this morning. As the coffee brewed, I took out my phone and called Gina.

"Where are you?" she demanded. "I've been trying to call you since yesterday."

"I'm sorry," I said. "I've had my phone off."

"I almost called your parents," she told me.

"I'm glad you didn't. I'm fine. Better than fine, actually. I'm upstate in a cabin."

"That doesn't sound like you," she said.

"I'm here with Bridgit." Gina let out a joyous sound somewhere between a cheer and a squeal that made me laugh. "Listen, I have a lot I have to tell you, but there are some things we need to figure out. I need to be able to spend less time in the city."

"What do you mean less time in the city? You are always in the city. You love the city," Gina said, sounding incredulous.

"I do," I confirmed, figuring this was the ideal opportunity to reveal the big news. "But I love Bridgit more. And our baby."

Gina gasped. "Your baby? Bridgit's pregnant?"

I told her the entire story, starting with chasing Steven to the cabin and recounting everything Bridgit told me. I didn't give as many details as she did, figuring those were things they could talk about if Bridgit ever wanted her to know, but wanting Gina to understand the whole thing. By the time I got to the part of Steven coming back into the cabin after his confrontation with his parents, Gina sounded emotional on the other end of the line. I finished the story and could hear her sniffling. This was much more than I was accustomed to from my spirited, tough-as-nails assistant, but it was a genuine reaction and I was touched to hear it. We'd been close for years, and I knew she and Bridgit had become good friends in the time she was there at the office. I was happy she was there for both of us.

"So, that's why I need to figure out how I'm going to do this. Bridgit is really settled here. She doesn't want to go back to the city, and I agree with her. I was born and raised in the city, but I don't want that for my baby. He deserves fresh air and space to run around and play that isn't concrete."

"And maybe it's time for you to have a slower pace in life?" Gina jabbed.

"Hell, no," I said. "But I do look forward to having more time with her and to seeing my child grow up. So, I won't be living my life in the office anymore. I need you to help me figure out how I can spend as much time as possible here with her, and also get my work done in the city."

"I can do that," she said.

I heard a door and looked up to see Bridgit coming toward me.

"Sleeping Beauty has risen," I teased. "I've got to go. We'll talk soon."

"Okay. Tell Bridgit I miss her and congratulations. And congratulations to you, too," Gina said.

Tears sprung to my eyes. That was my first congratulations, and I felt it go right to my heart. I hung up and turned back to Bridgit. She was in her pajamas, her hair was a complete mess of bed head, and she wasn't wearing a stitch of makeup. She grumbled and made little grunting sounds as she rubbed her belly, and if there had been even the fragments of questions left in my mind, they were gone. She was it. Bridgit was mine, and I wasn't walking away or letting her walk away. Not again. We weren't going to make that mistake another time.

I got another mug and poured her a cup of coffee. She sipped it happily, and even without the caffeine it seemed to wake her up.

"Who was that?" she asked when she seemed to have regained control over her language skills.

"Gina," I told her. "Talking about how we're going to work this out."

"I'm not going back to the city," she said.

"I know. I meant how it's going to work out with me here," I told her.

Her eyes filled with happiness, and she gave a slight nod. After breakfast, we got dressed and took a leisurely stroll down into the town so she could show me around. She brought me to the coffee shop, and I eagerly bought a cup of their darkest brew. I left happily clutching the biggest bag they would sell and the business card of the owner so I could add him to my list of suppliers. I had plenty of clients who enjoyed coffee, making bags a perfect addition to the thank-you gifts I liked to send after events, and I was always in the market for new products to offer. It wasn't exactly imported but having a selection of exceptional local prod-ucts created more diversity.

We spent the rest of the day together, but as evening approached, I knew I needed to leave. If I didn't pry myself away from her now and head home to take care of the things I needed to handle, it would just get harder and harder to go. Before I left, I gathered Bridgit into my arms and gazed down into her face.

"You have to promise me you're not going to run away again," I told her.

She shook her head. "I'm not going anywhere. I love my little cabin, and I'm not leaving the art store or Rhea."

I laughed.

"I hope I factor in there somewhere, too," I said.

She grinned and wrapped her arms around my waist.

"Of course you do. You're the best part," she told me.

I leaned down and kissed her softly. She sighed into the kiss, and I rested my forehead against hers.

"Just a reminder," I whispered and reluctantly stepped away from her.

Bridgit stood at the door waving as I drove away, ready to figure out the logistics for the company and get back here as soon as I possibly could.

CHAPTER 38

BRIDGIT

Andrei kissed me on the side of the neck, and I turned my face to him so I could give him a quick peck. He let out a sigh and walked out of the kitchen carrying the first of three huge bowls of popcorn Rhea and I were popping. She looked at me from the stove where she was cranking the handle of the popcorn popper and shook her head.

"You are seriously being mean to that man," he said.

"Mean?" I asked incredulously.

Steven came into the kitchen and opened the refrigerator, leaning in to take out drinks.

"Are you talking about how mean Bridgit is being to Andrei?" he asked as he shut the door and tipped back one of the glass-bottle sodas he'd gotten obsessed with over the last few weeks. He got them from a tiny market in town, and they always made sure they let him know when his favorite flavors were in.

I gasped and made a look of mock offense.

"What is going on with the two of you?" I asked.

"The question is what is going on with you?" Steven

asked. "Or what is not going on with you." He walked past me to leave the kitchen, leaning toward me before walking out. "And you are being mean."

I looked at Rhea, and she shrugged, finishing up the popcorn and tipping the cascade of fluffy white kernels into a huge mixing bowl. I took a glass measuring cup of butter out of the microwave and drizzled some over the top of the popcorn, then sprinkled it with salt.

"What are the two of you going on about?" I asked.

"You know exactly what we're talking about," she said. I stared at her with my best innocent look, and she tilted her head at me. "Come on, Bridgit. It's been two weeks since the two of you reconciled, and you still haven't had sex with him."

"How do you know that?" I asked.

It wasn't like I'd been talking about it with either one of them. Not that I was ashamed of our relationship, but we were exploring this new phase of just the two of us. At least, that's what I thought until I had both my best friend and my brother turn on me.

"You've got to be kidding. Everybody knows. He's pouting everywhere he goes," Rhea said with a laugh.

I shrugged and nodded.

"That's true." I smiled. "It is pretty cute, though."

"That isn't why you're holding out on him, is it?" she asked.

"Maybe, like, fifty percent."

She laughed again, and we grabbed the last of the snacks to bring out to the fire pit in the backyard so we could join the guys. Steven had already broken into the s'mores supplies and was carefully roasting a marshmallow over the flickering flames. He kept pulling it out and looking at it, evaluating the coloration before putting it back in and twirling it slowly. Andrei watched him like he was mesmerized by how meticulous he was.

"Impressive, isn't it?" I asked, nodding toward Steven as I sat down beside Andrei.

He wrapped half the blanket draped around his shoulders around me and nodded.

"Does he always take this long to toast a marshmallow?" he asked.

"Yes. He has to have perfect golden color from all angles," I told him.

"Just shove the thing in and light it on fire," Rhea said.

Steven looked horrified, and we all laughed. For the rest of the evening, I watched Andrei, thinking about what Rhea said. I didn't think I was still making him atone for anything. It felt like everything was good between us. At the same time, I did enjoy listening to him make sad jokes about his lack of love life, then grin at me. By the end of the evening, I knew I was done waiting.

When the flames burned down and the snacks were gone, Steve and Rhea went home. I took a bath to wash away the smell of the flames and met Andrei in the living room. He was setting up the couch to sleep, and I ran my hand down his back to get his attention. He turned around and gathered me in his arms, dropping his mouth down onto mine for a deep kiss.

I sank into the kiss, and his arms wrapped around my waist. I let him turn me and push me against the wall, his lips moving from mine to my neck. He pressed his body against mine, his thick erection nestled against my core as he let his tongue slide from my neck to my ear. I groaned softly as he nibbled at my lobe while grinding his hips into mine. My hands found their way to his back and slid to his ass, pulling him into me harder. He leaned forward with his hips to grind into me under my belly, and I moaned.

"Bed?" I whispered.

He nodded and scooped me up. I giggled at how weightless and delicate I felt in his arms, even now. Our lips crushed into one another again as he carried me down the hall and to my room. I reached down blindly to turn the knob and open the door. He carried me in and kicked at it to shut it, and the darkness of the room enveloped us. I floated through the pitch-black room to the bed, and he laid me gently onto it. He was being careful with me, and I appreciated the gesture, but I knew there was a desperation hiding behind those kisses. A need and a hunger to fuck me until my eyes rolled back and the sweat poured down his chest.

I felt it, too.

I scooted back in the bed until my head rested on a pillow, and I watched as his shadow, with just a small sliver of light from the window, undressed. I heard his zipper undo, and I salivated. I unbuttoned my pants and pulled them down and off me and opened myself to him, waiting for him to mount me, to enter me and fill me. To dominate me with his desire.

But when the bed sank under his weight as he climbed onto it, he did not rush. Instead he curled himself between my legs and trailed a line of kisses up my thigh. My skin was sensitive and tender, and each time his warm lips pressed against my skin, I felt a rush of goose bumps up my arms. He teased me, going around my core to kiss down my other thigh and then back up again. His tongue slid out and brushed the lips of my wet pussy, and then he repeated the action on the other side. Blowing a thin line of breath where his tongue had been, he made me writhe in the wait.

Then, dipping his head, he lavished me with attention.

His tongue slipped through my folds and circled my clit, encouraging it to come out as he slipped a finger into my tight hole. I gasped as he pushed it deep inside me and his mouth covered my center, tongue flicking at my sensitive pearl and bringing me immediately to the brink of an orgasm. I tried to focus on his fingers sliding in and out of me, and preparing me for his cock, and I noticed his other arm moving in the shadows. He was pleasuring himself while he pleasured me, and the thought of it drove me over the edge. I clinched my thighs around his head and vibrated as the climax overtook me.

I was in the throes of it when his mouth left me, and the cool air on my pussy made me cry out in surprise and petulant disappointment. I wanted his warmth, and I got it almost instantly. All the gentleness was past, and his hunger consumed him. His cock speared me, driving deep in me, and stars filled my vision and my voice left my throat.

My fingers dug into his arms, but he didn't seem to mind as he reared back and thrust into me again. I clenched my legs together around his waist and tried to settle into the thickness stretching my walls, filling me and driving the desire only deeper. He sat up on his knees, rocking into me at will as his hands reached up to clasp at my bra. I had torn off my shirt upon landing on the bed, but my bra was still on. He thumbed for the clasp in the center, and it unhooked under his grasp, letting my heavy, round breasts spill out of them.

Eagerly, he took one into his mouth, flicking my nipple with his tongue while his hand massaged into the other. My senses were so heightened, my body so sensitive and responsive to his touch, that I felt the wave of a second orgasm coming soon. I tried to breathe deeply, but I had little control. He slammed into me with a need to have me feel him, to know I was his and forever would be. He wanted to own me with his cock, and I was going to let him. I opened myself even further and sank into his thrusts, rocking with him. I pulled one arm around his neck as he switched breasts and began to suckle the other.

When they were both wet and perky, he sat back up, grabbing me by the waist and pulling me on top of him. We scooted to the edge of the bed, and I rested my knees as he let his hips fall just off the edge. His hands clasped on my ass as I sank another kiss into his mouth, and he thrust upward into me. The new position was eliciting an entirely unique sensation in me, and I was losing the ability to control the moans which now reverberated off the walls. His voice began to match mine, and our eyes locked on one another. His hips moved faster as he fucked me hard, his hands pushing my hips down with each thrust, so he impaled me deeper, filled me further. Our foreheads rested on each other as our eyes continued to search each other's.

Then, with a building roar, he exploded into me, and I came hard on him. We both rode the wave of a powerful orgasm, and he thrust into me until his cock was empty, and he lay back gently on the bed. I curled up on him and rested, my body glowing as I milked him dry.

When I felt like I could move again, I rearranged us so we could rest more comfortably. Andrei wrapped his arm around me and pulled me close. Even though we were sweaty and sticky, I didn't want to move. There was nowhere else I wanted to be.

CHAPTER 39

ANDREI

I woke up the next Saturday morning exactly the way I always wanted to. Naked, happy, and in Bridgit's bed. I didn't even bother to look at the clock. It didn't matter what time it was. I didn't want to leave the bed anytime soon. At the same time, there was so much more I wanted to do now. It was strange how much it felt like life had opened up to me. Forty years old, a self-made billionaire, and with a nasty divorce already under my belt, suddenly I felt like I was seeing the world through completely new eyes and finally experiencing life. I wanted it to do it all and share everything with her.

Bridgit cuddled closer to me, and I shared some of my ideas with her.

"What do you think about inviting my parents out to see the cabin sometime soon?" I asked.

"That would be really nice," she agreed. "I still haven't seen them since you told them about the baby, and I'd like to. It would be nice to get some advice from your mother. Considering she actually raised you as opposed to my mother, who handed me off to a nanny as soon as she could."

That explained a lot and answered many of the questions I had as soon as she told me about the way her parents treated her.

"You are going to be a fantastic mother. I can already see it. But how do you feel about having a nanny? I can hire one for you if you want one," I reassured her.

Bridgit shook her head.

"No. I don't want to do that. I want to take care of this baby. Especially considering Rhea is giving me such nice maternity leave from the store, I'll be able to do everything for at least the first few months of his life. After that, she said we could figure it out. If I want to, she'll let me bring the baby with me into work when you are in the city."

"Speaking of Rhea. I really want to invite Gina to come to the cabin for dinner. She should meet Rhea. I think the two of them would get along famously," I told her.

"I think they would too," Bridgit said. "In fact, maybe we should reconsider having the two of them in the same room together. The world might not be ready for us to inflict that partnership on them."

I laughed.

"You may be right. Those are definitely two strong personalities."

"We should still do it. It would be fun to see the two of them together. Besides, I miss Gina so much. I don't want to just be without her all the time now that I'm up here rather than in the city," she worried.

"She misses you, too. She checks on you every time I go into the office."

"Are you sure she's checking on me and not the baby?" she asked playfully.

Considering the piles of stuffed animals and other gifts I brought home with me from "Auntie Gina" nearly every time I went to the office, it was a logical question.

"You know what I found out yesterday?" I asked.

"What's that?"

"The next parcel of land over is available for sale," I told her.

"Oh, really?" she asked. "I didn't realize you were in the market for a huge slab of land."

"I'm not. But Gus might be. I've been thinking about encouraging him to come build out here. I'd like to have him next door."

I'd been missing my best friend and knew he would enjoy being out here as much as I did. The little town didn't have the Russian presence that the city did, and we would be hard-pressed to find a convenient place for our weekly lunches, but we could make do. I just wanted to have him closer.

"Before we start building a commune out here, do you think I could have a cup of coffee?" Bridgit asked.

I laughed and nodded, leaning forward to kiss the tip of her nose.

"Of course. You wait here. I'll be right back."

I got out of bed and headed for the kitchen. As I made the coffee, I thought about all my plans for our future. There were many of them, and every day it seemed I added more. But first, I wanted to bring her coffee, kiss her pale skin, and find any other way I could to serve her. I wanted to rub the belly that was growing bigger every day and feel for the kicks that were getting stronger and more frequent. These were moments I cherished, treasuring their simplicity rather than brushing past them and burying myself in work like I used to.

I returned to the bedroom and climbed back in bed beside her. I waited for Bridgit to take a sip of her coffee and set it aside, then scooted down toward the end of the bed. She giggled as I lifted her nightgown and kissed along the curve of her stomach. Covering it again, I moved back up her body and kissed between her breasts, running my fingertips up her leg. I wanted to make a play for more. Now that she had allowed sex again, Bridgit was pretty insatiable, and I was more than happy to enjoy the spoils. But as I lowered my mouth to hers and eased my body closer, a sharp knock on the cabin door broke the mood.

"Mail?" Bridgit asked. "This early?"

"Just ignore it," I said, moving to kiss her again.

She lifted her arms to wrap them around my neck and melt into the kiss, but there was another harder knock and my head dropped. I grumbled in frustration and pulled away from her.

"Who is that?" she asked.

"I don't know, but I'm going to throw them into the ocean," I said, backing off the bed and heading for my dresser to get dressed. "You stay right here. Don't go anywhere. I'll be right back."

She stretched herself out, tossing an arm dramatically over her head and bending one knee like she was putting herself on display. She was trying to be silly, but she still managed to be sexy as hell, and I was tempted to just yell to whoever was outside to go away. But that wasn't going to work out. A third round of knocks on the door was even louder and more insistent. Whoever the hell that was, it better be fucking important.

I was still dropping my shirt down over my head when I opened the door. A courier stood outside, gripping a large manila envelope in one hand.

"I have a delivery for Bridgit Holliday," he said.

"Sure," I said, reaching for it.

He pulled it back.

"It needs a signature."

"I can sign for it."

"It has to be her," he insisted.

Letting out a frustrated groan, I walked back into the bedroom and leaned over the bed to kiss her.

"I'm sorry, babe, but you've got to get up. The courier won't let me sign for your delivery."

"Courier?" she asked, sounding confused. "What is it?"

"I don't know. It's just an envelope."

She got up and threw clothes on before following me back to the door. She signed the form and accepted the envelope.

"Thank you," she said and closed the door as he walked away.

She stared down at the envelope, and I saw the color drain from her face.

"What's wrong?" I asked.

"It's from my parents' lawyer," she told me.

She looked up at me, then tore into the envelope. It dropped to the floor at her feet as she unfolded a letter. Her hands shook as she tried to read it, so I took it from her and let my eyes scan over it before reading it out loud.

"Bridgit Holliday, Mr. and Mrs. Holliday have rescinded their names from your bank account and have arranged for them to have individual designation. Effective immediately, you are hereby granted full access to the account and all monies contained therein. This amount is currently $1,989,000.56. If you have any questions, please don't hesitate to get in touch," I read, then scoffed. "Fifty-six cents. Give it to them for attention to detail."

"Holy shit," she muttered, her mouth falling open. "I wonder what changed their minds?"

She took the paper from my hands and stared down at it herself, shaking her head occasionally and laughing.

"You're a millionaire, babe," I said.

She looked up at me with an almost mocking look.

"Honey, you're a billionaire. What are you, jealous?" she asked.

I laughed and wrapped my arms around her, pushing her back toward the couch.

"Not at all. I'm happy for you. Now, let's pick up where we left off."

EPILOGUE

BRIDGIT - THREE MONTHS LATER

I was smiling so broadly as I signed the dotted line at the bottom of the contract it felt like my cheeks were going to split. It would have been worth it. This was one of the happiest moments of my life, and even though I knew there were more thrilling and deliriously happy events coming soon, I would always hold this one as one of my most trea-sured memories. I would always see it as the day I took complete control and secured my life for myself, my baby, and my family.

Finishing my signature, I added my initials to the places the attorney pointed out.

"And you're done," he said.

"That's it?" I asked. "Really?"

"Really. That's it. Congratulations."

With a pleasant smile, the attorney scooped up the papers, tucked them away in a folder, and waved before heading away. I grinned and accepted a glass of sparkling cider being held out to me by the original owner.

"Congratulations," Steven said.

I clinked the edge of my glass against his in a toast before taking a sip.

"Thank you," I said. "I still can't believe you wouldn't tell me you're the friend who owned the cabin. I mean, I've heard people use 'I'm asking for a friend' as an excuse, but this is a little extreme."

"I didn't want you to feel guilty," he said.

"Yes, because taking over the cabin of a nameless, faceless complete stranger is far less awkward than staying in my brother's cabin," I pointed out sarcastically.

"I didn't want you to feel like you were taking a place I wanted for myself to get away from Mom and Dad," he explained. "You know I've been thinking about moving out of the mansion and into my own place, and I didn't want you to think this was that spot and that you were taking it from me."

"That was nice of you. But I still don't understand why you bought it and never stayed in it. It's wonderful," I said.

"I know. But it's not exactly my style. I bought it as an investment property. You see, I wasn't completely lying when I said it was my friend's cabin. It really did belong to my buddy Malcolm before he got married and moved across the country. He thought about keeping it as a place to come back to when he visited New York, but he and his wife decided they would rather have an apartment in the city than the cabin. So, I bought it. Dad was more than happy to see me spending money on something he thought was valid, even though he'd rather me buy something closer to the city, or something bigger."

"Of course he would. But that does make sense why you were even more frantic than me when I saw Clark here," I said.

"They had already insisted on coming out here to look

for you when you first left and realized it hadn't been used in a while, so they were satisfied you weren't here. I honestly don't think they thought either of us were smart enough to move you, so they wouldn't have thought for themselves to check here again," he said.

"Nothing like the resounding endorsement of confident parents," I said.

"Yep. They figured you were hiding away somewhere in the city and they'd eventually find you. Especially once Mom got her hands on your phone number. But I knew as soon as Clark told them he saw you at the art shop, it would be all over. You knew they would come to town to find you, maybe go to your work, but I knew Dad would immediately know you were here at the cabin. I didn't want them to just spring themselves on you. Though, that kind of happened, anyway."

"You know I don't blame you, right?" I asked. "I know you did everything you could to keep them away from me."

"I know, but they definitely blamed me." He laughed. "Which is how we ended up in the Excommunication Club together."

"About that. I'd like to point out you totally broke club policies by waiting all this time to tell me about the cabin so I could buy it from you," I said.

"Well, I was going to surprise you and give it to you as a wedding present," he said. "But no. You had to insist on buying it."

"Aren't you glad I did? You wouldn't want to be my landlord for the rest of your life, would you?" I asked.

"Not particularly. Now I just get to be your neighbor."

He and I tipped our glasses together again and sipped on our cider. From my vantage point on the back deck of the cabin, I could just see the edge of the land where my new property butted up against the parcel Steven bought a week ago. The construction of his house was about to get underway, and when it was finished, we would be as close to next-door neighbors as could be in this area.

But he wasn't the only new neighbor I could look forward to as I settled into the cabin as my very own. Right at that moment, Andrei was over on the plot of land he'd picked out for Gus months before. Gus was signing the final papers to purchase the land, and then they were going to meet with the contractors who were ready to start on the spectacular cabin he'd designed.

We were finally going to have exactly what we wanted. All of us loved the area so much, and now we were going to have our own little compound where we could live close and see each other all the time. Gina came from the city to visit regularly, and Rhea was over several times a week. Just like Andrei and I guessed, the two women were fast friends and always seemed to be scheming something. I couldn't wait to see how much more our friendships would grow over the years, and to see them with our little son when he came.

Andrei and I were going to try to wait until the baby was born to find out if it was a boy or girl, but we didn't make it long. By the sixth month, we were both dying to find out. Our feeling about it being a boy was still strong, and both of us figured if we were wrong, it would be hard to get used to when I delivered a little girl. Finding out meant we could have the opportunity to get to know our baby before birth. But as it turned out, we were absolutely right, and since then we'd been even more excitedly anticipating the arrival of our sweet baby boy. Only a few more weeks and he would be in my arms.

I looked down at my huge belly and saw my engagement ring glinting in the late-evening sun. Like it always did, the ring made me smile. I loved that ring. It was perfect in every way, right down to the fact that Andrei designed it for me and chose the diamond himself. But even more, I loved what it represented. The proposal was everything I could have wanted—impulsive, sweet, and completely without fuss. Andrei and I were stuffed together into the tub with his hands pouring the warm water down over my belly and rubbing it across my skin as he asked.

We weren't in any rush to get married. I wanted to be his wife. In fact, I couldn't wait to be his wife. But right now, I was focused on my pregnancy and welcoming our baby. After that, I'd turn my focus to planning a wedding. The best part about it was everyone was so deliriously happy for us.

Well, almost everyone. My parents were still in the process of coming around. At least, that's what Steven said. Cutting him off didn't last nearly as long as it had with me. I didn't know if they'd come to the realization on their own or if it was Steven pointing it out that pushed them along, but soon after I received my letter releasing my bank account to me, Steven received the same notification. He later confessed he told them they would never meet their grand-child if they continued to mistreat me, and he wouldn't be on their side if they continued to mistreat us.

So far, I still hadn't spent any time with them. Maybe I would sometime soon, but if they couldn't be truly happy for me simply because I loved the man I was marrying, I didn't need them in my life right now. It would probably change when the baby came, but for now, I had everything I needed.

Looking up from my belly, I saw Andrei coming toward

me. I opened my arms to him, and he hugged me, then kissed me deeply, bringing his mouth to my ear.

"Welcome home."

The End